SILENT
INVASION

SILENT INVASION

CHRIS SHOCKOWITZ

ARPress
ILLUMINAVING IDEAS.
EMPOWERING VOICES

ARPress
45 Dan Road Suite 36
Canton MA 02021

Hotline: 1(888) 821-0229
Fax: 1(508) 545-7580

Ordering Information:
Quantity Sales. Special discounts are available on quantity purchases by corporations, associations, and others. For details, contact the publisher at the address above.

Printed in the United States of America.

ISBN-13   Softcover   979-8-89389-973-3
                        eBook   979-8-89389-972-6

Library of Congress Control Number: 2024918458

This book is dedicated to the estimated 800,000 people
who died in the Rwandan genocide.
May it never happen again!

ACKNOWLEDGMENTS

I'd like to thank the following people for helping me complete this novel:

Carolyn Shockowitz, for her feedback and encouragement
Arlene Robinson, for her feedback and ideas

My friends at Skill Synapse Media, for their many contributions

Patrick Snow, for his coaching and inspiration

Karen Schmautz of Sierra Springs Photography, for her excellent photos

Tyler Tichelaar, for his editing skills and guidance

Nicole Gabriel, for her design expertise and guidance

Susan Friedmann, my publisher, for letting me be part of the Aviva family

And to all my family, friends, and well-wishers, thank you!

CONTENTS

Since the 1950s, humanity has explored the many ways aliens could invade Earth, but the ugly truth is that no intelligent race need risk their own lives to kill humans while humans are still so willing to kill each other.

CHAPTER

THE JOURNEY BEGINS

Jeff Smith walked quickly into the outer offices of the high-tech lab located under the rolling hills of Virginia. He walked right past the receptionist in his haste to reach Alon's lab. One of Alon's assistants was chasing Jeff, saying, "Sir, you must wait in the waiting room. You cannot just walk into the labs! Sir!"

Jeff spotted Alon and said, "Hi, Alon. What did you find out?"

Alon looked at his assistant. "It's okay. Thank you for your help."

"Why do you always do that, Jeff?" Alon asked, half-joking as his assistant frowned and walked off.

"We are 100 stories underground in a maximum-security lab. If I couldn't be here, I never would have made it below ground." Jeff was a senior CIA agent in charge of ten other agents. He hated waiting and was used to getting what he wanted when he wanted it.

Alon just shook his head with a smile. He then got very serious. "Jeff, where did you get the material you brought me?" Alon had emigrated from Israel with his parents when he was a teenager. He was a full US citizen and a gifted scientist, but some in the upper ranks of the CIA still did not trust him.

"Alon, this entire operation is now class 11 secure. You know what that means."

"It is well over your pay grade," Alon said with a smile.

"And probably not over yours," Jeff said, smiling back. "But seriously, Alon, this is strictly need-to-know basis. No one can get this information without explicit authorization. Use me to request approval."

Alon smiled and spread his arms wide. "I agree."

Jeff looked around to ensure no one else was in the lab. "We found this material at a crash site, underwater."

Alon looked confused, "Underwater? That cannot be. There is no corrosion. The surface is perfect—as if it were polished yesterday. Did you clean it up? What was it part of? What kind of water? Ocean? Fresh?"

"Slow down, Alon. It's a long story. No, we did not clean it up. It was in the ocean, about five hundred miles south of Anchorage, Alaska, about five miles off the coast of Queen Charlotte Island. We don't know what it is; some salvage company found the wreckage while looking for a World War II submarine."

"The wreckage was confusing at first. There was a semi-circular pattern to the wreckage, but what we found were these flat, roughly triangular pieces like the sample I gave you, very neatly placed, each one slightly overlapping the next. The metal was in perfect condition. We thought it must be new, but the salvage company said it spotted it weeks ago and had just gotten around to this site. It was underwater at least a month. There is no telling how long it was there."

"There are other ways to tell," Alon said.

"You're right; I misspoke. That part of the ocean floor has no direct inlets from rivers. The only deposits are from sea creatures dying. Based on the lack of any significant deposits on top, we know it has been there less than 100 years. We also know the salvage company spotted it about one month before. So, we know the wreckage is between two months and 100 years old."

Alon was deep in thought now. Jeff decided to give him time to think.

Finally, Alon broke the silence. "Okay. Shall I share what I've found out?"

Jeff nodded.

"This substance is unlike anything I've ever seen before. After close visual inspection, I found nothing. No flaws, no cracks, no imperfections. Then I found nothing on its surface. No dust. No rust.

Not even bacteria were present on the entire surface. That was strange, so I attempted to slice off a sample to analyze chemically. Guess what. I could not cut off a sample. I tried saws, torches, and lasers. Nothing worked," Alon said as he raised his hands and dropped them at his sides in frustration.

"That's not possible," Jeff said.

"Exactly! The energy from the lasers and torches was just absorbed, and the surface never got hotter. The saws slid uselessly over the material without causing a single scratch. Hammer blows bounced right off the surface with no distortion. Then I decided to place it in a hydraulic press. I set up lasers to measure any change in the material's surface. I clearly warped it at eighty tons of pressure, but when I released the pressure, it was back to its original shape with no distortion at all."

"Wow! What did you do next?"

"I took that three-foot-long sample and placed it under some very powerful microscopes."

"How did you do that?" Jeff asked, amazed.

Alon smiled because Jeff clearly appreciated just how hard that would have been to do. "It wasn't easy. Eventually, I could analyze the structure of the metal and its composition."

"And?" Jeff asked, intensely focused on Alon's words.

"This material is not just metal. It's an intricate matrix of nanites."

"Nanites?" Jeff said incredulously. "I thought nanites were just a theory."

"No, there are some molecular machines, but they're very primitive. Nothing even close to this material.

"How could that be?" Jeff asked.

"Jeff, there's more. I believe these nanites behave the way they do because they're in a default state."

"What's a default state?" Jeff asked.

Alon struggled for words. "The default is when they have no other orders to reform into any other...configuration."

"What?" Jeff asked more confused than ever.

Alon took another deep breath and said, "Jeff, I believe that some intelligence can control the nanites to form shapes. In fact, the nanites could reform into anything. It's a smart material."

Jeff was stunned. "Do you mean to tell me that the sample in your lab could turn into a swirling set of knives that kills everyone in the room?"

"I didn't think about military applications. I was thinking only of construction and manufacturing." Alon put his hand on his chin and started thinking about it. Then he decided, "What you are saying is possible, Jeff, but only if an outside force acted to control the material. The material is smart but not intelligent. It could change into a knife if something ordered it to, but it couldn't spin around without some other force affecting it."

"Smart but not intelligent?" Jeff asked.

"Yes; it cannot think for itself. Something or someone would have to control it to make it do anything. Otherwise, it will sit in its default configuration and do nothing. What you found could have been a systems failure that caused a ship made of this material to fall apart into its default state and sink to the bottom of the ocean."

"But then wouldn't the remains be scattered?" Jeff asked.

"Yes. Perhaps it was sitting on the bottom when the failure occurred. Either way, I think there's a more profound question to ask: Could this material have been produced on Earth? I think the answer is no."

"Why?"

"First, no one on this planet has this technology. Second, the nanites themselves appear to be perfect spheres."

"What's so important about them being spherical?"

"Not spherical, perfect spheres. Anything produced on Earth is affected by the Earth's gravity. No manufacturing facility on Earth has ever produced a perfectly spherical object. It cannot be done because of Earth's gravity."

"Cars have ball bearings. Those are spheres, aren't they?" Jeff asked.

"They're spherical but not perfect spheres."

"Where else could it be produced?"

Alon motioned upward with his eyes as he said, "Perfect spheres can only be produced in space."

As Jeff headed back to Washington, DC, he mulled over how to communicate what he had learned to his direct superior.

He couldn't help but think, *How do I tell my boss that aliens left their footprint on Earth between two months and 100 years ago?* He blurted out "Bloody hell!" before he realized it.

His driver looked back to inquire, "Sir, are you all right?"

"Yes, thanks for asking."

The driver was perplexed but decided to let his passenger elaborate only if he felt the need.

Jeff decided to break out his laptop and write his report.

✴ ✴ ✴

An hour later, as Jeff approached Langley, he was almost done with his report. His shoulders and back were stiff, and he was tired, but as the car stopped in front of the main entrance, he moved quickly through security and the main campus quad area to Assistant Director Zachariah James' building.

Fortunately, James was there, even though he was on a phone call. Jeff paced nervously back and forth in front of his boss' desk.

As James hung up, he said, "Well, what is it, man?"

"Do you remember the material we found off the Pacific Coast, sir?"

"Vaguely."

"It may be proof that alien life visited Earth."

"Are you mad?" the director asked as he stood up.

"Sir, the material we found on the ocean floor is not metal. It's a structure formed by nanites."

"Nanites?" James asked.

"Yes, nanites. They're smart microscopic machines that are not intelligent but do react to commands. They can reshape themselves and move to some extent."

"Where did you get this fairy tale?"

"Alon's team did the analysis, sir."

"Alon is an Israeli. Why do you keep taking things to him?"

"He's the best there is, sir. There's more. These nanites are formed in perfect spheres. They're tiny, but they're perfectly round. Alon was adamant that a perfect sphere could only be produced in space."

"You have a report?"

"I do, right here, sir," Jeff said as he handed the micro-drive to his boss.

"Good. You're off this case, effective immediately."

"Sir?"

"I will have my own team verify this nonsense. In the meantime, I have an assignment for you."

"But, sir—" Jeff tried to interrupt but was cut off by his superior.

"I need your full attention on an interdiction mission. The target is Amber van Hosteen."

"Are you kidding me?"

"Silence. She is heading to Burkina Faso to investigate some companies. One of those companies is a CIA front. It's your job to make sure she doesn't link this company with her investigation." The director handed Jeff a file folder with a micro-drive attached.

"Sir, I know you don't like me for some reason, but this is not where I need to be."

"I decide where you need to be. How dare you accuse me of favoritism when making assignments? Now do your job and get out of my office before I bring you up on charges."

"Sir, I did not mean anything—"

"Silence. Is this micro-drive the only copy of your report on the Pacific material?"

"Yes, sir."

"Then get going." The director sat down and ignored Jeff.

Jeff walked out of the office and rested against the closed door to the director's office. His face was turning red. The folder in his hand was crushed as his grip tightened on it.

Then Jeff heard the director say, "We have a problem with this Pacific site." He could not hear the other voice reply. The director continued, "He'll be out of the way for now."

The director's secretary noticed Jeff and asked, "Are you okay, Jeff?" She liked Jeff, even though he had successfully evaded multiple invitations to drinks or dinner from her.

"Yes. I'm fine," Jeff said as he changed his demeanor, smoothed his suit, and approached the desk. "Not the best meeting this time around. Tell me, has our assistant director gone anywhere strange these last few months?"

"Strange? Not really. He goes to DC a lot for meetings and has lunch with his wife. That's about it. Why, Jeff?"

"Nothing. It was just something he mentioned. Thanks." Jeff gracefully exited the office and went down to his own.

Once he closed his door, Jeff threw the new file on his desk. He sat down and fidgeted with things on his desk while his mind raced. What had he stumbled upon, and what should he do next? If he disobeyed orders, his director could have him arrested for insubordination. He had already lied about not having another copy of his report. "I have to play my cards right or I could end up dead!"

The new assignment had him leaving the country tomorrow. "I'll play along for now but cover my ass."

Margo waved at Amber as she entered the cute little bistro in downtown New York. Amber's copper-colored hair usually made her easy to find in a crowd.

"Hi," Margo said as Amber took off her jacket and sat down. "You look great, Amber. You've got that look in your eyes like you have a really good story brewing."

Margo was Amber's best friend. They had met a few years after Amber moved from Vermont to the Big Apple. Amber had gotten her first solid reporting job at the *New York Post* and Margo had sat near her on the same floor. Although Amber had moved on to a bigger job at News Corp at 35 Rockefeller Plaza in the heart of New York, she still kept in frequent touch with Margo.

"Thanks, Margo. Yes, I do. I've been researching the activities of a few corporations that all tie back to a handful of really bad people. They have their fingers into everything from guns and diamonds to cargo freighters and political back office dealings."

"Oh, this is the same story you've been working on for a while now. The corporations were rigging elections in some African countries?"

"Yes, and a lot more it seems," Amber said with a grimace. "A network of holding companies appear to be hiding their wealth. But that can wait. How have you been?"

"I'm doing great. Work hasn't been too crazy, but I still haven't been getting my workout time in every day," Margo said as she patted her belly.

Margo was a workout fanatic. You could bounce a quarter off her stomach or her butt. Amber had been jealous until she found out how much workout time was required. They had worked out together for a little while, but Margo was just in far better shape than Amber.

"Sam has been away on business trips a lot this last month. We've only been together for six months, but I really miss him every time he leaves," Margo said.

Amber knew Sam was Margo's new boyfriend. "Is Sam away now?"

"Yeah, he is—for the rest of this week," Margo said. "Hey, maybe we could have dinner and catch a show one night this week?"

"I would love to, but I'll have to take a rain check. The story I've been working on will be taking me to Africa soon."

"Africa? Where in Africa? Will the cute CIA guy be following you there?"

"Burkina Faso is the country. It recently changed from a dictatorship to a democracy. It was a French protectorate. Its success at electing and keeping a government hasn't been stellar. Lately, people have been disappearing in the Northern provinces. They are 60 percent Muslim in the North, and there are rumors that Muslim groups are trying to push other religions out."

"How does that relate to your story?"

"Burkina Faso is one of the least developed countries in the world. It has few natural resources except gold. A lot of new money is flowing into the country from more than one of the holding companies I'm tracking. The company is building something, and I want to find out what it is."

Here the waiter interrupted to take their order.

As they ordered, Amber wondered why Margo always asked her about Jeff Smith. She had only seen him once on TV. He was the only one who had ever stopped Amber from getting a story, a quid pro quo scandal she was working on. Jeff had suppressed the key evidence she needed to prove a National Security Advisor was cutting deals. She hated him for it.

When the waiter left, Amber continued, "As for Jeff Smith, I couldn't care less if I never saw him again. He will not hide the truth from me."

"Are you telling me you don't find Jeff the least bit attractive?"

"He's fine if that's your type," Amber said defensively.

"Tall, dark, handsome, muscular, intelligent…" Margo said.

"Know it all, self-centered, egotistical…and what do you mean intelligent?" Amber replied.

"From the last story you told me, he seemed to be pretty clever. He'd have to be to outsmart you. You're one of the smartest people I know."

"Thank you, Margo, but I have no interest in him." Amber looked away. "I have no time for people who hide the truth."

Margo knew Jeff must have hurt Amber somehow to get that reaction. "That is just his job. Outside of work, he may be really sweet."

"I guess we'll have to wait and see," Amber said with a forced smile.

FOLLOWING A LEAD

After traveling from New York to Paris, Amber finally arrived at the airport in Ouagadougou, the capital of Burkina Faso. Her contact, a local Catholic Priest named Jean-Paul Mulifi, held a sign with her name just outside of customs.

"Hello, Amber, and welcome to Ouagadougou," Jean-Paul said warmly with a heavy French accent as they exchanged cheek kisses. Jean-Paul was a black African about 5' 5" and very thin with short gray hair. He was older, but his brown eyes were bright and his smile engaging.

"Thank you for coming, Jean-Paul. It's a pleasure to finally meet you. The work you've been doing with the poor in this country is incredible."

"Thank you, thank you. Come, I have a car," he said, then motioned to two young Arab boys standing behind him. "Grab the lady's bags."

Amber never thought of herself as tall, but at 5' 10" with two-inch wedges, she was taller than all the women and most of the men at the airport. Her red copper hair, light cream complexion, and bright green eyes made her unique among the Africans at the airport. Almost everyone was staring at her.

She turned back to her host and asked, "Where will we be headed today, Jean-Paul?"

"I will take you to the capital. There we have a room where you can rest. Tomorrow, we will head north to Djibo as you requested. We can stay at the church in that city and explore from there. My bishop is thankful to have a reporter with your reputation looking into the disappearances we have witnessed. International awareness can only help our people."

"I'm so thankful for your support, Jean-Paul. We will get to the bottom of this together."

They climbed into a white 2010 Toyota Land Cruiser Prado. Amber thought this vehicle should do well on city streets and dirt roads.

As they rode into the capital city, Amber noticed that most of the buildings were single-story earthen structures made with sun-dried mud bricks. It wasn't until they reached downtown that more modern buildings appeared in this city of 1.4 million. Amber spotted a large white church as they approached the city center.

"Is that where we're going, Jean-Paul?"

"Yes, but I will take you to your room first. You can then rest or sleep as you wish."

"Thank you!"

The church was plain but clean and well maintained. The main building was tall, rectangular, and had a large spire in the front with a huge cross on top. A smaller two-story wing branched off the main building to one side. It looked like a series of apartments with outdoor walkways. Jean-Paul drove to one of them and escorted Amber to a second-story room. The room was plain but very clean with stone flooring, a main room, and a bathroom.

"I hope this is to your liking?"

"This is very nice, Jean-Paul. Thank you for being such a gracious host."

"I will send a boy with lunch. The clock near the bed has accurate local time. Straight down the hall is a kitchen and dining area. I will meet you there at 5 p.m. if you wish."

"Thank you. I'll try to be there."

Amber felt good to be alone. She freshened up and began writing her thoughts on the trip so far. After half an hour, a young boy knocked on the door and handed Amber a tray covered with a towel. Under the towel were two bottles of water and a small casserole bowl with rice, lamb, and vegetables. The boy stayed and watched her for a few moments.

Amber tried the meal. "Mmm, this is good," she said as she turned toward the boy. He smiled and ran away toward the kitchen.

After eating, Amber went to sleep.

✳ ✳ ✳

Jean-Paul arrived at 9 a.m. the next morning with oatmeal for breakfast. He and Amber sat and talked about their plans as they ate. "Today," Jean-Paul said, "we will drive north for about six hours until we reach Djibo. We can stay at the church there and begin our investigations the next day. Does that sound good to you?"

"Yes," Amber replied, "but I might want to start talking to people this afternoon as soon as we arrive."

"The church has arranged interviews for you and will want to show you some locations."

"That's excellent! I'll still need to do some of my own investigating."

"As you wish. If you are ready, we should be off."

As they left the city, Amber could see miles of savanna with sparse trees and rolling grassland. As they went farther north, the terrain became drier and eventually hilly. The people they passed became a 50/50 mix of black African and Arab.

As they entered Djibo, most of the buildings were mud-brick construction. There were even fewer modern buildings. The church and a mosque were notable exceptions.

The church was a two-story building with a cross over the front door. Behind the church was a courtyard with a few other buildings. Jean-Paul drove straight into the crushed-rock courtyard and parked in front of a small office building.

"Please come with me," he said as he walked confidently into the building.

As Amber entered the building, she saw a waiting area with about ten people sitting, a small office area where two clerks were working, and another office to the side. Jean-Paul was at the office door waving at her to enter.

Behind the only desk sat a tall middle-aged Frenchman with thick, dark hair streaked with gray. He wore black glasses and a priest's black robe with a white collar. He looked unsettled.

"Maurice, this is Amber van Hosteen, the reporter from the United States I told you about. Amber, this is Father Maurice Cantin."

"Call me Maurice."

"Maurice is the one who reported missing families in the mountains near here."

Amber and Jean-Paul sat down while Amber asked, "Can you tell me more about what is happening, Maurice?"

"Until recently, there were a few families that just seemed to disappear from their land."

"Until recently," Amber prompted.

"Yes. Today I have a report of an entire town missing."

"That cannot be!" Jean-Paul exclaimed.

"Can we go see this town tomorrow?" Amber continued.

"It is remote," Maurice said. "It will take all day to get there."

"We can leave early," Amber suggested.

"I have about a dozen people for you to interview, Miss van Hosteen," Maurice said.

"Please, call me Amber."

"Amber, I can go and investigate this town tomorrow by myself," Maurice said. "I can return late, and we can discuss what I find."

"All right. I do have some other questions. A large amount of construction material is going somewhere in northern Burkina Faso. Do you know where it's going?"

"Gold mining has been on the rise here over the last few years. We are the fourth largest exporter of gold in Africa now."

"These materials do not make sense for a gold mining operation," Amber explained. "There are too many high-tech materials and electronics for a mining operation. Is there any place that stands out as having ultra-high security?"

"A new mine in the north has very high security," Maurice said. "The rumor is that the mine has found something other than gold. No one can enter, and few ever leave."

"I'd like to see this mine before I leave."

"How long were you planning to stay?"

"As long as necessary."

"Very well," Maurice said. "I have made arrangements for you to stay at the local hotel. We have very few accommodations here."

"I'm sure it'll be fine. Who are the people waiting outside?"

"Members of my flock with an issue or grievance to report. We help everyone we can. Two of them are from the town that disappeared. I was just going to speak with them."

"Can I join you in this discussion?" Amber asked.

"Perhaps, but we should not have too many people. It will scare them."

"I have business elsewhere," Jean-Paul said. "I can go. I will get your luggage to your room, Amber. I will be staying at the same hotel."

"Thank you, Jean-Paul," Amber replied.

Maurice got up to escort Jean-Paul out and bring two young women back to the little office. The women's clothes were dirty, as if they had just arrived after hard travels. The younger one could not stop twirling her hair. The older one, who was maybe eighteen or nineteen, just sat and stared at her hands.

"Young ladies, are you hungry or thirsty?" Maurice asked.

There was no reply.

"Please look at me. I am here to help you. Can you tell me what happened?"

The younger girl began to speak rapidly in French and cried as she spoke. Amber knew a little French, but she could not keep up with the rapid flow of words. When the girl stopped speaking, both girls looked at their laps and cried.

Maurice turned to Amber and said, "These girls were tending to goats their family owned. The goats got away from them and started to scatter into the hills when some large trucks approached. They did not want to get in trouble with their father, so they chased the goats and brought them back to their house. When they returned, everyone was gone. They stayed one night in their town, then came here for help."

Maurice went around the desk to comfort the girls. He was asking them in French for more information, but they had nothing else to share.

After the girls settled down, Maurice led them out of the office to a clerk. When he returned, he explained, "My staff will find them a place to sleep and a nun who can help them through these trying times."

"That is very kind."

"It is what we do for our people."

"Tell me, Maurice; isn't slavery still practiced in this part of North Africa?"

"Burkina Faso has outlawed slavery!"

"I know, but isn't it still practiced in some parts of North Africa?"

"Unfortunately, yes," Maurice admitted.

"On the surface, this sounds like slavers."

"They could never be so bold. They took an entire village."

"If I had to guess, they took these people to the new mine as workers."

"That is pure conjecture. We need to verify there was a disappearance before we raise alarms."

"Yes, it is only a guess. You know your country better than I do, but shouldn't we report this to the authorities?"

"The capital of this province is 170 km to the east. Our nation's capital is 190 km south."

"What about the local police?"

"I called them earlier today. They have not arrived yet. Our police force is very small. We only have ten officers in Djibo, a town of 22,000. I will get a police officer to join me tomorrow. I will go to this village and see what happened for myself. If it is as the girls say, the officer and I will raise the alarm. In the meantime, I have twelve people who want to talk to you tomorrow. You can use my office. When I return, we can decide on our next step. Agreed?"

"I agree. When should I come here tomorrow?"

"About 9 a.m. is a good time to start. My staff will let you in."

"Thank you for your help, Maurice."

"The pleasure is mine."

Amber walked out of Maurice's office and sat in the waiting area until Jean-Paul returned.

After going to the hotel to freshen up, Jean-Paul and Amber ate dinner together at the hotel restaurant.

"I was surprised," she told him, "that Maurice did not immediately take the disappearances to the police or other authorities."

"We are a small country, Amber. The local tribes do a good job of policing their own. Do you know what Burkina Faso means?"

"No, I don't."

"It means 'the fatherland of honest people.' I take great pride in that name."

"It is a wonderful name. I had no idea."

"We have over sixty native tongues, but we are united by the French language. Those girls could be running from an angry father or a failed marriage. We do not know. Communications in our country are not so good. We will find out the truth tomorrow."

"Then I look forward to tomorrow."

FINDING THE TRUTH

Amber returned to Maurice's office early to organize and prepare herself for multiple interviews. She snooped around Maurice's office but found nothing unusual.

After a long day with twelve interviews, Amber was studying her notes when Jean-Paul came into the office. "How did your day go, Amber?"

"Tiring. I'm seeing some disturbing patterns in these stories. Seven out of twelve had family members go missing when they traveled north for business. Two had property seized by the government. The other three are indirect stories of people missing. I mapped the locations of the disappearances. They're all along the road to Mali. I need to go north."

"I'm returning to the capital tomorrow," Jean-Paul replied. "I can arrange for a car and a driver, but we should wait for Maurice to return first."

"Any ideas on when that will be?"

"I would guess 8 p.m. at the earliest."

"Can you and I meet here before you leave tomorrow? Either Maurice will be back by then or he won't."

"That's fine. I can take you to the hotel now if you wish."

"That would be great. I'll take dinner in my room and work on my interview notes tonight. I'll see if I can find out anything else about this part of the world from my colleagues in the United States. I left my hotel room phone number on Maurice's desk and with the head clerk."

"All we can do is wait," Jean-Paul said with a smile.

There were no calls that evening. Amber met Jean-Paul the next day at Maurice's office.

"There is no sign of Maurice."

"I feel something bad is happening, Jean-Paul. I need a car."

"Are you sure you want to go there now?"

"Yes, I am. I can't find the truth sitting here. I was thinking last night that my driver should be Muslim. If there are religious issues at the heart of this, I can dress as a Muslim and hide my identity."

"As you wish. Please be careful."

Within an hour, Amber was on the road north with Malik, her Muslim driver. She also had a black dress to cover her body from the neck down, and a hood that covered everything except her eyes.

Amber's data gathered so far placed most of the disappearances around a small town named Diguel near the Mali border. They would stop at the village Maurice was headed to first. It was on the way to Diguel.

The trip was uneventful until they came close to the village. Amber put on her disguise just before trucks loaded with armed men forced them off the road. They were both scared, but the trucks did not stop.

"Is there a military base near here?" Amber asked Malik.

"No. Border guards only. Burkina Faso has small army near capital."

They continued to the little village and found nothing but empty houses, a few goats, and some chickens. As they explored the little village, it was as if the residents had dropped everything and run away. "There was food still cooking when they left," Amber observed. "The wash is still hanging on lines even though it's dry. Windows are open. Tools are sitting out as if they were set down in a hurry."

Malik was silent.

"I noticed crosses in almost every house. Was this village Christian, Malik?"

"I think so."

Amber took many photos and some video before returning to the car. As they started to leave, Amber saw a reflection between some buildings. "Let's drive behind those houses, Malik."

As they drove around the houses, they spotted a pickup truck like the one they were in with the doors open. No one was around.

Amber got out to inspect the Toyota truck. The keys were still in the ignition. She found paperwork written in French that looked like the registration. She walked back to Malik.

"Malik, can you read this paperwork? Is this truck registered with the church?"

Malik was nervous and looking everywhere. He was ready to drive away. He took one quick look at the paper and said, "That truck is owned by the church. We must go!"

"Don't leave me, Malik. We need to see if Maurice is here. He may be injured."

Malik said nothing. Amber took his silence as consent and started looking around the nearby houses. She could follow the tracks of two men exiting the vehicle. They appeared to enter a house. Amber went inside and found a patch of blood on the floor, but no sign of Maurice or the police officer.

Amber decided not to press her luck with Malik. She took a few more pictures of the village, then told Malik she was ready to leave.

Malik calmed down once they were back on the road—until another convoy of trucks forced them off it. After the last truck passed, he put his face in his hands and started shaking.

"Malik, what's wrong?"

"I cannot continue. I want to turn around now."

"Okay," Amber said slowly. "Let's go back to the village. I can take Maurice's truck and you can go home. Okay?"

Malik looked at Amber and said, "I do not want to go back to that village."

"Okay, just take me near the village. I can make it from there."

"You shame me with your bravery."

"There's no shame here. Let's just take it easy and go back near the village."

Malik turned the truck around and drove cautiously back to the outskirts of the empty village. "I will wait here for you, and then go home."

Amber grabbed her bag and walked into the empty village. The truck was where they had found it and the keys were still in the ignition. She closed the doors, started it up, and drove out to meet Malik.

He got out and put a gas can in the back of her truck, then waved and drove away.

Amber was on her own, but that didn't worry her. She drove north toward Diguel and looked for signs of heavy traffic or construction. She stopped at a crossroad about ten miles from Diguel and hid behind a small hill. The road looked worn and heavily used by large trucks. She waited for about two hours before a convoy of trucks pulling flatbed trailers flew by. Their cargo was in large boxes covered with a beige canvas. She jumped into her little white Toyota truck and followed the convoy.

For about forty-five minutes, Amber drove though deep canyons following the dust kicked up by the trucks before the convoy slowed down. Then she pulled off the road and climbed a rough shale hill with her camera. The trucks stopped in front of a barbed wire gate. Guards armed with AK47 machine guns were talking to the drivers and inspecting their cargo. The small convoy had ten trucks. One of the guards boarded each truck before allowing it to move forward into the facility. About ten minutes later, ten different trucks left the facility, each dropping off an armed guard as it left.

As the sun began to set, Amber decided to leave and spend the night at the empty village. It had food and shelter, and no one was there. She could also spend some more time investigating the village. She slid down the little hill, made her way back to her truck, and headed back the way she had come. The road was empty all the way back to the little village.

She found her way to a small house she remembered had food and candles. She closed the shutters, lit a candle, and made herself something to eat before falling asleep.

The next morning, Amber heard voices. She looked out one of the shuttered windows and saw two men with rifles. They were thieves stealing from the empty village. She could not understand what they were saying, but it was definitely not French. She had hidden the truck behind some hills near the village. She doubted these men knew she was there. The house she was in sat right in the middle of the village. She could not leave without being seen.

As the men approached her house, Amber became scared. She had no weapons and no way to escape, so she hid under the bed with a rough woven cloth over her. A man tried to kick open the door. When it failed to open, he shot the lock and kicked it again.

Amber fought to stop shaking with fear. Who were these men? What would they do to her if they found her?

The man kicked the door again, shattering the lock. As the door swung open, Amber froze in fear.

Automatic weapons began firing and rifles were firing back. The man at the door fired three times, then ran away into the village. Suddenly, the weapon fire stopped. Amber could hear feet walking toward her house. A man stopped in the doorway and said, "Amber, you can come out now."

She was still scared, but she really had no other options, so she crawled out from under the bed to see Jeff Smith standing in the doorway with a machine gun in his right hand.

"What the hell are you doing here?" Amber asked.

Jeff smiled and said, "How charming? I would have expected 'Hello' or maybe even 'Thank you.'"

"Why are you here?"

"We've been tracking you since you arrived in the country."

"We?" Amber asked as she dusted herself off.

"Let me introduce Dureau from the French Directorate-General for External Security and Emil from Burkina Faso Border Security.

"Thank you for your timely arrival, gentlemen."

"You're welcome," Dureau said with a bow. Emil just smiled at Jeff.

"We surprised the thieves," Jeff said. "They outnumber us and might return with more. We should go."

"Do you know what happened in this village?" Amber asked.

"No," Emil answered.

"The entire village disappeared," Amber said. "A priest from the church I'm working with came here to investigate and also disappeared. I have his truck behind the hill over there."

The men all looked at each other before Emil spoke, "I have heard rumors of other disappearances."

"I interviewed twelve people yesterday who all had family members or friends disappearing around this area. I followed some large trucks to a secure facility north of here. Look at these photos." Amber shared the pictures on her camera of the facility's front gates and of the convoy entering. "I believe this facility has something to do with these disappearances."

"Officials for this region visited that facility a few weeks back. They never returned," Emil said.

"We need to go," Jeff repeated.

"We should investigate the village," Emil said.

"Jeff is right. We can always come back with more men," Dureau said.

Emil looked at them a moment and said, "All right. You take the girl. I'll take her truck. Keys?"

"Now wait a minute," Amber said. "I'm not some cargo you can haul around."

"If we stay here any longer, we could all die. We need to go!" Jeff said as he grabbed Amber's arm.

Amber pulled away from Jeff and slapped him hard across the face. "I will not be manhandled," she stated.

The other two men snickered. Jeff gave them a look, asking for their help.

Dureau walked over to Amber and said, "Please, Amber, will you come with us to a safe place to talk? We really cannot stay here much longer."

Amber gave a cross look at Jeff and then smiled at Dureau. "I accept your offer. Please lead the way." She pulled her bag onto her shoulder, threw the truck keys to Emil, and followed Dureau to their black SUV.

Jeff looked over at Emil, wondering what had just happened. Emil laughed and walked off to find the church truck.

When they returned to their safe house, they would be in for multiple surprises.

BREAKING EGGS

After driving an hour, Amber and her companions arrived at a French safe house hidden in the hills. The outside was mud-brick construction, but inside were finished walls, stone floors, and all the comforts of home, including a television.

They sat at a large table in a dining room where Amber shared everything she knew. She finished with, "I believe that new mine isn't a mine. I think whoever is operating it is taking the local population as slaves for some reason. We need to get into that facility."

"Slavery was abolished in Burkina Faso," Emil said.

"True, but we know it still happens in these parts of Africa, my friend," Dureau said.

"Can you tell me more about the companies and materials you're tracking?" Jeff asked.

"I've discovered a web of corporations and holding companies all owned by a small number of very rich men. Your assistant director is on the board of two of these companies," Amber said.

"Well, that's news to me," Jeff said.

"What's odd is the number of electronic components and chemicals being shipped here," Amber said. "A mine might use some of these chemicals, but most of them are used in high-tech manufacturing, not mining."

"They could be building a factory of some type," Jeff suggested.

"Yes, but what exactly is hard to pin down," Amber said.

"Could it be arms or munitions?" Emil asked.

"I doubt it," Amber replied. "I compared bills of material for bullets, rockets, tanks, etc., and the list of materials doesn't add up."

"I think you are right about one thing," Dureau said. "I think we need to get inside that place."

"I was analyzing the photos, and I think I have a plan," Jeff said.

"Can we take a break?" Emil asked. "I am getting pinged by my boss." He had his cell phone out.

"Me too," Dureau said.

"So am I," Jeff said as he checked to see a priority callback request from his boss.

"Let's take a half-hour break," Jeff said.

"You can make yourself at home, Amber," Dureau said as he pointed down the hall. "The first bedroom on the left is yours if you want it. The bathroom is just down the hall. Any place you cannot go is locked."

Amber was thankful to get away from the boys for a while to gather her thoughts.

She was in for a shock when they reconvened.

"I have been ordered to terminate this operation and return to the capital," Emil said.

"I have the same order, but to return to France," Dureau said.

"This is crazy!" Amber exclaimed. "Did you share the disappearances?"

"Yes," both men said.

"They did not care," Dureau said.

"I was told I would be fired if I did not leave immediately," Emil said.

Then everyone looked at Jeff. "I had a similar order, but I objected to it and raised the concern that this could be a national security risk. Only the Director of the CIA can overrule me now, although I may have just ended my career," Jeff said with a forced smile.

"They ordered me to leave, but they did not deny the use of this facility. You may use it as long as you are here, my friend," Dureau said.

"Thank you, Dureau," Jeff said.

Once the shock wore off, Jeff said, "I still have a plan for entering this facility. Notice how the guards in these photos inspect the cargo and the cab but not under the trucks."

Dureau looked at the photos. "You are right."

"I can get under one of those trucks, hang from the I-beam frame, and hide until I get inside," Jeff said.

"It could work," Dureau said. "If you fall, you are dead, my friend."

"There is that," Jeff said with a smile.

"I'm going with you," Amber said.

"You are going back to the capital and flying home," Jeff said. "News Corp has closed the story."

"What?" Amber said. "How do you know that?"

Jeff pointed at himself and said, "CIA, remember?"

"Well, unlike you, I can just not call in and finish the story," Amber said. "Listen, Jeff Smith; this is my story, and I am going in there with you or without you."

Jeff looked at Amber for a full minute before saying, "All right, but if you die, it's your fault, not mine."

"I've faced tougher challenges than this," Amber said. She was scared, but she would not show that to Jeff Smith.

"Then it's decided," Jeff said. "We leave tomorrow."

Jeff said goodbye to his team. Amber noticed that Jeff and Dureau were good friends, not just coworkers, by the way they said goodbye. Once everyone had gone, Jeff started cutting up some furniture.

"What are you doing?" Amber asked.

"I'm fabricating our cover for tomorrow."

Amber watched as Jeff stretched out the leather from the chair he butchered on wooden stakes. He formed it into the shape of a shield and covered it with glue. He then went outside and covered the glue with rocks and dust. When he laid the shield on the ground, it blended in so well Amber could hardly tell it was there, even when she looked right at it.

"This is an old Indian trick to hide in plain sight and surprise an enemy. We'll use it to get close to the road and wait for our trucks to arrive."

"That's pretty cool."

"Thank you. I think that's the first nice thing you've said to me."

"Don't let it go to your head."

The next day, Jeff and Amber waited at the cross street where Amber had earlier seen the trucks. After a set of trucks went by, they followed at a safe distance and parked behind hills near the gate but out of sight. After the trucks they followed went in and another set of trucks left, they snuck up along the road behind their shields. Once they were close enough, they lay down on the side of the road with the shields on top of them and waited.

After two hours in the hot sun, trucks finally arrived. Guards boarded the trucks, but before they started moving, Jeff gave the signal and he and Amber rolled under a truck, leaving their shields behind. They used a leather strap to loop over the I-beam frame and hung by their wrists. They found places to rest their feet as the truck started to move.

Amber was really feeling the pain in her wrists and arms as the truck started to pick up speed. The road below had changed from worn pavement to crushed rock about the size of a dime. The truck rode much more smoothly, but a lot of dust made breathing difficult.

In less than five minutes, the truck slowed down and stopped, then started and stopped in a rhythmic pattern. Jeff saw a spot where the trucks moved close to some cargo crates. He released his hands and feet, then lay on the ground, looking around. He motioned Amber to do the same and said, "We move now."

Jeff rolled out from under the truck behind the crates. Amber followed shortly after.

"The trucks are going to that building. Do we try to go there?"

"No. There'll be a ton of guards in there. Besides, we can't see where they unload from here. I think our best bet is to go into that building through a side door."

Amber now noticed the enormous building to their right. It had to be five stories tall. The hills blocked their view of its length.

They moved quietly through piles of empty crates to a point about twenty-five yards away from a door of the building. A very bored guard was standing in the sun by the door. As the guard turned his back to the crates to pick up a water bottle, Jeff sprinted at the guard and knocked him into the building. The guard fell unconscious. Jeff checked the door. It was locked. He searched the guard's body for a few moments until he found a set of keys. Jeff unlocked the door and slowly peeked inside. He then dragged the guard inside and motioned for Amber to follow. Amber ran as fast as she could. She couldn't help but notice how much slower she was than Jeff.

They entered the building into a long, well-lit hallway. No one was there except them and the guard. Doors were evenly spaced all the way down the hall. No signs or labels were on the doors, just numbers.

Jeff quickly checked a few doors, only to find them locked. He threw the guard over his shoulder and went down the hall quickly, checking doors as he went. Eventually, one opened to reveal a maintenance room. Some electrical panels were against the back wall. The other two walls had shelves with various supplies on them. Amber noticed that some shelves held outfits that looked like medical clothing, the kind a doctor or nurse would wear. They then heard a noise in the hall and people talking in English. Jeff was in the room tying up the guard, so Amber closed the door enough for it to look closed, but she peeked out through a tiny opening to see what was going on in the hall.

A man dressed in a white lab coat with a Belgian accent was saying, "Where are my new specimens that resisted the process?"

A woman in a blue lab coat with a Spanish accent replied in an apologetic voice, "I am sorry, Doctor; they all died last night. I thought you knew."

The doctor put a hand on the woman's shoulder and said, "Do not worry, my dear. You cannot make an omelet without breaking a few eggs." Their voices trailed off as they passed through double doors at the end of the hall.

The door to the room they had exited was closing automatically but slowly. Amber ran over to the door to catch it before it closed; she quickly looked inside. Nothing was there except for some office furniture and a gurney with what appeared to be a body on it, but it was covered with a light blue sheet.

Jeff came into the room and closed the door to the point where it looked closed but was not fully shut. He moved a chair to block it from closing. They then both moved to the gurney.

Jeff removed the sheet. A black African female in her early thirties lay there naked. There were no signs of wounds or trauma. Amber thought the woman's face did not seem quite right, but she could not place exactly what was wrong. Amber told Jeff, "A doctor and a nurse were in the hall talking about a specimen that was resistant to a process. I don't know what they meant."

While Amber examined the body, Jeff started looking around the room. It contained no paper. No computer. Nothing but office furniture, the gurney, and the body. Jeff looked at Amber and shrugged his shoulders.

"We can use the medical clothing in the storage room to dress as a doctor and nurse," Amber suggested. "We should be able to move through this place without an issue."

"Did the doctor and nurse have badges?" Jeff asked.

"Not that I saw."

They made the room look just like they had found it, then moved back to the storage room. Amber saw the guard tied to a pipe leading into an electrical panel.

They checked the clothing and found sizes to fit them both, but they both had to be doctors in white. The nurses had to be small in this part of Africa.

Before they exited, Jeff said, "If we get into any trouble, just follow my lead. I may not be able to tell you what I'm going to do before I do it."

"I'll follow your lead," Amber said.

They moved quickly down the hall to the double doors. As they passed through them, they found themselves at the crossing of two halls. Amber said, "The others went right."

"I think we need to go straight to reach the main building," Jeff said. Amber nodded agreement and they moved forward.

They passed through another set of double doors into a larger hall that went right and left. A little off to the right were two guards in front of a set of double doors that seemed to lead into the main building.

Jeff grabbed Amber's hand and walked straight toward them. She was scared, but she did not let it show. The guards looked at them but did not stare or seem upset. Maybe Jeff had guessed right that seeing doctors in the building was a common occurrence. Jeff smiled at the guards as they were about to pass and suddenly threw himself into them. One was knocked unconscious by hitting his head against the door with a solid thud. The other was knocked down. Jeff jumped on him and knocked him unconscious.

Jeff tried to open the door, but it was locked. He frantically searched for keys on their bodies. Amber noticed the keys hanging from a ring on the wall as they approached. She grabbed them and handed them to Jeff. He smiled and unlocked the doors after a little fumbling.

Jeff looked inside quickly and gave the "all clear" sign. They each grabbed a guard and dragged them through the doors, then shut the doors behind them. "That went better than I expected," Jeff said. Amber gave him a surprised look but decided not to say anything.

They pulled the guards to the side and started to notice the gigantic room they were almost in. The entire inside of the building was open space. Amber wandered toward the room's center when Jeff grabbed her and pulled her back. "Let's make sure there are no more guards first," he said. Amber saw the logic in that.

On the ground floor, lots of beams, pipes, and machinery were on both sides of the room down its full length. It was about three football fields long and five stories tall. It was like the inside of a pyramid. The "floors" had large glass enclosures suspended from a conveyer belt moving along the walls. One "floor" moved in one direction. The next "floor" moved in the opposite direction.

Jeff found electrical wire and tied up the two guards. He then joined Amber in examining the room from behind equipment, but he was looking for enemies while she studied the room.

After a minute of study, Amber asked, "Do you hear that sound?"

Jeff listened and then noticed the room's ambient noise. It was composed of machinery sounds, vibrations, and something he could not describe. "I can't place that sound," he said. It felt scary, like being in a Halloween haunted house.

"We need to get to the next floor for a better look at what is moving along these walls," Amber said.

Jeff looked around and found ladder rungs built into the walls. He climbed up one about halfway, then signaled Amber to follow.

When they got to the next level, they saw the other side of the room more clearly, but the near side was obstructed by a thin sheet of metal. Amber saw long rows of large, inverted glass test tubes. A framework of some sort was inside each one. When they found an opening on their side of the room, they saw the same giant glass tubes, filled with smoke or gas. The odd sound was definitely coming from inside the tubes, but for some reason, it seemed louder farther off to their right and quieter to their left. Each tube hung from a conveyor belt arm that attached to frames that extended into the glass tubes.

They decided to climb higher to see if anything was different above them. The next floor was the same, except the tubes were running in the opposite direction. Jeff noticed a poisonous warning label near the base of the glass tubes. The gas was thinning a little, but it was still too hard to see what was inside, so they climbed up another floor.

This floor was identical to the others, but this time, they noticed a device that connected to the tube and injected some clear liquid. As they walked a little way, they could start to make out what was inside the tube. Jeff saw it first, and his face turned ash white. Amber had a harder time making it out, but then suddenly, she moved her hands to her mouth. Her eyes grew wild with panic, and she started to run away, straight off the three-story walkway. Jeff grabbed her just in time to prevent her falling.

Amber was in a full panic attack. Flailing and panting, she screamed out, "Oh my God! There are people in there!"

Jeff subdued her, gently hugged her, and said in a calm voice, "I know. Just breathe."

"That sound," Amber said, holding her ears. "It's people moaning in pain." She tried to claw her way toward the tubes, saying, "We have to free them."

Jeff held her firmly and whispered to her, "Just breathe. Calm yourself. We will do what we can once we are calm."

Thousands of people were dying all around them. They were locked to a steel frame, injected with chemicals, and forced to breathe poisonous gases. The situation's inhumanity overwhelmed Amber. She looked up at Jeff while covering her ears, then buried her face in his chest and cried.

She was not sure how long she cried, but Jeff was right there with her the entire time. Finally, she could remove her hands from her ears without breaking down into tears. She focused on how to get information about this building to the rest of the world. Steeling her nerves, she broke free of the fear that had overwhelmed her.

Amber wiped the tears from her eyes and looked up at Jeff. For the first time, she noticed he was crying too. They were lying down against the outer wall, curled up together.

"We need to free these people," Amber said.

"We can't."

"Why not?"

"The gas they're in is toxic. They're already dead. If we free them, it will kill us too."

"How do you know?" Amber asked.

"There are markings on these tubes. See the skull and crossbones at the bottom."

Amber pulled away and stood up. She straightened her clothes and said, "Their leader must be in this facility. There must be a control room somewhere."

"We've been lucky so far, Amber. If we push our luck, we may not make it out of here alive. It's our job now to report back with what we've seen."

"We need something more than our word to convince anyone that this place actually exists. We need hard evidence," Amber said. "I'm going to take pictures while you look for a control room."

"If I had to guess, it looks like they're coming in from that end at the ground floor, snaking upward through these levels, and the top level delivers the result at the same end but the opposite side of the building. If we climb to the top level and head that way, we can see what happens at the end."

Amber nodded her head in agreement and said, "Let's climb."

It was hard work climbing to the top floor on small, steel ladder rungs, but they moved quickly. They both sensed they were running out of time. They followed a gangway in the direction the tubes were heading on the top floor. The dead and dying bodies were easily seen through a thin haze of gas. They tried not to look at them, but then Amber noticed lines running from the bottom of the victim's legs to a collection container at the bottom of the platform each inverted test tube was resting on.

Amber then noticed the emotions running through her: hate, fear, dread, anger, and a deep fatigue. She was a wreck, but she stayed focused on reaching the end of the gangway.

Only then did she hear Jeff saying, "Stay focused. Keep alert. We just need to reach the end of this walkway. Try not to look at the people. We can stop this only if we make it out of here alive."

Amber was not sure if Jeff was saying this for her or for himself. Either way, he was a real pro. He had probably saved her life. "Thank you, Jeff," she said.

Jeff stopped to look back at her, confused. "For what?"

"For keeping us focused," she said. "Now let's keep going."

They picked up the pace and jogged most of the way to the end of the building. Jeff was right. The input and output were both coming from the same place. They slowed and approached stealthily as they neared the end.

There was still no sign of anyone in the building. No maintenance crews. No operators. No janitorial staff. Nothing besides the dead and dying.

The tubes moved at the same pace as they approached the wall at the end of the building. They passed through a dark passageway as they lost elevation rapidly. An observation platform was near the opening. Jeff and Amber approached it cautiously.

They peeked out the side of a giant window. They saw the entire operation running below them. Amber examined the process closely. A few men wearing gas masks were moving around machinery lined up in assembly-line fashion. There were four assembly lines. The tubes descended and were transferred to another conveyer system. Then the tubes gradually turned on their sides, with the humans inside facing up. An arm extended out to grab hold of the glass test tube. The last of the gasses seemed to be sucked out of the tube. When the arm gave a quarter turn, the tube disappeared under the floor.

"That's not the ground floor," Amber said. "The tubes are going under the floor."

"I see it."

Only the frame, the base, and the person inside remained. The entire base then rotated to the other side of the conveyor so that the victim was now facing down. He hung there limp and lifeless. Amber's hands started shaking, and her eyes were tearing up as her fear, anger, and empathy combined to almost overwhelm her. She sat back to wipe her eyes, clasped her hands together, and steeled her nerves. Once she was calm, she went back to observing.

Then Amber noticed a small container dropped from a platform into a metal chute in the floor. It rolled down under the floor. Amber tapped Jeff and pointed. "See that slot in the floor?" Jeff nodded. "Do you see the containers dropping from each one as it passes?" Jeff nodded again. "I noticed something attached to the legs of the people inside the capsules. Whatever this operation is doing, I think that container is the intended result. We need to get one."

Jeff went back to the gangway to look at a passing capsule. He then went back to Amber at the observation window and looked at the small containers dropping through the floor down a metal chute. "I think you're right," he said.

After dropping the capsule, the conveyor started to turn. Its human victim was hanging out over the floor. At the apex of the turn was a large bin that came up out of the floor on another conveyor. The frame released the victim, who then dropped into the bin. Twenty-five victims dropped into the bin before the conveyor cycled a new bin to replace the full one. The frame then turned upright and disappeared under the floor.

Amber said in disgust, "This is all so clinical. So mechanical. Who could do something like this?"

"There are a lot of automated manufacturing facilities in the world," Jeff replied. "Japanese and German car plants, food processing and computer chip manufacturing in the United States. But this is… elegant."

Upset by this remark, Amber asked, "What?"

"Look at it, Amber. It is so simple, so well-orchestrated," Jeff said. "It's difficult to make things simple. If you look at it objectively, it is very well designed. We just need to find out what it's designed to do."

Amber had to admit Jeff had a point, but she was still angry. "Let's find a way downstairs to figure out what's in that container."

"We need to get out of here soon. Those guards are going to be found sooner or later," Jeff said.

They backtracked along the gangway until they found a ladder leading down. They quietly moved down level by level, looking for an entrance at each one. On the first floor was a door. Jeff tested it and found it locked. Fortunately, he had kept the keys from the entrance door, and to his surprise, they worked. These people really did not understand security.

As Jeff peeked inside, he saw a large room with a door on each side. Each door had a window in it, except for the one leading to the large factory they had just exited. As they peered through each window and checked the doors, they found them all unlocked. The right and left doors led down long halls. The one straight ahead led down a shorter hall to double doors.

"Let's go straight," Amber said. "The assembly lines we saw have to be straight ahead and above us, I hope."

"Let's just play the doctor card and walk right in like we own the place. If we get any surprises, follow my lead."

Amber did not like the plan, but she did not have a better one, so she nodded agreement.

When they walked through the double doors, Amber started talking as if they were colleagues discussing a patient. "Doctor, when I looked at the test results, I was surprised to find it. We need to check the process output to validate the results."

Jeff was looking around the long narrow room. Once again, everything was automated, and no one was there. After confirming the room was empty, they started looking for the opening in the floor. They found the metal chute leading into a hopper that processed each canister one by one. A disk was spinning slowly at the bottom of the hopper. With each revolution, it would grab and align one canister and move it into a machine next to the hopper. Jeff reached in and grabbed a canister. He pulled a plastic baggie from a hidden pocket inside his shirt and put the canister inside.

As they moved toward the door, Amber said, "We have what they were producing, but we don't know why, or who is doing this."

"I don't think we'll find that here," Jeff said.

"Why not?" Amber asked as she grabbed Jeff's arm and stopped him.

Jeff held up the canister in the plastic bag and said, "Because this place is too automated. Anyone smart enough to build this is smart enough to run it from somewhere else. Our best chance to find out who is doing this and why is to follow the trail this leads us down."

"Okay," said Amber, "but let's get a look at the other end of this factory if we can. It might tell us something."

"Honestly," Jeff replied, "I don't want to see it. Besides, it's probably just the reverse of what we saw. They probably gas people to make them unconscious. The platform with the frame comes out of the floor; they strap people in and put the test tube thing on top to seal them in. We really have to go."

Amber thought about it. Her instincts were telling her to investigate further, but Jeff was probably right about the need to leave soon. They had to get the canister analyzed and figure out what they were doing.

She reluctantly said, "Okay, let's go."

Jeff was leading them to the opposite side of the factory building. He noticed the trucks entering on one side and heading out the other. He wanted to position them near the exit and find a point where they could hide until they made their move.

On their way out, they walked into a hallway with a doctor walking alone right toward them.

THE GREAT ESCAPE

Amber flinched involuntarily when the doctor entered the hallway and looked right at them. Jeff was calm and unaffected. He walked confidently down the hall like he owned it.

The doctor continued to look at them curiously but did not seem alarmed. He said, "Hello" as he approached. Jeff and Amber nodded back at him and continued walking by. "Hello," he said again. They stopped and said, "Hello."

"I am Johan," the doctor said. "You must be new here."

"Yes, we are," Amber said as she smiled. "We are a little lost to be honest. This place is so big."

"Yes, well, it can be confusing. I have to run to my lab to check on something, but it will be quick, and I can take you where you are going," Johan said. "Follow me."

"Thank you," Amber said politely. "Lead the way."

After Johan passed, Jeff gave Amber a look that said, *'Lead the way.' Are you kidding me?*

Amber mouthed back, *Follow my lead.*

Jeff was not happy, but they were committed.

Johan's lab was close by and he was eager to get there. As he unlocked the room, he said, "It will be just a moment." The room was filled with equipment and what looked like scientific tests, but there were no people there other than them.

Amber took the opportunity to start asking questions. "Johan, what do you do here?"

Johan was checking some equipment and making small adjustments. "Oh, a lot of this and a little of that," he said, chuckling.

"No need to be shy; we all do important work here," Amber replied.

Johan finished what he was doing and went to a cluttered desk to get something from a drawer. Just then, Jeff dashed around the desk to grab Johan's hand. In it was a short-barreled revolver. Jeff disarmed the man easily, claiming the revolver for his own.

Now with the revolver pointed at Johan, Jeff said, "Once again, Johan, what do you do here?"

Johan was briefly scared. Then he stood tall and proudly said, "I am the head of research at this facility, and you are trespassing."

Jeff laughed and said, "Trespassing? The crimes you are committing go far beyond trespassing."

Johan looked a little pale for a moment. Then he said, "The people running this facility have created one of the most technologically advanced research centers in the world. We know more about the human body than anyone else on the globe."

"Do you really need to kill so many people? How does this research require the deaths of thousands?"

"It does not," Johan said. "I do not know why they are doing that."

"Then why are you here?" Amber demanded.

"Because I am able to do research that no one else can do. I have a dedicated staff that is blissfully unaware of what is going on here. We are creating the building blocks to improve the human genome. We have the basic research nearly complete to find a cure for many diseases like cancer. We can even cure the common cold if given enough time. This facility is amazing."

"Is it worth the price?" Amber asked as she shook her head.

"This knowledge is worth any price. This facility will enable me to bring a new age of medical science to the world. It is revolutionary."

"What are they extracting from those dead bodies, Johan? What is this?" Jeff asked as he held up the canister.

"The owners of this facility have a set of rules. None of us know what they are doing or why. I can swear to that," Johan said with confidence.

He looked at his watch and added, "Look outside in about ten minutes and you'll get a sense of who the owners really are."

Amber and Jeff looked at each other but said nothing.

Jeff stepped forward and knocked Johan unconscious with a right cross to the chin. Johan fell to the floor and did not move.

"I really wish I could have done that," Amber said.

Jeff smiled and said, "I'll teach you."

They looked around the room quickly but found nothing they could use or carry with them. They returned to the hall and ran down their original path. They reached a door at the end of the hall. Jeff put his hand on the door and felt warmth. That meant it was an outside door facing the afternoon sun. They were right where he wanted them to be.

"I'm going to play the doctor card again," Jeff told Amber. "Stay inside until I signal for you to exit."

Amber nodded and leaned against the wall next to the door. As Jeff went out, she peeked out the door, which she held slightly open.

Jeff stepped outside to find a guard sitting in the hot afternoon sun. He was surprised and stood up, but he did not grab his rifle. Jeff looked around as he said, "Hello." Jeff saw no other people, so he grabbed the rifle and hit the guard hard in one smooth, swift move and dropped him to the ground. He dragged the guard inside, took his keys, and locked the door after Amber came out. Jeff grabbed the guard's rifle and they moved quickly into another cluster of discarded cargo crates.

They heard the trucks, but it took them a few minutes to find their way. Jeff saw a spot near the truck's exit path where they would stop at a crossroad. They were going to have to get closer to the building exit than he wanted, but there was no choice if they were going to exit the way they came in.

They moved back through the crates and ran to the edge of the building where a number of vans were parked. Jeff told Amber, "We are only going to get one shot at getting on a truck. See how they are stopping as they approach the cross street. We need to get under and ready in about five seconds. Can you do it?"

"Do I have a choice?" Amber joked. Jeff stared at her with a serious expression. "Okay, I can do it. I will do it."

Just then, there was a strange noise. It was strong but not loud. It reverberated in their chests like they were standing next to a big bass drum. Suddenly, a yellow light appeared from the other side of the big building. As they moved to get a better view, they saw the light moving up into the sky. It started off fast—faster than anything Jeff had ever seen before. It moved faster as it rose into the sky. As it vanished from sight, it had to be moving at thousands of miles per hour.

Amber took a few pictures before the light disappeared. She asked Jeff, "What was that? A rocket?"

"If that was a rocket, we would be dead from the exhaust gases," Jeff said. "That was no rocket. Its propulsion system is like nothing I've ever seen."

"Is it Russian?" Amber asked.

Jeff gave a short laugh and said, "The Russians can't make that." He cut Amber off and said, "No, it's not one of ours."

Confused, Amber asked, "If it's not Russian and not one of ours, then who made it?"

Jeff looked up into the sky and said, "That is a very good question."

Amber looked up into the sky and realized what Jeff was saying. She looked scared and shaken.

Jeff took her by the shoulders and said, "We need to get out of here. Follow me."

As they moved closer to the entrance, another van pulled up, parked, and the driver ran inside the doorway with a package. The van was close to where they needed to be and provided perfect cover.

They made their move then, running behind the van and timing their jump to the next truck. The truck stopped, they rolled under, threw their hand straps over the I-beams under the truck, and Jeff got his feet up just as the truck started to move. Amber was too slow, and her feet slipped from the metal box she tried to rest them on. Her feet were dragging as the truck picked up speed. She was scared and didn't know what to do.

Jeff yelled, "Try holding one foot down while you put the other one up!"

When Amber gave it a try, it worked. She was able to get her foot high enough to find a perch until she could bring the other one up to its final resting place. Her shoulders and wrists hurt like they were on fire, but she held on for dear life.

The truck slowed at the gate, then came to a stop as the guards left the trucks.

Jeff told Amber to get ready. He signaled. They both dropped and rolled off the road, into a dirty gulley. They lay there motionless and covered in dust until the trucks left.

Jeff grabbed Amber's arm and led her through the dust kicked up by the trucks toward their car. After a few minutes of walking, Jeff said, "We're free and clear." Amber was rubbing her wrists and working her tortured shoulders to relieve the pain.

They moved quietly back to their car and followed a safe distance behind the trucks, back to the main road, and their safe house. They drove in silence like zombies for the first forty-five minutes. Their minds were so overloaded they just needed time to process all they had seen.

Amber was the first to break the silence. "I can't believe what we just saw. A UFO, thousands of people being mechanically murdered, and fanatic scientists indifferent to it all. I want to look at these pictures, but I'm afraid to."

"I'm going to have a tall stiff drink before I do anything else."

"I don't drink. My father was an alcoholic. He wasn't a nice man."

"I'm sorry. I hope you don't mind if I do."

"No. I just won't be joining you."

"The agency taught me to face my fear and be calm when everything around me is falling apart. I don't think I've ever had to draw on those skills more than today."

"I fell apart in that room today. I was overwhelmed."

"I've seen some horrible things over the last seven years. I've done things…but none of them compare with today. Nothing could prepare you for that. You recovered quickly and focused on the job." Jeff held up the metal container they took from the facility. "You led us to this."

"I hope it's enough."

"I've been thinking about the facility. We saw twenty-five people going into each bin when we were at the observation window. I'd say about four bins fit on one truck. There were about 100 trucks going in and out each day. That makes it 10,000 per day."

They were both quiet for a few minutes. Amber sat with her hands over her face and her elbows on her knees. Jeff couldn't tell whether she was crying. He gave her some time to sort through her emotions.

Amber was overwhelmed by what she had seen, but she fought to regain control of herself. If she let the despair she was feeling overtake her, she would not be able to do what needed to be done to bring the news of this atrocity to the rest of the world.

Taking control of her emotions, she said, "What do we do next?"

"We analyze the data and report back to our superiors."

"I can construct a timeline of events and detailed descriptions of what we saw and did."

"Really? That would be great."

"It's my specialty," Amber said.

"I'll start with an analysis and key messages for my report."

"Key messages?"

"The salient points. The details that matter most. It's how we communicate in the agency. Analysts pour over the details. The leaders just want the key messages."

"Do you think we did the right thing leaving that scientist alive?"

"He was no threat to us once I knocked him out. Besides, I have his full name from a paper on his desk. I'll add it to my report," Jeff said with a smile.

Amber returned the smile, and then they rode the rest of the way in silent thought.

They were ready to get to work until they spotted armed men around their safe house.

NO SAFETY

As Amber and Jeff approached the safe house, it was getting dark. Instinct told Jeff to slow down and turn off the headlights. As they rounded a hill, they could see armed men in front of the safe house in the distance and enough vehicles to suggest there were more inside.

Jeff used the emergency brake to slow down without brake lights and rolled to a stop behind a hill. He lowered the windows and listened for pursuit. No engines had started, and no tires were crunching over the rocky road.

"Who are they?" Amber asked.

"I don't know, but I'm going to hide the car and go get a better look on foot."

Jeff slowly rolled their car between some hills that hid it from the road. He then opened the back of the SUV to grab binoculars and a pistol.

"Take this, Amber," Jeff said as he handed Amber the pistol.

"I really don't like guns."

"Get over it. This is the safety. Aim. Fire. Just like that." Jeff forced the pistol into Amber's hand and said, "Stay here."

Amber took the pistol and seriously considered pointing it at Jeff for a few seconds.

Jeff climbed the hills nearby to get a better view and zoomed in on the men around the safe house. They were Burkina Faso border police, and they were armed with AK47s and shotguns. He could not see if Emil was there. They looked like they were staying put for the night.

Jeff slid down the hill and went back to the car to talk with Amber. He sat in the driver's seat and said, "It looks like Burkina Faso border police are waiting for us to return."

"What do they want?"

"It's not a welcoming committee. They're either here to arrest us or execute us."

"Execute? Why execute?"

"They're too well armed for an arrest warrant."

"Where do we go then?"

"I'm going to assume Burkina Faso is no longer friendly territory. I'd say we head to Mali, then fly to Algiers."

"Why Mali?"

"It's nearby, somewhat lawless, and I think we can buy some passports there."

"Why do we need passports?"

"I'll bet yours is in the house."

"Damn it! My phone and my computer are there too," said Amber.

"Also, the first rule when things go bad is to assume the worst. I'm going to assume someone here knows where we went and wants us dead. So we need to change our names and get to a safe place. I know I can find help in Algiers."

"Okay, then how do we get to Algiers? It must be 1,000 miles away."

"More like 1,200. We can take back roads across the border and drive to Timbuktu. It's only 170 or so miles away. From there, we get passports and fly to Algiers."

"Okay. How do we find these back roads over the border?"

"The CIA provides," Jeff said with a smile as he took out a detailed map with several routes highlighted. "You're my co-pilot. We're here," he said, pointing, "and need to follow this route."

Amber's voice was thick with sarcasm as she said, "This should be fun!"

Their route was tedious and tiring, but the border crossing went smoothly. They eventually found their way to a major road in Mali and drove north to Timbuktu. They only stopped for food, gas, and bathroom breaks, usually on the side of the road.

Jeff knew a little about Timbuktu and found a small cash-only hotel on the outskirts of town just as the sun was setting. After checking in and getting the key, they went into the small hotel room. It had a double bed, a desk, a closet, and a bathroom.

"Yes, a bathroom," Amber said. "Is this my room?"

"It's our room."

"I hope you like the floor."

"I'll probably be gone all night. I'm going to look for passports. I need a good photo of you."

"Use the News Corp website. They have headshots and bios on every reporter. I used that picture for my passport."

"Great! You still have the gun I gave you?"

"Yes, unfortunately."

"Keep the door locked and don't let anyone in. We should assume whoever wanted us dead in Burkina Faso will still be looking."

"With a network of multinational corporations and spaceships, they must have spies too. I get it. I'm planning on taking a shower and going to bed."

"I'll try to be back by morning. Goodnight."

"Before you go, there's one piece of this puzzle I can't work out. Who were the men at that facility? They couldn't be the Burkina Faso Army, and they didn't look like locals."

"They had to be a private army. Mercenaries most likely."

"I thought that too, at first, but would some random mercenaries murder thousands of people like that? I don't think so. They had to be some kind of fanatics to do that."

"I see your point."

"And that doctor. He seemed to be blinded by science. He knew what was happening but didn't care. The ends justified the means. I think there's some greater cause these people are lining up behind. They must have some motivation to do these horrible things."

"We can talk more about it later. For now, I have to go. Goodnight."

✳ ✳ ✳

Amber couldn't remember where she was when she woke up the next morning. Jeff was nowhere to be found. She started to panic, worried that she had been left stranded. She looked outside the window upon a strange city. Then she took three deep breaths to calm herself and think. She remembered the long drive, the hotel room, and Jeff leaving. After settling her nerves, Amber decided to take control of the situation and get ready for the day. If Jeff returned, great. If not, she would figure things out as she always did.

After getting dressed and ready for travel, she looked in the mirror at her hair and laughed. What a mess. She had to comb it out for close to half an hour to get it untangled and somewhat in order. "I am going to need a trip to a salon," she said to herself. She heard some noise in the room and cautiously cracked open the bathroom door. She saw Jeff carrying a bag and came out into the room. "What did you get us?" she asked.

"Breakfast and passports," Jeff said, flashing the Algerian passports.

"Thank you for the breakfast," Amber said. "What's the plan for today?"

"We eat, go to the Timbuktu airport, and fly to Algiers."

"Veronica Mason?" Amber asked after reading her passport.

"It's based on some online research," Jeff said defensively. "And a little improvisation."

Amber stared at the name a few minutes before closing the passport. Jeff could tell she did not like it.

"I know nothing about Algeria. What happens if someone asks me questions?" Amber asked.

"That's about to change. We're going to Algeria next. If anyone asks lots of questions, just say you grew up in the US. You're visiting for the first time."

"Why Algeria?" Amber asked.

"It's easy for an Algerian to get into France, and some American soldiers took Algerian wives after World War II. Their children still have Algerian citizenship, so they're used to seeing Americans with Algerian passports."

"Who are you?"

"Alfred Mason, your husband."

"My husband?"

"Couples clear customs easier than singles. We don't have to kiss for them or anything."

"Okay, let's get this over with."

"That's the spirit," Jeff said sarcastically.

They left their guns and most of their belongings in the black SUV. Jeff set a time-delayed signal that would trigger CIA satellites to find the car.

Jeff knew there was a flight in a few hours. They bought tickets and boarded the plane without incident.

Amber was scared and could not eat or sleep, while Jeff slept the entire flight. Amber had to shake him to wake him up before they landed.

They cleared customs and grabbed a taxi to a market deep in the city. As they exited the cab, Amber started noticing the clothes people were wearing and how they interacted with one another. They were going to need new clothes to blend in. Amber also noticed that all the men and most of the women were staring at her. She was going to need to hide her hair and eyes.

Jeff led them down a labyrinth of small streets and back alleys. It felt like they were moving in circles until they finally stopped at an old hotel. They approached it from a back alley.

"Wait here while I get us a room," Jeff said.

Amber waited in the building's shadow cast by the afternoon sun. There was almost no foot traffic near this building. One main entrance led into a central courtyard. She guessed there were many ways out of the building's back and sides. The building was three stories high with shutters currently all opened. The paint was light pink or faded red. The coloring wiped off on your hand, leaving a light powdery layer like a table with dust on it. She was wondering how old the building was when Jeff returned.

They went up to the third story to the last room on that floor. The hotel suite had a table, chairs, and a couch in one room and a separate bedroom. The bathroom was also not connected to the bedroom.

As they entered the main room, Amber said, "It felt like we were going in circles on the way here."

"We were. Let's face it; you stand out in a crowd. I was making sure we weren't being followed."

"Isn't that a little paranoid?"

"Paranoia keeps me alive. Someone might follow you just because you're a beautiful foreigner and sell that information to anyone who is looking. We need to be paranoid."

"All right. I noticed our clothes don't fit in here, and I need to cover my hair and eyes so I don't stand out so much. I want to go shopping."

"Okay, but not just yet. I need to make some contacts first. Can we go this evening?"

"Sure. I want to start writing about our adventures so far anyway. Can we get some paper from the front desk?"

"I'll take care of it on my way out."

Jeff returned with twenty pieces of paper and two ballpoint pens. He then left.

While he was gone, Amber worked on writing down all their experiences and analyzing her notes.

✳ ✳ ✳

Jeff returned after dark with their dinner and several bags.

"What did you get?" Amber asked as she looked through the bags. "Ammonia, bleach, mothballs?"

"I will be making some explosives. Nothing too dangerous."

"Oh, good. I thought all explosives were dangerous. What is this, a harpoon gun?"

"This will set a spike with a cable attached into any building." He walked into a bedroom and opened the window. Several smaller buildings surrounded the one they were in. An alley in the back ran between the buildings. "We can look out this window, see what we are up against, pick a building to fire the spike into, and slide down the cable to safety." Jeff finished with a smile.

"Okay," Amber said. She couldn't help but think this was all a little crazy, but Jeff had saved their lives more than once.

"I also have something far more important. Information." Jeff smiled again. "I'm going to meet with some people at the market. They should be able to help me get in touch with the CIA. I'll leave you here with most of the money and this." He showed her a 9-mm pistol. "Fully automatic. Just unlock the safety like this, point, and pull the trigger. It's very effective at close range. And it'll punch through these walls so be careful where you point it."

"I really don't like guns," Amber said.

Jeff put the gun in Amber's hand. "We're targets, Amber. You need to protect yourself if the worst happens. If I'm not back by nightfall tomorrow, you need to pack up and move on."

Jeff's words stunned Amber. She had thought the worst was behind them, but now she was realizing this journey had just begun, and the dangers were just as bad now, if not worse.

"Okay," was all she said.

"Keep that near so you can grab it quickly," Jeff added.

Amber just shook her head in agreement. Her eyes were tearing up.

"What's wrong?" Jeff asked.

"I don't know. I guess I thought we were out of danger. I'm scared. Every time you leave could be the last time I see you," Amber said.

"I can't promise you I'll return. I'd be lying if I made that promise, but I will do my best to return, and that is no small thing."

"If I went to the market to get some local clothing, would that be a problem?"

"You should wait for me to return. If I don't, you should leave and not come back here. It won't be safe," Jeff said.

"Take care of yourself, Jeff," Amber said with a forced smile.

Jeff returned the smile. He packed up a few things into his small backpack, slung it over one shoulder, and left their room.

Amber checked the street and alley a few times, and then decided the best way to spend her time would be to continue writing their story.

Writing required focus, which helped Amber not to become obsessive over how long Jeff was gone, though she did find herself frequently checking the clock.

Amber also noticed a change in the way she was thinking about this journey. It was now *their story*, not her story. Was she developing feelings for Jeff?

WHY MAYO?

When Amber woke the next day, she again couldn't remember where she was. Jeff was gone. She started to panic until she looked out the front door and saw the courtyard below. She was in Algeria. She calmed herself and started to wonder if she was going crazy. This was the second time she had woken up not knowing where she was. The stress was getting to her.

She decided the best thing to do now was to focus on the story. She grabbed a piece of bread leftover from dinner and starting pacing around the room as she spoke to herself.

"Here is what we know so far: A network of corporations is generating a great deal of wealth for a few owners. Jeff's boss is on the board of directors for at least two of these companies. They are shipping materials to an alleged mine in Burkina Faso, but the materials do not make sense for a mining operation.

"Fanatics are kidnapping people in northern Burkina Faso at this mine and killing them to produce this." She walked over to the canister they had taken from the facility and looked at it as she turned it in her hand.

"I have no idea what this is or why they're making it. We know this facility launched a vehicle of some sort into space. The propulsion system was unlike anything my CIA friend has ever seen.

"Our allies from France and Burkina Faso were ordered to drop everything and return to their offices immediately. The CIA gave Jeff the same order, but he refused.

"Armed men from the Burkina Faso border police came to our safe house to arrest us or worse.

"For these things to happen, there must be a conspiracy between these corporations and at least three governments. There must be some entity coordinating these activities for them to happen so fast. There is a link between all of these actions, but what is it? Why isn't that space launch all over the news? Burkina Faso cannot afford a space program."

Amber sat down and started analyzing the data she had. She worked until she ran out of paper late in the afternoon. She had eaten all the leftovers and was getting hungry for dinner.

She was considering going out to eat and shop when she heard a knock at the door.

"Amber, it's me," Jeff said in a low voice in the hall.

Amber cracked open the door, then opened it wide when she saw it was Jeff and he was alone. "You made it back," she said with a smile.

"I hope you like falafels," Jeff said.

Amber noticed his face was red on one side and his knuckles were bleeding. "What happened?"

"Local thieves, I think. Nothing I couldn't handle. I have some good news and some bad news."

"What's the good news?"

"I got in contact with Dureau. We're going to meet up with his team in the Balearic Islands."

"That's north of here in the Mediterranean, between North Africa and Spain."

"Right. You know your geography. We're going to find an inn on one of the smaller islands until I can make contact. The town is called Mahon today, but in the 1600s, it was called Mao. They claim it's where mayonnaise was invented."

"Really?"

"Really!"

"Why are they going to help us now when they couldn't before?"

"Well, that's the bad news. I'm no longer employed by the CIA."

"What?"

"And you're no longer employed by News Corp."

"What?"

"We both have bounties on our heads greater than $1 million."

Amber sat down and stared out the window for a few minutes.

After a minute, Jeff asked, "Are you all right, Amber?"

"Is there anything else I should know?"

"Someone placed a private contract on you. Private hit men look for stupid mistakes. Credit card charges, phone calls, air travel, or bus travel under your name. Do not use your real name and they will not try very hard to find you. I, on the other hand, have multiple nations looking for me."

"At least we know where we stand. This doesn't explain why Dureau is now helping us."

Jeff was impressed with how quickly she had recovered from the news. She was completely calm and in control. "There are strange things going on in his government. He believes the same thing is happening in the United States, and he wants to resist it."

"What kinds of strange things?"

"He didn't say, but he will when we meet him. We leave tomorrow morning at 10 a.m. by boat. I believe you wanted to go shopping."

Amber smiled and said, "I could really use a shopping trip right about now."

They packed Jeff's small backpack with some money and weapons before heading out into the city. Jeff expertly navigated the side roads and back alleys to the market. Amber knew what she was looking for. She bought big sunglasses that seemed popular with the locals and a light gray scarf to cover her hair. After picking out a few outfits, she helped Jeff pick out some new clothes. They found a small restaurant with private alcoves built into the walls. They were able to relax, eat, drink, and talk. This was the first normal meal they'd had together. They enjoyed each other's company.

After dinner, they made their way back to the hotel. Jeff made the same three circles where he doubled back on their path to ensure they were not being followed. Once they were back in the room, Amber went to the bedroom to try on her new clothes while Jeff sat at the table and started cleaning and inspecting the guns.

When Amber came out of the bedroom, she wore the local clothes she had just bought, a white head covering with big sunglasses, a light blue top, and slightly darker trousers.

"How do you like it?" she asked.

Jeff looked up from his work briefly and said, "That should work just fine tomorrow." He then went back to work on the next gun.

His lack of interest was annoying and reminded her how self-absorbed he was.

Amber decided to go to bed early. The travel and stress were catching up to her. When she decided to check on Jeff one more time before going to bed, she found him making explosives.

"What are you planning to blow up?" Amber asked playfully.

"I'm shaping these charges to create a distraction in the hallway if anyone approaches that door, and I'm making a breaching charge for that wall, so we can move to the room next door if needed."

"How will you know who's at the door?" Amber asked. "It could just be the landlord with a question."

Jeff threw her a small device and said, "Turn that on."

Amber played with the device until she found the on switch and saw a small screen light up. It was a camera with a small display screen. A small flexible tube and the video screen showed whatever the tube pointed at. "Wow, that is so cool!" Amber said as she pointed it at Jeff. "This doesn't have a gun in it or anything, right?"

Jeff laughed. "No, we don't have enough money for anything like that, but I like the idea."

"Is all this really necessary?"

"I hope not."

"Well, I'm going to bed. Try not to blow us up," said Amber.

The next morning, they woke early. Jeff had spent the night on the couch.

As they finished packing, Amber heard some strange noises outside. She checked the hall camera and saw six armed men dressed in black moving down the hallway. She called Jeff.

Jeff looked at the hall camera and said, "Time for Plan C." He quickly took the explosive wiring and ran it into the bedroom. He moved the bed to reveal a large circle outlined in plastic explosives.

"Under my bed?" Amber exclaimed.

Jeff looked at her and said, "It's perfectly safe. Run to the bathroom now and cover your ears. Open your mouth and breathe out when I say 'Now.'" He then ran back to the triggering device, wired in the new contact, and hit the firing button. He ran to the bathroom and yelled, "Now!"

At that moment, they heard shouting coming from the hallway outside their door. It was in Arabic, so they could not understand the words, but it sounded like a request to surrender or else.

Three blasts all went off at the same time. One blew a hole in the bedroom floor, one in the wall to the apartment next door, and one blasted the men in the hall from the top of the doorway.

Amber was stunned, and her ears were ringing, but she followed Jeff when he pulled her arm to leave the bathroom. Jeff had a rope tied to the bed. He dropped their bags through the hole, then handed Amber the rope and motioned her to climb down. She was starting to recover and moved as quickly as she could. Jeff pulled the bed back over the hole as he climbed down with three bags dangling from his shoulders. They were in the bedroom of the apartment below theirs. It was empty, but it was a mess.

Jeff went to the window and opened it. He took the harpoon out of one bag and fired a spike into the wall across the alley just above an open second-story window. "I'll go through first," he said. "You'll have to carry this backpack." He put the pack on her and gave her the leather straps she would use to slide over. She wrapped them around her wrists and moved toward the window.

Jeff was in the windowsill and sliding over with two bags strapped to him. He crashed into the window, breaking it and making a hole for Amber. Jeff came back to the window with a pistol at the ready. He looked at the rooms they occupied just above them, then signaled for Amber to go. She was scared and still a little shaken from the blast, but she did not hesitate when he signaled. She set the strap and leapt out, sliding toward the window. The spike was a little off to the right side, but Amber noticed it too late. Her hip hit the window's edge as she went through. Her landing set her spinning, and she hit her head on a table leg.

She was hurt and lay still in pain for a few seconds. Jeff came over and knelt next to her, his weapon still at the ready. She finally heard him speaking to her.

"Amber, can you hear me? Say something!"

"Ouch!" was all she could say.

"Can you stand, Amber? We have to get out of here," Jeff said.

"Let me try." Amber rolled onto her uninjured side and slowly tried to stand. She found she could stand, but her hip hurt more when she put weight on it. She then felt pain on the side of her skull. She touched her head for a few seconds, but her hand didn't come away with any blood.

Jeff lifted her chin and looked into her eyes. He didn't see any signs of concussion. "I think you'll be okay if you can walk," he said.

Amber gave it a try. It hurt badly at first, but she got better with each new step. Together, they quickly exited the building and moved into the crowded streets. Fortunately, they had their new clothes on and blended in with the crowd. Jeff hid the pistol in his pants.

"I'm sorry you got hurt," he said.

Amber looked at him through her large sunglasses and said with a little smile, "Too bad we didn't leave earlier."

Jeff admired her toughness.

They moved as quickly as they could through the streets. Jeff steered them toward the market where he caught a three-wheel taxi. They piled in and traveled through the maze of streets and heavy traffic until they were close to the wharf. Jeff made it look like they were stopping at a restaurant. The doorman even had the doors open for them as they exited the taxi, but they turned and walked on toward the wharf.

Jeff had traveled to the wharf the day before to make his contact. A good-sized sailboat was waiting at the pre-decided pier. Amber waited on the wharf walkway while he checked out the pier and the boat. After he made his down payment, he signaled her to join him. They immediately went belowdecks into a small cabin. They could feel the boat moving shortly after they entered the cabin.

Jeff checked Amber's head wound and found it was just a bruise. It would be tender for a few days, but without any permanent damage. He then looked at her hip. There was a massive bruise, and it was tender as he probed the wound, but her bones were fine. They just needed to do something about the swelling, so Jeff exited the cabin to talk to the captain.

He came back with a bucket of ice.

Jeff smiled and said, "I have some plastic bags. You can put them on your hip to reduce the swelling." Jeff made up the first bag of ice and helped her on to her side, bruised side up. "A drink is actually a good idea, for the pain. I'll see what I can get."

Jeff left the room to speak with the captain again. He returned with a local brand of rum.

Jeff poured two glasses of rum, handed her a glass, and toasted her. "To a speedy recovery." Jeff drank, but Amber did not.

"I don't drink, remember?"

His face was serious as he said, "I'm sorry. I forgot. Today was rough. I was really worried when you hit the window frame."

"I'll do better next time."

"No, it's not that." He searched for the right words. "I thought I might have lost you."

She smiled and said, "I'm like a bad penny. It takes more than a window frame to get rid of me."

The boat traveled through the night and anchored at a small natural cove at one of the smaller islands. The Balearic Islands were a famous haven for pirates, cutthroats, and brigands. Conquered by the Moors, the English, the French, and now owned by Spain, the islands' government found it difficult to manage the comings and goings of anything outside the main harbors across so many islands covering such a large area. The islands were also famous for beautiful rocky shores and ocean views.

When they woke up the next morning, Amber had a terrible headache. Jeff half-carried her out to the open deck for some fresh air, aspirin, and coffee. She recovered quickly as she took in the beautiful seascape and rocky shorelines.

The boat weaved its way expertly between the smaller islands and into a cove that was invisible from the open ocean. The captain came to talk with them as they ate and explained that they had to time their passage to avoid Spanish naval patrols and satellite surveillance.

Jeff asked how they could make their way to the town of Mahon. The captain explained that they would need to walk a few miles to the only town on this island and take a water taxi to Mahon. It was a two-hour journey by foot and the water taxi ran at 2 p.m. each day.

A small motorboat dropped them at the beach with their belongings and a crudely drawn map of the trails they would need to follow. Amber was sore, but the trail was relatively flat with few obstructions. They made their way to the town in a little more than two hours.

The community was small but friendly. Jeff and Amber shared their cover story about being on holiday from Algeria; Amber had grown up in the United States and moved back to Algeria a few years ago. They booked passage on the 2 p.m. water taxi to Mahon on the island of Menorca, one of the four big islands in the Balearic Islands.

The trip was beautiful. They entered a large natural inlet with homes dotted across the rocky shore. As the inlet narrowed, they then entered a small port. They exited the water taxi and the port without incident. They were then free to explore the small city of Mahon, or Mayo, depending on whom you talked to.

They took a taxi. Amber was surprised to find that the driver spoke English. He explained that the English had occupied this island before it was taken over by the French and then the Spanish. The nation that owned these islands today seemed to matter little to him. Jeff negotiated to find a small inn close to water but out of the way. When he implied it was a romantic getaway, the driver loved it. After seeing a few places that were too high profile, they finally came upon an inn near the water but off the beaten path. Small but not tiny, it would do.

Once they were finally in their room, Amber and Jeff both dropped to the bed to rest in a quiet place. It was peaceful. After five minutes, Amber broke the silence, saying, "It feels good to just lie still with nothing to do and nowhere to go."

"Nothing to do today," Jeff said. "Tomorrow we meet my contacts. Stephan is the person in charge. It's important you remember his name in case we're separated."

Amber sat up. "Why would we be separated?" she asked.

"No reason," Jeff said calmly. "It's just a precaution."

"Okay. I think I need a nap," Amber said as she lay back down on the comfortable bed. "After everything we've been through, I just need to stay still for a few hours."

"No problem," Jeff said as he got up. "I'll go looking for food and supplies while you rest."

Amber, already drifting into sleep, said, "Just tell me the next time you put explosives under my bed, and no more spike shooters. I've had enough flying between buildings for one week."

Jeff smiled. As he started to leave, he said, "I'll tell you everything."

As the door closed, Amber thought, *Jeff can be charming when he isn't blowing things up.* She rolled over on her good side and fell asleep.

✳ ✳ ✳

When Amber woke, Jeff had returned with two duffel bags of weapons. He was working on a device as she got out of bed.

"Hi," Jeff said with a smile. "I'm rigging a device for the door to delay intruders, and I have an escape route planned out back. I'll show you how to work it all once I have it rigged, and we'll go over the plan."

Amber shook off her sleepiness and sat down at the table. Still tired, she rested her head on her hands as she took in everything Jeff was doing. "You're diabolical," she said.

Jeff looked up, unsure how to take that comment.

With a smile, Amber said, "Don't worry. Diabolical is good."

Jeff smiled back and kept working. "I was able to make a one-way signal to my contact today. I should get something back tomorrow. We may be here for a few days. You should do some shopping tomorrow and explore the islands a little."

"Really?" Amber asked excitedly.

"Really, Really," Jeff said. "If you took a tour or went to see the sights, you would fit right in with the rest of the tourists. I think it's safe."

"I noticed a brochure for day tours at the front desk," Amber said.

"Man, nothing gets by you, does it?" Jeff said.

"What do you mean?" Amber asked.

"I mean you notice everything and remember it. Hair styles, shoe colors, people's behavior, how they walk, and all kinds of things I never notice."

"It's all part of being a reporter. I did a lot of human interest stories on people and places in my first few jobs. You had to notice the details and convey the way people felt or what the place felt like to really connect with your readers. You just train your eye to look for details."

"You are far better at it than anyone else I know, and I know spies," Jeff replied.

"Thank you, Jeff. I'm going to get cleaned up. We should grab dinner in thirty minutes or so."

"Okay," Jeff said and returned to work.

The rest of the day was uneventful. They had fish and chips at a nearby pub and turned in early.

The next morning, after a typical European breakfast, Jeff stayed at the hotel to wait for his contacts and guard the canister, while Amber joined a tour to Mt. Toro. The mountain was the tallest on the island and had several archeological sites. The tour also stopped off at various touristy locations along the way for everyone to shop and eat.

When Amber returned, she found Jeff sitting at the table. His hands were at his side and he was doing nothing. "Jeff, this tour was so fun. First, I met this seventy-year-old couple who was married for fifty years. We talked about their life in Spain, their family, their adventures. It was a great story. Then we stopped by this disco built into a cave that was used by shipwrecked buccaneers in the 1600s."

She then noticed Jeff was tense, so she stopped talking. A man stepped out from the hallway behind Jeff and pointed a gun at Amber.

NO EASY ANSWERS

The gunman was shorter than Amber, 5' 6" at the most. He was nicely dressed, but his clothes were torn. When she looked into his dark eyes, they caused her to freeze with fear—they were so cold and sinister.

"Please take a seat on the couch, Miss van Hosteen," the gunman said with a French accent as he motioned with his pistol toward the couch.

He knew her name and somehow had gotten the best of Jeff. This was bad. Amber thought fast and said, "Where are my manners? Can I get you something to drink?"

He wasn't going for it and sounded angry as he said, "Move to the couch or I will shoot you where you stand."

As Amber moved toward the couch, she was frantically thinking of options. She had left her pistol in their room that morning. There was nothing close by she could grab. She moved enough to see Jeff's hands were handcuffed to the chair legs. Then she noticed movement outside the window behind the man. On the roof of the next building was a man with a rifle. He was motioning Amber to move to her left. It was Dureau! Since the couch was to the left, she moved quickly and sat down.

Simultaneously, Amber heard what sounded like a small rock punching a hole through the window and saw a three-inch hole erupt from their mysterious visitor's face. His head jerked forward as blood and gore sprayed into the room.

Amber felt sick immediately, but she fought back the sensation. She stood up, unsure what to do.

Jeff flipped the chair backwards on the floor to move his body so the new gunman would not have a clear shot at him. He struggled to break the chair and free his arms, but the chair was too sturdy. He motioned his head toward the dead man and said, "Amber, get down and find the keys."

Amber dropped to her hands and knees immediately and crawled over to the dead man, now face down on the floor. She found the keys in their would-be captor's chest pocket and turned to free Jeff. Just as she got the first handcuff off, the front door burst open. Jeff sprang up into a fighting stance, standing between Amber and the new threat, holding the chair as a weapon. He then seemed to recognize the man in the doorway and said, "Stephan?"

"I'm glad we got here in time. I'll have to explain later. We need to go, now!" Stephan said.

Jeff looked at Amber and said, "You know the drill. Let's grab and go."

Jeff took the keys from Amber and unlocked the handcuff from his other hand while Amber started to pack bags quickly. They were headed out the door in less than two minutes. They exited the building and headed toward one of Jeff's planned escape routes. As they turned a corner, Amber saw Dureau placing a gun case in the back of a white Renault Captur five-door crossover. They placed their bags quickly in the back and got in. Stephan was driving and Dureau was in the passenger seat, while Jeff and Amber got in the backseats.

"Keep your heads down until we are out of town," Stephan warned.

Amber was all too happy to comply. She laid her head in Jeff's lap as Jeff leaned over her protectively.

"Thank you for the timely entrance, Stephan. Were you the marksman, Dureau?" Jeff asked.

"The pleasure was all mine, killing that traitor," Dureau replied.

"What do you mean by 'traitor'?" Jeff asked.

Dureau explained, "His name is Stiles. He was monitoring our communications for some time. When you contacted us, he had our director reassign us to another case and left to find you. We suspected him of several crimes but had no hard evidence. We backtracked to where he was going and found out he was going after you, here.”

“Do you know about my status with my government?” Jeff asked.

“Yes,” Stephan answered. “It is unusual for the French government to assign our agents to clean up another country’s mess. Even more so for an American. I know you, Jeff. I want to understand what is going on and why someone wants to kill you.”

“I have a summary in my bag,” Amber said, “and a lot of documentation on what is happening.”

“It’s going to be a little difficult to believe,” said Jeff. “The implications are large. It affects my government and may affect yours too. Do you have a safe place we can go to talk?”

“We are on our way there now. It will take about forty-five minutes,” Stephan said.

After a few moments of silence, Jeff asked, “How is Shay doing, Stephan?”

“Shay was killed three weeks ago on a routine fact-finding mission in Africa,” Stephan said. “I still cannot believe he is dead.”

“I’m sorry,” Jeff said. “I know you were close friends.”

“He went to Angola to research some strange things going on there,” Stephan said. “He ran into a stone wall. When he reported he would need more time, he was urgently reassigned to Burkina Faso. He checked in per standard procedure when he landed, and we never heard from him again. There was no follow-up. No investigation. It was like he never existed. It’s been like this ever since our unit was assigned a new director.”

“If you haven’t heard from him and there was no investigation, why do you think he’s dead?” Jeff asked.

“You knew Shay, Jeff. You know what he was capable of. No one could imprison him for more than a day.”

“We came from Burkina Faso,” Jeff said.

“I know. We can talk freely once we arrive.”

They drove on in silence until they arrived at their destination.

They turned off the main road and drove down a hard-packed dirt road for about one mile. They then turned off onto another dirt road for another half mile and finally ended up at a tomato farm.

"Really, a tomato farm?" Amber said.

"What better place? Who would look for international fugitives on a tomato farm?" Dureau replied.

Dureau got out and opened a barn door as everyone else stayed in the car. Once the car pulled in, Dureau closed the door and turned on the lights.

Amber was surprised to see the barn's finished interior. It had a rough finish and a concrete floor, but it was rather nice for a barn. There was one large open space and three doors to their right that led to enclosed rooms. One door was open, and Amber could see a lot of communications equipment in it. A fair number of crates and other equipment were along the opposite wall from the rooms and what looked like a conference room table at the end of the barn.

They all got out of the car and headed to the table with their gear. Walking to the table, Amber noticed a typical refrigerator and a large freezer next to a cooking surface and sink.

They all dropped their gear near the table and sat down. Dureau offered them food and drinks. Amber was the only one to take any refreshment—a glass of water.

Stephan started the discussion. "There's only one other person at this facility. His name is Chesney. I trust him and Dureau with my life. Strange things have been happening in our Agency the last two months."

"The French Directorate-General for External Security?" Jeff asked.

"Yes. Odd assignments, unexplained deaths, random case reassignments." He then gave Jeff a very intense look and said, "I want to find out what happened to Shay, so I am very interested in your story. Please, share everything."

Jeff looked at Amber and nodded in agreement. She pulled out her summary and started to share. It was a story briefing like what she would do at News Corp.

No one interrupted her, but her audience's body language went from discomfort to disbelief as she spoke. She described conditions in Burkina Faso when she arrived, her investigations, and the "mine." She told them about her and Jeff's trip to the mine—who and what they found inside. There were no interruptions, so she talked about their escape. When she described the spaceship launch, Stephan could contain himself no longer.

"My God! This is unbelievable!" Stephan exclaimed. "Why did you say a spaceship, not a rocket?"

"It didn't fly like a rocket," Jeff said. "And the propulsion system was like nothing I've ever seen. It didn't expend hot gas. We would have died if it did, and the light it gave off was yellowish, not orange or red. It did not give off a lot of heat like you would expect from a rocket."

"If I imagined what an angel would look like, lifting off the Earth, that is what it looked like to me," Amber said.

The two Frenchmen looked at each other and back at them, not knowing what to say. After a few moments of silence, Amber went on. She described their exit from Burkina Faso, their trip through Mali and Algeria, their escape from Algiers, and the trip to Menorca.

When she was done, the two Frenchmen were silent for a long time. It took them a little while to collect their thoughts. They then peppered Amber and Jeff with questions for over an hour. Amber showed them the extensive documentation she had written on their journey and their conclusions.

After the questions slowed down, the group moved on from the clarification of facts to discussion about their story's implications.

"To summarize," said Dureau, "some unknown party has set up a high-tech factory in the middle of Burkina Faso to kill thousands of people each day."

"Yes, but they are not completely unknown," Amber said.

Stephan sat up and said, "What do you mean they are not completely unknown?"

"I went to Burkina Faso to follow a lead on a story," Amber said. "Some very bad men were involved in selling weapons illegally, smuggling, human trafficking, and worse. Each one seemed to be working for an organization called the 'Hand' or the 'Hidden Hand.'"

"Where did you get that name?" Stephan asked.

"It wasn't easy. I was digging for weeks through shell companies, legal entities, and subsidiaries. Each one of those leads led to a dead end. Then I got lucky. I found a person, a whistle blower.

"This person reported that her company had a shipping and logistics subsidiary that was handling cargo illegally. She thought the company was knowingly aiding smugglers. She reported this to the US FTC and local law enforcement. Once investigations began, a federal agency came in and took over. She never heard another word after that. She came to me and I started investigating her story.

"Every time I got close to something interesting, the lead would dead end. But I did notice references to this 'Hand' or 'Hidden Hand' organization. When I would ask about it, people would get quiet, like they were scared. One person said, 'If you like your head on your shoulders, you do not want to know about that.'

"Naturally, that piqued my interest, so I dug twice as hard for leads. Then I found a second subsidiary of this corporation moving a lot of material to Burkina Faso."

"I tried to contact the local government, but they were of little help, so I made my own contacts, oddly enough, through the Catholic Church. You heard the rest of the story," Amber concluded.

Stephan was listening intently. After a few moments of thought, he said, "Shay was in Angola investigating arms smuggling. He was reassigned to investigate this 'Hidden Hand' as a possible link to the smuggling."

"This Hand organization is bad news and covers its tracks well. I cannot find anyone who has talked to a member of this group. I was starting to think it didn't really exist," Amber said. "Can you find out more about the 'Hidden Hand,' Stephan?"

"I have been trying to ever since Shay disappeared," Stephan said. "I also keep running into roadblocks and dead ends, as you say. What little information there is was reclassified to a higher security level than mine."

"I thought you were the highest level there is in France," Jeff said.

"No more," Stephan said. "Ever since my unit was reassigned by this new director, my access has been reduced and he added his lackeys to my team. Stiles was one of them. What were you doing before they fired you?"

"Some pretty routine stuff," Jeff said. "The only thing out of the ordinary was this crash site underwater. We found some exotic materials. When I reported on it to my director, he reassigned the case and sent me to Burkina Faso. When I got the recall order from him, I declined on the grounds that I thought it was a national security issue. On the next contact, I found out I was terminated. We were attacked shortly after that in Algiers. There is also a one-million-dollar contract on me."

"One million no more, my friend. It is now ten million. Someone wants you dead," Dureau said.

"Can you tell me more about this material?" Stephan asked.

Jeff took a deep breath. He was now sharing classified information without authorization, but what the heck. He was fired anyway. "A marine salvage company was surveying for shipwrecks when it stumbled upon this site. There were three-foot-long metallic ingots. They were underwater less than 100 years, but we could not place the date exactly."

"Why couldn't you place the time underwater?" Stephan asked.

"It was odd, but there was no corrosion from being exposed to seawater. The marine salvage company spotted the site a few months earlier, but it had only just gotten back to it. That area of the ocean floor gathers sediment slowly. Without any metallic corrosion, we could only set an upper limit based on the amount of sediment covering the site," Jeff explained.

"Anyway, they were in a pattern, neatly laid out in a semi-circle. They were shaped oddly, smooth on the outside with a bulge in the middle that formed a kind of a triangle with an obtuse apex. In addition to zero corrosion by seawater, the surface could not be damaged by saws, lasers, or torches," Jeff said. "I had a sample taken to one of our best labs. I forgot how many tons of pressure they used just to distort the shape, and it would always bounce back. They ran an analysis under an electron microscope and discovered that the material was made of nanites."

"Nanites?" Stephan asked. "I've only just heard of experiments with this technology. It could not be 100 years old."

"There's more," Jeff said. "The scientist told me these nanites were perfect spheres. That means they could only be manufactured in space."

"That is not possible," Dureau said.

Jeff raised his hands. "I know. I know. That's what I said, but he assures me it could not be produced on Earth due to gravity warping the shape."

Dureau shook his head but said nothing more.

"One more thing," Jeff said in a very serious tone. "My lab believes this material can transform itself into any shape, on command. They're still working on the details of how it might work. The head of this lab believes the ingots are in a 'default' shape."

"So, I just talk to it and it transforms into anything I want?" Dureau said sarcastically.

"No," Jeff replied. "They think it is some form of high energy signal on a very short wavelength."

"You are serious?" Dureau asked.

"Dureau!" Stephan said with a stern look. Dureau remained quiet.

Stephan took the opportunity to summarize, and Dureau started writing as Stephan spoke. "Let us take stock of where we are now and not jump to any conclusions. We have a material of unknown origin that is technologically advanced, yes?" There were no replies, so he continued. "We have an advanced manufacturing facility in Burkina Faso with a technical staff of medical specialists and the ability to launch something into space.

"Once inside, these unfortunate souls are rendered unconscious, strapped into a frame on a circular platform, and a glass dome, shaped like a large test tube, is placed over them. Yes?"

"Yes," Amber and Jeff said together.

"But," Amber added, "we never really saw that part of the operation. We don't know for sure how they did it, so it's our best guess."

"Noted," Stephan said as he nodded to Dureau. "Some gas is pumped into the glass dome that you believe is poisonous."

"Yes," Jeff said. "A sticker with the international symbol for poison, skull and crossbones, was on the outside of each frame."

"And a liquid was being fed intravenously into the legs of each victim?" Stephan asked.

"Yes, but there was one going into one leg and one coming out the other leg," Amber corrected.

"You believe the liquid pulled from the victims was gathered in a canister of some kind?" Stephan asked.

"Yes, we have a sample of this liquid," Jeff said.

Jeff took the metallic object out of their backpack and set it on the table. It was circular, about four inches in diameter with a flat bottom and tapering to a point on top. The top looked like it was melted and made from a different type of metal than the base.

"Do you have any idea what's inside?" Stephan asked.

"Not really," Amber answered. "We know it's some type of liquid that was being extracted from the victims. We need to analyze it to understand what it's made of and reason out why they're doing this."

"Yes," Stephan said. "This is the only tangible link you have to support your story."

"There was the space vehicle launch as well," Jeff added.

"Yes, but until we can verify it, it does not support your story," Stephan clarified. "We should split the sample up into three separate containers. I can take one back to a French lab to analyze. Dureau can take another to his contacts in Spain, while you take the third back to the United States. That way, we can spread the risk of losing any single sample and have the labs compare their findings."

"It's a good plan, Stephan," Jeff said. "I'm just not sure it's safe to open this thing."

Stephan looked to Dureau.

"The hospitals here use a medical lab on this island for blood tests. They also perform 'specialty medical treatments,' for a price," Dureau said. "They could handle this and package it safely without contaminating the samples."

"I'll need to stay with the sample everywhere it goes until we have the three separate samples," Jeff said.

"I would expect no less," Stephan said with a smile. "Dureau, work out the details for our visit to the lab."

"I'm on it," Dureau confirmed.

"We also need to make copies of this documentation and get it distributed to everyone who will listen," said Amber as she picked up her summary pages.

"That will not be easy, Amber," Stephan said. "The media in France is being controlled. Major news events are happening in the world, but no news agency reports on them."

"What do you mean?" Jeff asked before Amber could.

"This situation in Burkina Faso, for example. You'll find nothing in the news," Stephan said. "Armies are being armed in backward countries with no political purpose as far as we can tell. In the past, we would have shut this down instantly. Now, my superior ignores it."

"I need to see what is happening in the US," Amber said. "News Corp fired me. I never thought to question if anything else strange was happening back home."

"We need to move quickly," said Jeff, getting up. "The information we just shared is already days old. I feel it's about to affect a lot more people. Dureau and I can go find this lab and get the samples packaged while Amber makes copies of our documentation and starts researching the best way to get this information distributed."

"Stephan, one of the reasons I looked for you was to get in touch with space-tracking resources. The French have some of the best tracking systems in the world, and I know you monitor more than just Europe," Jeff said.

"This is true," Stephan replied.

"First," Jeff continued, "I need to find out if anyone can spot a launch in Burkina Faso. If not, why not? If so, why are they not doing anything about it? Second, where are those launches going?"

"Jeff, you realize you're not the agent in charge here?" Stephan said.

Jeff took a moment, then said, "Yes, of course. I'm sorry. Old habits."

"I just had to make that clear," Stephan said. "Having said that, I think your plan makes sense. You and Dureau should focus on the samples while I explore confirmation of the space launch. I will see if I can answer your questions. What are Amber's qualifications?"

"She has no formal training or experience in our line of work, but no agent other than me has ever deflected her from her goals. You heard the research she did and the leads she dug up herself," Jeff said.

"Then perhaps it would be best if Amber worked with Chesney to determine how we get this story published. I believe the mainstream media is going to be problematic," Stephan said.

"If you're right, Stephan," Amber explained, "there are still too many smaller publishers for the government to cover all of them. A thousand smaller publishers can do just as well as one major media player."

"I like your thinking," Stephan said, smiling. "You and Chesney can work on making electronic copies and readying them for distribution while finding contacts to send them to. Also, make some physical copies for us. Each sample should have a physical copy with it. We can also make a few more to place in safe places around the world in case things do not work out as planned."

Amber looked at Stephan, then Jeff, and said, "You two are the same. You're always planning for the worst."

"'Plan for the worst and you will never be surprised,'" said Stephan, quoting some unknown author. "This is important in our line of work."

Jeff and Dureau nodded in agreement.

"Do we have enough facts to start talking about conclusions?" Amber asked. She was getting frustrated with Stephan's process.

"Perhaps," Stephan said. "Are there any other relevant facts that anyone needs to share?"

After looking around the room and seeing everyone shake his or her head 'no,' Stephan said, "Now we can move on to the list of possible players in this story. Who benefits from these facts? Who would want to do these things?"

"Blood-sucking aliens from outer space?" Dureau said.

Stephan laughed, and then explained to Amber and Jeff, "He always says that for everything as a joke. This time, who knows? But seriously, who benefits and who would want to do these things?"

After a moment of thought, Jeff said, "The companies building this facility would make a lot of money."

"Yes, very good. Who else?" Stephan encouraged the group.

"The scientists in the facility," Amber said. "The one Jeff and I spoke to was a fanatic. He said, 'Any price is worth the knowledge we gain here' or something close to that."

"Yes, the scientists, the construction companies, the equipment manufacturers, all the angles involved in the facility," Stephan added. "Now, what about the space launch? Who could do this and why would they?"

"Twelve nations have the proven ability to launch anything into space," Jeff said. "The United States, France, Britain, Germany, Russia, China, Israel, Iran, Pakistan, Japan, North Korea, and India. No other nation has ever done so until now. France, Britain, Germany, China, Pakistan, and India have only launched missiles and satellites, nothing manned."

"Based on our limited resources, Jeff, you are the expert on the US and Russia. Who benefits from doing this?" Stephan asked.

"I don't know, but I can find out," Jeff answered with determination.

"Very good. Now, what about your situation, Jeff and Amber? Jeff was a very senior US agent in the CIA. A decorated war hero. Who benefits from terminating him?" Stephan asked.

Amber caught the reference to Jeff being a war hero. She made a mental note to follow up on that.

"I don't know, but I can find that out too," Jeff said with even more determination.

"Okay, and Amber, you are an accomplished reporter based on what Jeff says. Who benefits from firing you from News Corp?" Stephan asked.

"I don't know, but I can find out," Amber replied with the same determination.

"It's difficult to draw accurate conclusions without understanding all the facts, who the players are, and their motivation to perform these actions, yes?" Stephan asked.

"I really like the process you led us through Stephan, but I cannot help but draw one conclusion," Amber said. "These events appear to affect more than just one country. What is happening to you in France, to thousands of people in Burkina Faso, to Jeff and me—it's all related to something bigger than any one nation. There is a conspiracy here, and I think the people behind it are the real players behind all of this. I think their name is the 'Hidden Hand.'"

"Each of us during our lives has built prejudice toward something," Stephan replied. "You may like the color blue or a certain political party or not like croissants."

"That is impossible; everyone likes croissants!" Dureau exclaimed.

"Enough with the jokes, Dureau; I'm making a point," Stephan said, kindly but firmly. "You may have a prejudice toward this conspiracy theory and you may be right, but it is only your idea without proof. It is our job to connect the threads of truth through the players in this story to the people, organizations, or governments behind all this. I accept your prejudice. Now bring me the proof."

"This is what I'm good at, Stephan," Amber said with confidence.

"What about the site with the metal ingots?" Dureau asked.

"Yes, who could manufacture this material? Why would they manufacture it? Why was it left on the ocean floor?" Stephan asked.

"Who could manufacture it?" Jeff asked. "No one on Earth. Why make it? What was it used for? We have no idea. Why would something that valuable be left on the ocean floor unguarded? We have no idea."

"I will not accept easy answers to hard questions. 'No one on Earth' is the easy answer. If not someone on Earth, then who and why?" Stephan said.

"How do I figure that out?" Jeff asked.

"A good question. Start thinking about it," Stephan replied. "So will I."

Jeff was a little angry with that answer, but he started to think about it.

"Then I believe we have a list of actions. Jeff's original plan with my recommendation is actionable and defines our short-term list. Longer term, we need answers to the open questions we just talked about. Dureau will complete his notes and give each of us our tasks," Stephan said as he looked around the room. "Are we agreed?"

Everyone nodded in agreement. Then Dureau said, "First, I am having a croissant."

Stephan laughed and got up as he shook his head.

Then Chesney ran into the room and said, "There is an American spy satellite focused on our location."

HUNTING MOTIVATION

"Did you deploy the countermeasures?" Stephan asked Chesney following his surprising statement.

"Yes, we're radio silent. Only passive sensors are active. The infrared deflector is up and running. This barn looks like there is a cow and two horses in it now, but I don't know if I did it fast enough." Chesney looked worried, which seemed to upset Stephan and Dureau.

"All we can do now is wait for the satellite to pass." Stephan said. "Bring up the perimeter cameras. If we're attacked, at least we can see them coming."

"If we're attacked on the ground," Jeff said.

"If there is a missile on its way here, we will know it in a few minutes," Stephan said.

"How will we know?" Amber asked.

"We will be dead," Dureau replied.

Chesney and Dureau were watching video screens of the security cameras in one room while Jeff and Stephan were looking at sensor readings in another room.

Amber was alone at the table, scared to death. Her hands started shaking.

After five minutes that seemed like an hour, Stephan and Jeff came out of their room. Stephan said, "The satellite will be out of range in twenty minutes."

"There's no ground attack," Dureau said.

Jeff saw Amber's hands shaking and ran over to sit with her. He put his hand on her back and said, "If someone were going to attack us, it would have already happened. We're safe for now."

"You scared me half to death," Amber said as tears started to form in her eyes.

"I am sorry," Chesney said as he entered the room. "I will make it up to you tonight. I will make my world-famous stew."

"When the satellite passes," Stephan said, "we need to split up and move to our secondary location. Chesney and Amber can go to the new safe house. Jeff and Dureau can go to the medical lab, while I go into town and work on verifying the space launches. Are we agreed?"

Everyone agreed and started packing up their gear. The group split up into teams and went to work on their assignments. Before Amber had met Chesney, she had expected him to be a young technical support person. Instead, he was in his sixties.

"I expected our technical support to be much younger," Amber remarked.

"No one expects a spy to be old," Chesney replied. "Being old lets me go places and observe things without being noticed. I did not start using computers until I was forty. I just love it."

He also seemed to know everything they talked about even when he was not in the room with them. Amber was going to keep a close eye on this one.

They drove for forty-five minutes to an orange orchard. The farm had two farmhouses. They drove to the one farthest back from the road and parked in an empty three-car garage. The four-bedroom, ranch-style house had a back bedroom filled with equipment and computer screens. Chesney went straight to work starting up the computers and adjusting monitors as Amber watched.

Chesney proved to be excellent at gathering information. They pulled together lists of possible news agencies around the world, categorizing them for their effectiveness at communicating their story and the level of credibility they would have with readers. If all they did was get the story out in tabloid newsstands, it would do nothing for the people of Burkina Faso. They made a great team.

They prioritized their list of news agencies and started calling. By late afternoon of the next day, Monday, they had twenty-two news agencies ready to run their story on Wednesday. They felt good about how much they had accomplished.

✳   ✳   ✳

Jeff and Dureau showed up that afternoon, and Stephan arrived before dark.

They had a status meeting before dinner that night where they all reported on their progress.

Stephan called the meeting and ran the agenda. He said, "We have all had a day to make progress. Who would like to go first?"

Amber quickly raised her hand. When Stephan nodded to her, she began, "Chesney and I have made great progress. Our story has been picked up by twenty-two news agencies with good reputations and broad readership. Our story starts running this Wednesday."

"Are there any actions left to take, or are we all set?" Stephan asked.

"There's nothing more we can do but wait for Wednesday," Amber replied. "And Chesney has been a tremendous help. I could not have done it without him."

"Amber is kind," Chesney said, "but she overstates my role. Once she told those agencies she left News Corp to go freelance and they could have this story for free, they were sold. Only a few of them declined."

As Amber started to say more, Stephan cut her off by saying, "You both did well. Thank you. Who will go next?"

Dureau spoke up. "We had to spend some money to get the lab to cooperate, but we split the samples under vacuum seals and repacked it into heavy glass beakers with ground glass seals. It seemed to work fine. Their initial analysis of the liquid shows an organic acid of some type. We kept the original container for analysis too."

"Excellent. It would appear we have two successful missions completed. I will speak to the third," Stephan said. "When I began researching our missile-tracking capabilities, I ran into a stone wall, as you say. The security classification was increased beyond my level. However, I have many friends and was able to make contacts with people I know."

"French missile tracking is second only to the Americans' system, but only due to the number of satellites and sensors they have. The quality of our systems is just as good, if not better," Stephan said proudly. "We do, in fact, track North Africa. The Americans do not. They focus all their attention on the nuclear powers. No country in Africa would have the technology to fire a missile on the US, even if it tried. France, being closer, is not so lucky."

"I have one friend in particular who was involved in discovering the launch data from Burkina Faso," Stephan continued. "At first, they thought there was a satellite malfunction because the data was so odd. They then saw that these launches happen regularly every three days from the same point. And they are not just launching. They are landing."

"Landing where?" Jeff asked. "There are no runways long enough in Africa to land a space vehicle. Are they landing in a lake?"

"They appear to be landing in the same place they take off from," Stephan said. "And there is more. They tuned their satellites to track this anomaly. They found the launch ends and the landing begins from the same point in space: the L2 Lagrange point.

"They checked and double-checked this data, not believing it was real. When they finally reported this data to their superiors, they were issued a gag order. They would be convicted of treason if they shared it. Then the security levels of all missile-tracking data was raised."

"This is incredible!" Amber said.

"We can add one more fact to our list," Jeff said. "We know that a space launch and landing occur every three days between the Earth's L2 Lagrange point and the facility Amber and I visited."

"We also now know that someone in the French government is working with the same people who built that facility," Stephan added.

Dureau, immediately becoming defensive, said, "I cannot believe our countrymen are working with these people."

"There must be someone in a high position in the military to make security clearance changes and suppress those reports, Dureau," Stephan said.

"We can make a list of names and see where it leads," Jeff suggested.

"I'm not authorized to spy on my own countrymen. There is another agency for this," Stephan said.

"Is there anyone there you trust?" Jeff asked.

"No," Stephan said. "Maybe. I do not know."

"I can do it," Jeff offered.

"No, not now. You would end up dead in France when we need you in the United States. You have your mission to work out. I now have another."

"Fine. Then I need to find a way to see what is at the L2 Lagrange point. You can add that to my list," Jeff said.

"We also need to get you back to the US," Stephan said.

"How?" Jeff asked.

"Your military has a protocol for the dead. If we say we caught and killed you, plus marked the remains as unviewable, we could slip you into a body bag in a locked coffin. You would take a military transport for a ten-hour flight back to Atlanta or Virginia. We would arrange for someone to let you out and escape. You would be on your own from there," Stephan said.

"Can you really do that?" Amber asked.

"Yes, I have done it before," Stephan explained. "We can make the arrangements tomorrow."

"Wait, I'm not thrilled with being in a coffin for ten hours," Amber said.

"You will have oxygen, heating, and cooling. Just take a ten-hour nap," Stephan said.

"Guys, I am not doing this!" Amber said.

When no one answered her, Amber got worried!

That evening, they discovered Chesney's stew was famous for good reason. Most of the team got a good night's sleep while Jeff found someone with a telescope who was willing to use it that night. They looked for satellites and found a few. They found nothing at the L2 Lagrange point. Jeff returned disappointed well after midnight.

✳ ✳ ✳

The next day, the team planned for Jeff and Amber to return home. They had to orchestrate the process to ensure that Jeff and Amber did not run out of air in their coffins. They could also get heatstroke or freeze to death while confined. Fortunately, the Frenchmen had already worked out the details. The biggest problem with the plan was the mental effects of complete isolation for long periods of time.

The plan was for Stephan to call in to his superiors to inform them he had been recruited by Stiles to find Jeff and Amber. When they had found Jeff, he had killed Stiles. Stephan and Dureau had then chased Jeff and Amber for two days before they cornered and killed them. Bodies of foreign nationals were usually returned to the nation of citizenship promptly.

The team spent the day locating and transporting the necessary equipment to the airport in Mahon where they set up shop in an aviation hangar.

"These simple wooden coffins with breathing masks will be fine for the low altitude flight to Marseille," Stephan said. "It will take about three hours. Once we arrive, I will escort these coffins to the medical examiner's office. His son worked for me. We can trust him. In his office, we will transfer you to new coffins, complete with air, heating, and cooling. He will certify and seal the coffins. I will take you to an American military plane that will fly you to the US."

"What happens once we land?" Amber asked.

"An officer at the base will take possession of the coffins and let you out," Stephan said. "I cannot tell you more than that."

"I'm really worried about being confined for ten hours," Amber said. "Plus, wait time on the ground arriving and departing. It could be fourteen hours."

"We can drug you, so you sleep the entire way," Stephan replied.

Amber looked at Stephan for a long time before saying, "Can I decide when I enter the coffin?"

"Of course," Stephan said. "The clock starts when I make the call to my superiors. We want you on the ground as little time as possible to minimize unforeseen complications."

The team agreed. They slept in the hangar that night. Stephan sent the message to his superiors at 2 a.m. that he had killed Jeff and Amber at midnight. At 4 a.m., they got into their coffins and were sealed in. The coffins were loaded on board the rented twin engine aircraft. Dureau and Stephan boarded the plane with the pilot. The plan was set into motion. Chesney contacted the US Army and French Navy bases to arrange transport of the "special" dead US citizens back to the United States.

The private plane arrived in Marseille at 8 a.m., and the US transport would arrive by 10 a.m. Stephan flashed his credentials and pushed the Naval Airmen to move his coffins quickly to the medical examiner's office. Each coffin was loaded on a separate metal cart and pushed by a French Naval Airman. One wasn't paying attention when a forklift backed into his cart and knocked the coffin to the ground. The wood cracked loudly as it hit the ground. The coffin was barely holding together. The forklift driver and the airman started arguing.

Dureau's heart skipped a beat.

Stephan smoothly stepped forward and ordered everyone to be silent. "These people are dead. You cannot hurt them, but they will smell really bad if you stand around and argue. Stand up the cart. Carefully put the coffin on it so it does not crack open, and let's get this mess to the medical examiner's office now."

The sailors stopped arguing and did as Stephan directed. When the coffin was safely back on the cart, Stephan and Dureau looked at each other and let out a sigh of relief.

Once safely in the medical examiner's office, Jeff and Amber were released from their confinement.

Jeff was holding his shoulder when he emerged and said, "That hurt. What happened?"

"A forklift hit you," Dureau said. "The man pushing your coffin was careless. When I heard that crunching sound, I thought the coffin would burst open."

"So did I," Jeff said with a grunt of pain.

"You have forty-five minutes to rest, use the bathroom, and get ready," Stephan said. "Your new coffins and suits are here." Stephan walked over to two polished metal coffins. "They are state of the art. They will monitor your temperature and breathing. You put on this body suit, we plug you in, you climb into the body bag, and we set your helmet, and seal you in."

Because of Jeff's experience, no one noticed how stressed Amber was when she exited her coffin. Amber's father had been an alcoholic. When Amber was a child, her mother would hide her in a closet when her father got mean and tried to beat them. She was terrified of small dark places. She spent most of the next forty-five minutes staring at the coffin.

When the time came to suit up, Amber had made a decision. "Stephan?"

"Yes."

"I can't do this. You're going to need to drug me."

"Very well. You must suit up first."

They put on their body suits and sat in the coffins. Their suits were connected to six tubes before they laid down in the body bags that were zipped up to their necks.

Amber was already starting to panic before they put the full face-covering helmet on her. She was starting to breathe heavily when she felt a pin prick in her shoulder and the world went dark.

Stephan and Dureau marched the new coffins, with the medical examiner's seal on each, to a hangar near the runway. The US Army C-140 cargo plane from Aviano air base in Lipa, Italy, landed on time at 10 a.m. Stephan met the pilot of the plane in front of their hangar where he transferred ownership of the sealed coffins to the US Army. They were now US army property.

"Farewell Jeff," Stephan said as the plane taxied toward the runway.

Just then a Jeep rolled up with a French Army general in the passenger seat. He stepped out to look around. He spotted Stephan and marched up to him.

"Are you the one with the remains of two US fugitives?" the general barked.

"General, the cargo is signed for and loaded on that US military transport plane. It is their property now."

The two men started a heated debate. Stephan kept the general engaged until the plane had lifted off the runway. Then he said, "General, our discussion is pointless. The plane has left the runway. Unless you plan on shooting down an American transport plane."

The general, seeing the plane in the air, frowned at Stephan and went back to his Jeep.

Stephan now knew two things: 1) His friends were safely on their way to the United States, and 2) He had found at least one senior-ranking military official working against them.

Stephan turned to Dureau and said, "I hope our friends do not run into trouble when they arrive."

FEELINGS

Jeff had been on many military transport planes before, so he knew when they were getting ready to land by the sounds of the slowly declining airspeed noises and the feel of the landing gear dropping into place. Big cargo planes ride rough, but the flight had been uneventful as far as he could tell. He hoped Amber was still sleeping.

After landing, they taxied for a long time before they finally stopped. The cargo sat on the plane for over half an hour before they began unloading. Jeff was eager to get out of his coffin, but he did not know what to expect—a helping hand or a firing squad.

When the pallet finally stopped moving, Jeff lay in silence, waiting for the sound of the coffin opening. He had to pretend to be dead in case there would be some sort of inspection before their rescuer could free them.

Jeff heard the second coffin open first. He was worried about Amber. He hoped the sedative Stephan had given her had carried her through the entire trip. She seemed to have issues with tight places.

When his own coffin opened, the body bag was unzipped immediately. Jeff found himself staring into the face of a big US Air Force Captain. His eyes were having a hard time adjusting to the light. The captain said, "David R. Samuelson, Captain US Air Force at your service, son." He then continued to unzip the body bag and help Jeff out of it. Jeff was sore and stiff from the long ride, but otherwise in good shape.

Captain Samuelson continued, "The pretty lady in the other one is passed out. She's breathing but not moving at all."

Jeff sat up and looked around the warehouse they were in. He saw no one except the Air Force captain. "Thank you for your help, Captain. We gave her a sedative to help her with the journey. I can wake her up."

The big captain helped Jeff out of the coffin. It took a minute to work the stiffness out of his joints. They walked over to Amber. The body bag was already unzipped. Jeff carefully took off Amber's headgear. He then took the revival agent out of his coverall pocket and placed it under Amber's nose. She shook her head and started to wake.

Amber held her head in her hands and started blinking until she could focus her eyes on the man standing over her. When she saw it was Jeff, she smiled and jokingly said, "Are we there yet?"

Jeff laughed and said, "Yes, we are. How are you feeling?"

"Like a truck hit me, then backed up and did it again," Amber said slowly but clearly.

"Meet Captain Samuelson. He's our contact. I assume we're at Pope Field in North Carolina?"

"That's right, son," said the captain.

"What's our plan to exit the base, Captain?" Amber asked as she sat up and looked around.

"I'm going to dress you up as two Air Force enlisted, get us in a Jeep, and drive right off the base. I have a backpack and some clothes your size, but that's it. I should never see you again after today, understood?" the captain asked.

"Yes, sir, Captain," Jeff said respectfully. "We're going to need some privacy while we change."

"I'll be right over there. Holler when you're ready," the captain said.

Jeff used the time to retrieve money hidden under a false bottom in the coffins. He and Amber approached the captain when they were ready to go. Jeff was the driver and Amber was in the backseat with the backpack while the captain sat in the passenger seat.

The captain gave them directions as they drove through the base to a side gate. The guards on duty at the gate saluted the captain and looked over the vehicle. The lead guard asked in a friendly voice, "Where you headed today, Captain Samuelson?"

"I have to head up to Virginia for some briefings and paperwork. You know, the usual, Kip," the captain explained in return.

"Try to have fun, Captain, and bring us back some chocolate ice cream. This base has been eating vanilla for far too long," the guard said.

"I'll see what I can do about that, son," Captain Samuelson replied as the gate opened. They then drove off down the road.

That was too easy, Jeff thought. He then asked the captain, "The Military Police at the gate seemed to think you could get them ice cream?"

"Well, of course I can. I'm the requisition officer for the base," Captain Samuelson explained.

Jeff knew from his time in the military that the requisition officer was responsible for logistics and supplies. He brought everything from food to ammunition into the base. That explained why he could get cargo from anywhere moved so easily.

"What will you do with the coffins?" Jeff asked.

"We already swapped them with empties," the captain explained. "Stephan is going to take a lot of heat for that, but it gets you here free and clear."

"I'm curious, Captain, why did you help us?" Jeff asked.

The big captain looked at Jeff and said, "Because fine young men like the ones at that gate are dying for no good reason. Stephan told me you mean to help stop it, and I trust Stephan. Do not prove me wrong or I will be on you like a chicken on a June bug."

Jeff shook his head in agreement like he knew what the captain was talking about, but in truth, he had no idea. He doubted Stephan would either.

Captain Samuelson directed them to a small town where he stopped. "End of the line, folks. This town is small, but there's transportation to everywhere. It's a military town, so two airmen walking around together will not attract attention here. You'll need to lose those uniforms eventually, though. Make sure no one else ever uses them. Cut 'em up if you have to. Good luck!"

Jeff helped Amber out of the backseat and turned to say thank you, but Captain Samuelson was already driving away.

Amber surveyed the street and quickly came up with a plan. "We can go shop in those two stores." She pointed toward a clothing store and a hardware store. "We can change; get what we need right now. I'll buy shears to cut up these uniforms and we can dump them in that dumpster." She pointed at a cinderblock wall that likely had a dumpster behind it.

Jeff, having gotten used to Amber's keen observation skills, just said, "Let's do it."

The store was a good pick. It had casual clothes for men and women. Jeff even liked what he bought himself. They each bought two sets of clothes and two new backpacks. They then went to the hardware store where Jeff bought an odd combination of things. Then they crossed the street and hid in the dumpster area. Amber cut up their uniforms while Jeff strapped a hunting knife to his leg and made something.

"What's that?" Amber asked.

Jeff looked up and said, "Simple mustard gas. Just combine chlorine, ammonia, and a reagent. Until we have better weapons, this will delay anyone following us for a while."

Jeff made two jars of the liquid and put them in each pocket of his hoodie. Amber looked at Jeff with his glasses and hoodie, then thought 'Great, my partner is the Unabomber.'

When Jeff was done, he looked around and said, "Let's see if we can get a bus to Virginia."

"And the latest newspapers," Amber added. "What was Captain Samuelson talking about? 'These fine young men dying for no good reason.' What's that about?"

"I don't know," Jeff replied.

Amber gave him a questioning look and said, "You acted like you knew exactly what he was saying."

Jeff started them walking down the street and said, "If that was his reason for helping us, I didn't want him to think we had no idea what he was talking about; then he may have changed his mind and turned us in."

Hmm, Amber thought. *Good thinking.*

"I saw a bus headed to the right. We can walk up to the next intersection to see if the bus station is in that direction."

"Why don't we just ask someone where it is?" Amber asked.

"If we talk to someone, we'll draw attention to ourselves and then they'll be more likely to remember us. What if we grab today's newspaper and it has your face on it? People will remember you if they talk to you," Jeff said.

"Oh, I thought it was just the guy thing. You know, how guys don't like to ask for directions," Amber joked.

Jeff gave a short laugh as they rounded the corner. They could see a bus station two blocks down the street. They booked tickets to Arlington, Virginia. One stop before Washington, DC. They had some time to kill so Amber bought one of every newspaper they had.

There was no mention of her story in the *Wall Street Journal*, the *New York Times*, the *Charlotte Post*, or the *Charlotte Observer*—nothing. She finally found a very short story in the *San Francisco Chronicle* on page 8 titled, "Reporter Dupes 20." The story explained how Amber van Hosteen, former employee of News Corp, had coerced several small newspapers around the world to print an outlandish fictional story she had tried to pass off as fact. The list of governments renouncing the story was impressive.

As Amber and Jeff talked about the implications of the coordinated effort required to shut her down, the picture became bleak. "The only way this type of coordinated effort across countries could happen this fast is if some central intelligence network coordinated a response," Amber said angrily. "No legitimate news agency will ever want to talk to me again after this."

Jeff, putting his arm around Amber to comfort her, said, "This does actually tell us something we didn't know before today."

"That these assholes ruined my career," Amber said with tears of frustration in her eyes.

Jeff hugged Amber and said, "I'm sorry about that, but we need to look at the bigger picture. It means this 'Hidden Hand' thing may be real. It means there's an international organization that can manipulate the flow of information worldwide. It means that Shay's killer, the facility in Burkina Faso, the space traffic to and from the L2 Lagrange point, and shutting down this story are all related. The same people who want us dead are messing with your career and Stephan's French intelligence unit."

"This is a lynchpin that ties them all together," Amber said.

"Exactly! We're headed to Virginia, so I can get this sample to a lab there," Jeff said as he patted his backpack. "Our job is to save the world. What happens to us doesn't matter if the Hidden Hand doesn't win," Jeff said in a soft voice.

Amber looked at Jeff with amazement and said, "Who says things like that?"

"I do," Jeff said in a determined voice.

"You're a hero," Amber said as she hugged him back. "But we really need to change these glasses. You look just like the Unabomber. It's creepy." Amber made him get up and walk over to a small shop to buy a new pair of glasses.

As Jeff bought new glasses, Amber thought about what Jeff had just said. The members of the Hidden Hand were not simple thieves and murderers. These people committed crimes against all of humanity, and she would devote her life to bringing them to justice, no matter the cost.

Amber didn't know it then, but her career was a small price to pay compared to what would come next.

HOME OF THE NOT SO BRAVE

As the bus pulled into Arlington, Jeff explained his plans. "I'm going to stake out one of my ex-employees. He can get the sample to our lab through all the security checks. If I can convince him to work with us, we should have the answers we need in a few days."

"I'd like to use a library computer and publish my stories under an alias. There is more than one way to get the word out and people listening," Amber said.

"That's an excellent idea," said Jeff, "but we need to think about the timing of using that approach."

"What do we do until then?" Amber asked.

"We can rent a room for cash at some out-of-the-way place. An inn or bed and breakfast should work out fine," Jeff said. "We can also buy a car for cash from a private party. That will give us a few months' transportation with no questions asked. If we look around town, we're bound to find a car for sale somewhere."

"Okay, so we explore town, get something to eat, buy a car, and find a bed and breakfast somewhere on the outskirts of town," Amber summarized. "I like that plan. Tomorrow, while you're looking for your former employee, I can check up on recent events and try to figure out what our captain friend was talking about."

"Sounds good, but be careful," Jeff cautioned. "Be sure to follow the protocols I shared with you, so no one backtracks to us here. We need a few days minimum to get the lab results. I'm going to look for Mike tonight. He'll be at work during the day, and I can't reach him there."

"Okay," Amber replied. "I feel like some Mexican food."

"In Virginia? Good luck with that," Jeff said with a laugh.

Amber took Jeff's hand and said, "You know this town better than I do. Surprise me."

They had a great meal made from Virginia-raised beef and local produce. After, it didn't take them long to find a vehicle for sale. They bought a 2012 Buick Park Avenue from an elderly gentleman whose wife didn't like the car. The registration sticker was good for nine months, and a big four-door car with Virginia plates would not be out of place in Washington, DC. They found a room for rent in a guest house in the back of a lot surrounded by trees. Breakfast was included, and they could rent week to week.

Their cover story had Jeff looking for work in DC while Amber was trying her hand at being an author. They were not sure how long they would be in the area and needed to rent for a few weeks at most. The older couple who owned the property loved their story. Having found everything they needed, Amber took time to rest while Jeff set off to find Mike.

Jeff knew where Mike lived, but he also knew his apartment in Bethesda, Maryland, would be watched. Mike was a creature of habit. He complained every Friday about how he hated doing laundry in the laundromat on Thursday night and talked about how he was going to play darts with his friends at their favorite pub on Friday night.

Since it was Friday night, Jeff drove to the pub to find Mike. He parked a block away and walked to the street corner where the pub was located. He immediately spotted a black four-door with two men in it talking. Jeff checked for the typical surveillance signs to determine if it was a two-man or four-man team. It looked like a two-man team, but they were being lazy. Jeff spotted them too easily. He kept walking around the corner and hid down a side alley. He worked his way around to enter the building through the back door.

The back door opened to a hallway with bathrooms on one side and a door to the kitchen on the other. Jeff entered the main bar area and sat down at a high table in the back near groups of people. He could see Mike playing darts with several other young men. He could not spot anyone else watching Mike. The men were drinking beer, so all Jeff had to do was wait for nature to do its work and follow Mike to the bathroom to talk. Jeff kept track of who went to the bathroom and when they left so he would know how many people would be in there with Mike when he went. He nursed a beer himself as he pretended to read a newspaper.

Eventually, nature called, and Mike ducked out of the dart game to head to the bathroom. Jeff left his newspaper on the table and followed him. He knew one other person was in the men's room.

Mike went to a stall while Jeff went to the urinal. As the other man in the room finished and left, Jeff went over and locked the door, then waited for Mike to finish.

As Mike came out of the stall, he looked up and saw Jeff with his arms crossed, leaning against the sink. His face turned white.

Jeff wasn't sure what the agency had told Mike about him, but it must not have been good. Jeff raised his hands to show he had no weapons and said, "Mike, it's okay. I'm not here to hurt you."

Mike gave a sigh of relief and put his hand to his heart. "First, I heard you were a rogue agent. Then that you were dead. Now you're here and I was scared. I'm sorry, Jeff."

"No need to be sorry," Jeff said. "We don't have much time; you're being watched."

"Watched! Me?" Mike exclaimed.

"Shhh, keep it down," Jeff said in a low voice. "I was framed. I'm not sure who did it, but I think it was our director."

"No way, man. He was really upset when you left for Africa. The next thing I knew, he was calling you a rogue agent. I was reassigned," Mike blurted out.

Jeff said quickly and quietly. "We need to talk. Go back and play your game with your friends. Head home when you normally would. Once you're home, sneak out the back door and I'll meet you there."

"I don't know, Jeff. You were a great boss and all, but there is some bad shit happening. People have died," Mike said with a worried expression.

"This isn't about me, Mike. America—hell, the world—is at risk, and it's our job to stop it," Jeff said with passion.

"Whoa. Okay," Mike said. "Your intensity is scaring me a little, dude. I don't want to be the next person not showing up for work, you know."

"What do you mean?" Jeff asked. Just then the doorknob turned, and someone was knocking on the door.

"Hey, let me in, man!" someone said in an irritated voice. "I gotta pee." Mike started toward the door to unlock it.

"Wait, Mike. Who didn't come to work?" Jeff asked.

"Half your old team, man. The rest were shipped off to assignments in the middle of nowhere or reassigned like me," Mike said. "I think we're getting shuffled around so we won't notice who's missing."

The knocking grew louder. Jeff hurriedly asked, "You know about the shipwreck I worked on, right?"

"Yeah."

"That material was alien in origin. I've seen one of their ships. Our director is covering up their presence."

"Holy hell!" Mike said.

The banging got louder. "I need your help, Mike. Our country needs your help. Can I count on you?" Jeff asked.

"Yeah. Yes. Hell, yes! Just don't get me killed. I'm only an analyst, right?" Mike said.

"I won't get you killed. Now I'll go in a stall while you open the door. Wipe your nose like you were doing something illegal and say you're sorry as you exit. Don't look him in the eye. Got it?" Jeff said as he headed for the stall.

"Yeah," Mike said and smiled at Jeff. "It's good to have you back, boss."

Mike opened the door. A very large man was standing there looking very unhappy. "Sorry, man," Mike said as he wiped his nose with the back of his hand and sniffed.

"Freaking druggy," the man said as he passed.

Jeff waited for the man to finish his business and leave. He then left the bathroom and headed out of the building, returning to his car. He drove to a place near Mike's apartment and waited. When Jeff saw Mike pull into the parking area, he also saw the car tailing Mike park on the street. Jeff left his car and went to wait near Mike's back door.

Jeff hoped Mike remembered some counter-surveillance techniques from his training and applied them now. When Mike turned on the rear porchlight before exiting the building, Jeff knew he did not remember a single thing.

"Mike, lights!" Jeff whispered.

Mike looked around confused. "What? Lights? Oh, yeah," he said, then turned off the porch light and crept down the stairs like a cartoon burglar.

Jeff could only shake his head. Once Mike had made his way to the shadows, Jeff took him by the arm and led him to Jeff's car where they sat and talked.

"I need to know everything that happened from the time I left for Africa until now," Jeff began. "Keep it short but hit all the highlights."

"Right," Mike said. "The director started reassigning people the day after you left. He had us running all over the place doing useless surveillance or analysis. After Bill stood up to him about the useless work, the next day he didn't come into the office."

"Did he take the day off?" Jeff asked.

"Nobody knows. He just never came back to work again." Mike looked a little scared. "Then we were told you would be reassigned. They never brought a new guy in. They just started assigning us to new teams. As far as I know, Jennifer and I are the only people from our old team who are still around."

Now it was Jeff's turn to get angry. He took a deep breath and said, "I'm sorry to hear that, Mike. What happened next?"

"You're sorry to hear that?" Mike said. He was upset, almost to the point of panicking. "Dude, I think they're dead, and you're 'Sorry to hear that.'"

Jeff grabbed Mike by the shoulders and said, "Mike, look at me. I need you to focus. They may be dead or just shipped off to who knows where, but that doesn't mean we should give up. We need to get the bastards who are doing this out of our government."

"But...but," Mike stammered, "it's our assistant director—and people above him. We're screwed if we do anything."

"You're wrong. We're screwed if we do nothing. Your friends and coworkers may have died for nothing if we do nothing," Jeff said with conviction. "You know me, Mike." He nodded his head. "You know I keep my promises." He nodded his head again.

"I promise you that you will live, and I will avenge our team if you do exactly what I say," Jeff continued.

Some of the tension left Mike's body and he seemed able to focus. "What do you want me to do, boss?"

"I need you to take this sample to Alon." Jeff held up the canister he had brought with him. "Have it analyzed and determine its purpose." Mike looked a little confused, so Jeff clarified, "What could it be used for?"

"Well, that's easy," Mike said. "Alon loves me. His lab assistant wants to kill me, though."

"Can you do it Monday?" Jeff asked.

"Yeah. I can for sure," Mike said.

"Here's a list of phone numbers. Call me at the next number on this list each day at 2 p.m.," Jeff said, as he handed Mike a list of five phone numbers. "We will only use each of them once. I'll use the rainy day code words. If anyone asks about the calls, you are working some leads on a case. Do not use your office phone, cell phone, or our names on the call."

"Okay," Mike said.

"So, what else happened while I was away?" Jeff asked.

Mike looked around and then back at Jeff. He swallowed hard and said, "I think there was a coup."

"Where?" Jeff asked.

"Here, Washington!" Mike said.

Jeff was shocked. "There was nothing in the news."

"I know," Mike said. "There were tanks on the White House lawn. Helicopter gunships were firing on troops with Stinger missiles firing back. It was crazy. They said it was right wing activists blowing up car bombs, but people saw it. It was our troops firing on each other."

"Three Army Generals and an Air Force Colonel died, man, plus a few hundred more. They covered it all up. There were some videos and social media posts, but they all disappeared." Mike's tension grew as he spoke.

"No one is doing anything about this?" Jeff asked.

"No, man. No one I know of," Mike said.

Anger was growing steadily in Jeff. First, his team had been murdered. Now, a coup had been completely covered up and no one was doing anything about it. Since when had America become a country of cowards? This was going to change.

"Mike, I need names," Jeff said. "I want to talk to people who saw this coup. I need names of the people who died and the people announcing the details of the coverup." Mike was looking more worried. "Do not take any big risks. Just tell me what you know and what you can easily find out."

They talked for another hour. Jeff was pulling every detail he could out of Mike and making a list to follow up on. Mike was scared, and part of Jeff couldn't blame him—by the sounds of it, the country was changing from a republic to a dictatorship. The average person just didn't know it yet.

Jeff wanted to confirm everything Mike was telling him. He had excellent analytical skills. He had a lot of data on this coup attempt and even more on the government officials involved. Only a few elected officials were involved, but they were in influential roles like House and Senate committee leaders. Most of the people involved were administrative staffers—the non-elected officials who ran government offices like the CIA and FBI. Combine that with a handful of senior military leaders and the power they controlled was impressive. Jeff was going to keep Amber busy with this information.

Jeff knew Mike well. He had an impressive analytical mind, but he was emotionally immature. Jeff had to inspire this young man to keep him focused on a clear goal and reward him along the way. He had to trust Mike with a little more information.

As he was about to leave, Jeff said, "Mike, I know this whole situation is scary. I can only guess what you are feeling right now, but I believe the human race is in danger. Forces we do not yet understand are attacking the very fabric of our democracy. You have a very rare opportunity right now." Jeff held up the canister with the liquid in it. "This liquid was created in a factory in Africa. It kills thousands of human beings every day."

"No way," Mike said.

"I saw it with my own eyes," Jeff confirmed. "Machines dropping dead bodies in bins that were loaded onto trucks to be hauled away like trash. They treat people like raw material used in a manufacturing process. It was…inhumane."

"That's unbelievable," Mike said.

"When Amber and I escaped from the building, we saw a ship launch into the sky. Its drive system was not like anything I've ever seen before."

"No way! What was it like?" Mike asked.

"It was a bright yellow light without any heat or fire. It was fast. Too fast to be one of ours," Jeff answered.

"Oh my God!" Mike said excitedly. "Can you confirm it?"

"I was working with agents from another country," Jeff said, not wanting to share who or which country yet. "They confirmed the launch and tracked traffic to and from the L2 Lagrange point."

"No way!" Mike was amazed by Jeff's story. "The L2 Lagrange point is where the gravity of the Earth and the sun balance, so something can sit there forever without using any energy."

"That's right," Jeff confirmed.

"Wait, Amber, the reporter," Mike asked, "is she with you now?"

Jeff winced. He did not want to share anything about Amber or her whereabouts in case he was caught. "No," he lied. "We split up in Africa. I have no idea where she is now."

"There was a huge news story just like the one you're describing now. It was published in a lot of papers all over the world. Then the story was discredited the next day by our own president and leaders all over the world. There was huge buzz on social media."

"Mike, I took this liquid from that factory. I traveled ten thousand miles to bring it here—to bring it to you because I know you're the best analyst in the agency," Jeff said.

"Wow! Really?" Mike said.

"Yes," Jeff continued. "I need this liquid analyzed to find out what it is and why someone is creating it. Why go to all this trouble? Why create a factory in Africa and corrupt our government? We need to understand who these creatures are and what they want—why they just didn't bombard us into oblivion from space. They must have a reason to go to all this trouble, and you're the man I'm trusting to find out."

"I'm on it, boss," Mike said with conviction. "This is so crazy, and I can't tell anyone about it, can I?"

"Definitely not," Jeff said firmly as he handed the glass beaker over to Mike. "This is 'need to know,' and I decide who needs to know. Right now, it is you, me, and Alon. No one else."

"Got it, boss," Mike said. "Wow, so Amber's story was real after all. Man, this is wild."

"Now go home, get a good night's rest, and follow your same routines," Jeff said. "Do not do anything out of the ordinary and think before you talk about anything even close to this. Got it?"

"Got it, boss," Mike said as he got out of the car and turned with a smile. "And boss, it's good to have you back."

"It's good to be back," Jeff said, returning the smile.

As he watched Mike head back home, Jeff couldn't help but wonder whether he had just made this young man a hero in future history books or sent him to his grave, joining the rest of Jeff's team. Only time would tell.

FIND ANOTHER GAME

Jeff took the usual precautions driving home that night, and he snuck into the house without waking Amber, who had already gone to sleep.

The next morning, Jeff woke to Amber bringing him breakfast in bed. "Good morning," she said with a sad smile.

"Good morning, and thank you," Jeff said. "What's wrong?"

"Well, I just shoveled two months of work into a trash bin," Amber said, sitting on the bed and tossing a tablet aside. "According to every media source on the globe, I'm right up there with the Antichrist."

"Screw them," Jeff said. He rubbed her arm. "They're afraid of what you're saying. That's the only reason they'd go to such trouble. You're an incredible reporter and they can't control you."

She smiled at him. "Thanks." But then her smile faded. "I just worked so hard for so long. Not just on the story, but my career. I never thought the pursuit of the truth could end this way. Guess you didn't suspect you'd hooked up with Pollyanna."

"Amber," Jeff said as he turned to face her and grabbed her shoulders. "You know these people are wrong. You know what we found out has to be shared with the world."

"But how, Jeff?" Amber asked close to tears. "How can we share the truth when our own government is against us? When people are afraid to share the truth?"

"Remember the man who stood in front of the tanks in Tiananmen Square?" Jeff asked.

"That's different," Amber said.

"Remember the French freedom fighters from World War II? They faced greater challenges than we have, and they were only fighting over politics, not the extermination of thousands of people," Jeff said with a mixture of passion and concern. "We cannot change the past, but we can change the future."

"But everything we've tried has failed," Amber said as she looked into Jeff's eyes. "They seem to hold all the cards."

"Then we need to play a different game," Jeff said with conviction.

Amber stared into Jeff's eyes for a few moments, thinking. Then she smiled and said, "Play a different game. You're a genius." She jumped off the bed and went to her desk.

"Hey, the genius over here would like some coffee," Jeff said, half-joking. He really did want more coffee.

"You know where the coffee is," Amber shot back.

Jeff smiled. He decided to eat and get cleaned up before sharing what he had learned about the coup.

Jeff put the plates from breakfast in the small kitchen and sat down next to Amber, who was busy working. "What are you doing?" he asked.

"I'm playing a different game," she said as she turned to face Jeff with a smile. "Up until now, we have been trying to report the news. The powers that be are shutting us down. So…instead of trying to report the news, we'll make the news."

Curious, Jeff asked, "How?"

"Reporters are a predictable bunch really. There are thousands of them, and they're always looking for stories. What we need to do is float pieces of our story out there for reporters to find. They'll then research it and report on it. Once we get enough pieces out there, they'll paint the picture for us, and there's nothing anyone can do to stop it, short of shutting down all news and social media everywhere."

"That's brilliant!" Jeff said.

"It was your idea—play a different game," Amber said as she turned back to her work.

"Well, I have another story for you, and it's a big one," Jeff said ominously.

"What is it?" Amber asked with concern.

"When I met with Mike, there was some very bad news," Jeff said. "He said a military coup was attempted in Washington."

"What?" Amber asked.

"There were tanks on the White House Lawn. US military forces were firing on each other. Helicopter gunships were firing on men with Stinger missiles and they were firing back."

"There was nothing in the news. There's nothing online. Who could cover that up?" Amber asked in disbelief.

"It would appear they covered it up by saying it was radicals setting off bombs, not troops fighting in the streets," Jeff said.

Jeff pulled out a notepad and dropped it on Amber's desk as he said, "I have names, dates, who died, and a few other details in here. I think your anti-disinformation strategy will work really well on this topic, and people will pay more attention to it since it's very close to home."

"I can't believe it. A coup, here? The people who started it must have known something was wrong and didn't agree to go along with it," Amber said. "Anti-disinformation strategy? I'm going to look that one up."

"The government is covering up the coup with disinformation, telling people lies that are close to the truth but misleading. The strategy you described is countering their strategy, so it is anti-disinformation," Jeff explained.

"Wow! Okay. We could use this to our advantage. I could feed personal interest stories on the people killed. I can get civil rights reporters onto the killings and any other rights abuses. I'll need to do a little research."

"Okay, but be sure to wear your scarf and glasses. We're close to DC and you're easily recognizable," Jeff said. "I need to go shopping."

"Let me guess—guns and explosives," Amber said.

"You know me too well," Jeff said with a smile.

✳ ✳ ✳

The weekend passed quickly. Jeff acquired weapons for both of them. He created an escape plan with multiple rendezvous points. Then he went and surveyed the damage caused by the coup in Washington, DC.

In the meantime, Amber had done an impressive amount of research and come up with several startling conclusions. They compared notes Sunday night over a dinner of Chinese takeout.

"I need to share the escape plan," Jeff said. "It's pretty simple."

"You're not going to destroy this lovely old couple's rental house, are you?" Amber asked.

"No," Jeff said defensively. "I didn't rig any explosives to the house."

"I hope not to need an escape plan this time," Amber said.

"I hope not to need it every time, but hope is not a plan," Jeff said.

Amber shook her head and said, "I have some interesting information. Our friend, Captain Samuelson, had a nephew who was killed in the fighting."

"What side was he on?" Jeff asked.

"Hard to tell," Amber replied. "There was no clean delineation by service or unit that I can tell. The soldiers seemed to follow either their direct superior or someone higher up. It was chaos, and I don't have military records to figure it all out."

"When I checked out the DC area today, I could see where repairs had been made to buildings and streets. The coup was only one month ago, and everything was already repaired. Did you have a chance to look at the pictures I left you?" Jeff asked.

"Yes, I need to check that area out myself. The repairs do not fit the cover story," Amber said as she picked up the pictures.

"How so?" Jeff asked.

"See this picture here," Amber said as she showed Jeff a picture of a high-rise apartment building. "Why would terrorists blow up a bomb on the fifth story of an apartment building? That was caused by a missile being fired from the ground and missing its target in the sky."

"Also, see here," Amber said as she held up another picture. "These marks on this building were caused by a helicopter blade as it dropped to the ground. All this damage was from the helicopter crash landing."

"How do you know all this?" Jeff asked.

"I've seen war zones before. I've seen helicopters shot down and missiles hitting buildings. It's grizzly business, but war leaves different footprints than car bombs or natural disasters."

"Sometimes I forget how observant you are. What else did you find out?" Jeff asked.

"I've found three major themes I think we can exploit as our anti-disinformation strategy," Amber said as she shuffled through some papers. "One is directly refuting the government's story. This will appeal immediately to anyone who does not trust the government, and several organizations will take this data and run with it. The problem is most of them are not credible and lack broad readership, but it does put the data we want in print almost immediately. Some of those details will cause other reporters to investigate.

"The second theme," Amber continued, "is indirect but leads back to the first. We write on the people who died in the coup. We build them up as heroes and then add breadcrumbs that lead back to the facts we want to question. For example, how did a terrorist murder a two-star general with an M-16 bullet? I'm crafting stories that would make it into major media that tie back to the details of the first approach. For example, I could do a personal interest story on Samuelson's nephew. I can paint him as a hero protecting his country and work in the anomalies in the government's story we want people to question. Why did he die versus how did he die?"

"How do you know we can get the details in the story we want to highlight?" Jeff asked.

"Sometimes we won't, but sometimes we will. We need to create a volume of stories to improve the odds. I can also ghostwrite for another reporter. Smaller newspapers do this all the time. It's the only way they can afford to get enough stories to publish," Amber explained.

"I thought your name was no longer trusted," Jeff said.

"Ouch," Amber said jokingly. "I'll use a fake name. That shouldn't be a problem. I even have a few alter egos I've written under from the past."

"Probably best not to use those. Anything that can be traced back to you would prove you're still alive. We don't want anyone to know you're still around, and we definitely don't want people to think you're in the US," Jeff said.

"Okay. I can work with that," Amber said. "The third theme is difficult and crafty. We basically write stories that support the government's story, but we write them in a way that highlights the flaws in the government's story."

"Like terrorist bombs versus missile blast holes?" Jeff said.

"Yes, or our country is secure, but three generals died," Amber said. "If we cannot protect a general, what chance does the average citizen have? Those types of anomalies in a story will drive some people nuts; they'll investigate it just because it's in their nature to do so. You should see some of the obscure things people found while I was at News Corp."

"I have six basic stories ready to go now. Two of each. I also have five data sheets ready to go. I can start sending them out tomorrow when the library opens," Amber said.

"Excellent!" Jeff said. "Wow, you move fast. It's important not to send everything from the same place. It would point right back to where we are. We can send them in batches from places two or three hours away. We should also print it versus sharing handwritten text."

"I'm ahead of you on that, but two or three hours each day on the road.... I can't write if I'm driving. I can create another two or three stories every day if I have that time," Amber said.

"I can do most of the driving," Jeff said. "I really don't have much to do until Mike gets back to me anyway."

"Great!" Amber said. "I want to do some work on the Africa story too. I can do something similar on the human suffering angle and tie it into other stories on the alien spacecraft."

"Good idea," Jeff said. "I guess we have some free time until tomorrow then."

✳ ✳ ✳

The next day, Jeff left early to drive to post offices in different states to mail Amber's stories. He created a pattern in case anyone could trace the source of the mail so it would look like they were in Delaware and sending the stories out of post offices in states bordering Delaware. He could reach locations in Virginia, West Virginia, and Maryland before he had to stop to receive Mike's first check-in call. He would travel to Pennsylvania and New Jersey tomorrow.

At five minutes to 2 p.m., Jeff pulled over at a place with good reception and waited for Mike's call.

At 2:02, the phone rang. Jeff picked it up on the third ring. Jeff spoke the code words immediately, "It looks like another rainy day." He then looked at his watch and started timing the call.

Mike replied, "Rain is good and bad." Then he continued, "I have the package delivered but no results yet. All we know now is that this is an organic acid built off specific protein chains only found in human DNA."

"That is more than we knew yesterday," Jeff replied. "Anything else?"

"Yeah, our old assistant director, he got a new job. He was moved to a role in the FBI. It's not very clear what he's doing or even his new title."

"Hmm. Okay," Jeff replied. "See what you can learn when the opportunity arises. This call is over."

Jeff hung up the phone and thought for a few minutes. Did they move the assistant director because he was doing a good job or a bad one? If he had been doing a good job, moving him to the FBI was a very bad thing. Jeff removed the SIM card in his cell phone and replaced it with another before he started driving home.

Jeff spent some time thinking about the organic acid. What would an organic acid do for these aliens, and why would they go to such lengths to obtain it? The African situation had to be labeled a genocide eventually. Amber had estimated that more than one hundred thousand had died by now. This would have to be one of the bloodiest events in history. Of course, it was smaller than the 6 million Jews killed by Nazi Germany or the 75 million who died in World War II. Had the aliens been involved in that somehow? UFOs were not really a thing before the 1950s, were they?

Jeff was going to have to spend some time researching these questions. Next, he was going to pick up Amber and go visit the "terrorist" bomb sites in Washington, DC. He took notes in his personal shorthand so he would remember to follow up later.

When Jeff pulled into the driveway thirty-five minutes later, Amber was ready to go. She saw him pull up and ran out to the car after locking the door. She had a big smile for Jeff and started talking even before buckling her seatbelt.

"Hi, Jeff. I've had a great day. I have three new stories written. I walked to the library and found out the most interesting things. I need a little more data, but I think I found a link between multiple companies all over the world working with a corporate holding company. It's the same company I was researching when I went to Africa. I don't know what it means yet, but I'm sure I'm on to something. I have documents being shipped in tomorrow."

"You didn't tie them to your name, did you?" Jeff asked.

"No, I actually got this sweet old lady to do it all for me," Amber said. "I felt bad lying to her about my situation, but I helped her with a few things too. What did Mike have to say?"

"Mike said our mysterious liquid is an organic acid made from specific protein chains only found in human DNA," Jeff said.

"Wow, what do they use it for?" Amber asked.

"We don't know yet. It may take a few days to figure that out, but I was asking myself the same questions as we did in Africa. Why do this and do it this way?" Jeff asked. "Then I started thinking, when were UFOs a thing? Were these aliens involved in other bloody conflicts like World War II or the Jewish concentration camps?"

"I hadn't thought of that angle," said Amber. "Have they been screwing with us for ten years or a thousand years?"

"Maybe they're like our pirates," Jeff hypothesized. "A group acting outside the laws of their race to make money somehow."

"Maybe human DNA is an aphrodisiac to aliens like a Rhino's horn is in some cultures," Amber said, and they both laughed.

Then they looked at each other and shook their heads. That would just be too weird.

"Anyway," Jeff said. "Can you do some research on when UFOs became a thing."

"Became a thing?" Amber asked.

"You know what I mean. When did they become popular? Was there evidence of them before modern times?" Jeff clarified.

"I did a personal interest story on a UFO victim back when I was doing that kind of work. I did a little research. UFOs became famous in the West shortly after a doctor or businessman in Washington State reported flying objects moving at high speed, skipping across the water in the 1950s," Amber explained.

"Wait, where in Washington State?" Jeff asked.

"In the ocean off Puget Sound somewhere, I think," Amber answered. "I don't know exactly where, but he reported several crescent-shaped objects moving at thousands of miles per hour, skipping off the water like saucers. The interesting thing is that the press focused on the saucer part, not the crescent-shape of the object. So now we have 'flying saucers' as a term because of how the press reported the incident. Isn't that amazing?"

"You know that material I talked about with Stephan and his team? It was found at the bottom of the ocean off the coast of Canada. It was resting on the bottom in a semi-circular shape. That could be a crescent," Jeff said.

"Wow!" Amber exclaimed. "We had a sign, but no one knew what to do about it. You know, the UFO conspiracy theory people would eat this up. It would be all over the news and tabloids so fast. It could be in television documentaries within a few months."

"And leave breadcrumbs leading to the Africa launches and the traffic to and from the L2 Lagrange point?" Jeff added.

"Now you're catching on," Amber said.

Jeff smiled and said, "Who would have thought that everything happening to us is all related in some way? We just stumbled into it."

"Hey, maybe you stumbled into it, but I went to Africa following leads," Amber said defensively. "I was researching some really bad people for months before you came along."

"I thought I saved you?" Jeff said defensively.

"Three men with machine guns blazing isn't what I'd call saving. You could have killed me. What would you call it?" Amber asked, getting a little defensive.

Realizing where this conversation was going, Jeff decided to use charm rather than argue with a master debater, so he said, "A good reason to be slapped?"

Amber burst out laughing and couldn't stop for a few moments. Then she said, as she continued to laugh, "You should have seen your face when I hauled off and slapped you. I'm not sure, but I think the other men laughing at you was probably the worst part."

"It did hurt my feelings," Jeff said jokingly.

"Shut up," Amber joked back.

"It was pretty embarrassing, and I couldn't shave the next morning," Jeff said.

"Shut up," Amber said.

"I do have some other news if we are good on the UFO thing for now," Jeff said.

"Changing the topic, are we?" Amber said.

"You did say shut up," Jeff said.

"Like that ever works," Amber said, rolling her eyes. "Seriously, I'll work on the UFO angle tomorrow. I'll gather some more data from you later today. What's the new news?"

"My old assistant director was replaced," Jeff said.

"Is that bad news or good news?" Amber asked.

"I don't know. I've asked Mike to snoop around. We'll look at the actions he takes and see," Jeff replied. "I was more concerned with where they sent him. He now has a role in the FBI. We don't know what role yet."

"I can't help you there. Government agencies like the CIA and FBI are a tight-lipped group," Amber said.

"You really don't have a mole in some government agency?" Jeff asked.

"No," Amber said. "I never have. Is that why they assigned you to follow me around?"

"They assigned me because more junior agents failed to stop you," Jeff said. "I thought I drew the short straw until I found out how hard it was to stop you from getting a story. You're good."

"Thank you, Jeff," Amber said. "That really means a lot to me."

"You're welcome! We're close to the first bomb site. I'm going to park around the corner so we can walk around the sites. The White House grounds have been closed to the public, so we can't do more than look at those from a distance."

Amber wore a scarf and sunglasses. Jeff wore his hoodie and sunglasses. They walked around town, stopping at stores occasionally to shop, and inspected the "bomb sites" as they slowly walked to the next store or public building.

Amber's sharp eyes immediately picked out where walls were patched from rocket fire, explosions, and bullet holes. The cover story provided by the government painted a picture where four cars entered Washington, DC with bombs in them. One blew open the gates to the White House while the other three exploded at various sites around the city. This cover story would only make sense if the damage on the ground reflected that an explosion of some type had occurred, including damage from shrapnel. The bullet holes high up on a tall building only made sense if someone had been shooting at an object in the air.

Amber could map out one scene where a group was firing at an object in the sky, likely a helicopter, and it was firing back based on the damage patterns. The helicopter moved across the sky and got hit. Its blades stuck the side of a building before the helicopter plummeted to the street and exploded. She also pointed out that bombs leave craters in the ground. These "bomb sites" do not look like car bomb craters. They are too shallow, and the damage is directional, like when a plane crashes and leaves a long gouge in the Earth rather than one that is equal in all directions from the center.

Jeff was impressed. He took pictures of the repaired buildings and streets as they went. As they approached the White House, Jeff stopped Amber and turned around immediately, dragging her with him.

"What is it?" Amber asked.

Jeff put his arm around Amber and walked quickly. His eyes were down toward the ground, but he was scanning ahead and to both sides as they walked. "They were stopping people on the streets," he explained. "Move your eyes and not your head as you look."

Amber looked and said, "They're stopping men with hoodies."

Jeff looked around again and said, "You're right. When we turn this corner, I'm going to lose the hoodie."

Jeff led them to a garbage can near a corner store. As they turned the corner, he took off the hoodie and stuffed it into the garbage can, making sure the garbage covered it. "Time to get out of here," Jeff said.

Then a man in a dark suit, probably an FBI agent, stepped out of a doorway about twenty yards in front of them as he spoke into his radio. He was looking straight at Jeff.

Immediately, Jeff pulled Amber into the store next to them. They ran through the store toward the back. Customers dropped their bags and scattered out of their way.

"Keep running and hide until I call you," Jeff said as he stopped and hid in a changing room just off the main path.

The FBI agent entered the front of the store cautiously and saw Amber running toward the back. He sprinted toward the back of the store to catch her.

As the agent approached Jeff's hiding place, Jeff stepped out and hit the agent in the throat with the palm of his hand. The agent went down hard on his back and was out cold. Jeff took the agent's radio, cell phone, and gun and then sprinted toward the back of the store. He was listening to the radio when he found Amber.

"They know I'm here. They're using cameras in the streets. Damn it. I should have known. We need to take the back alley behind the buildings so they don't see us. Let's go."

They exited the back of the building and sprinted toward their car. They stopped running when they reached the sidewalk of a cross street. Then they calmly walked across the street to the next alley. As they walked, Jeff checked the cell phone. He could not unlock it, so he wiped it clean and dropped it in the back of a truck starting to drive away. They worked their way around delivery trucks and people working until they found the parking lot where they had parked. It looked clear, so they dumped the FBI agent's gun and radio in a garbage can after wiping it clean of fingerprints. Then they got into their car and drove away.

Neither of them said a word until they were safely outside the city. Jeff was driving toward Maryland in case they were being tracked. He ran the usual process of driving in three concentric circles looking for anyone following them. This time, he also parked in a parking lot and checked the sky for aerial surveillance. Satisfied they were not being followed, they headed to their temporary home in Virginia.

"Does this change our plans? Should we do anything differently?" Amber asked now that the stress of their situation had abated some.

"I'm not sure. I need time to think," Jeff replied.

"Okay."

"I keep putting you in danger," Jeff blurted out.

"What do you mean?"

"In Algiers, when we ziplined from our building and you bruised your hip," Jeff said, "it was my mistake that put the bruise on your hip."

"It was also your forethought that got us out of there alive," Amber said. "It was my stupid mistake that got me injured, not yours."

"I almost killed you under that truck in Burkina Faso," Jeff said, looking at Amber. "I almost got you killed today."

Amber put a hand on Jeff's shoulder. "We're in this together, Jeff. If I die, I die fighting the bastards who are messing with our government and our world. I know the risks, and I'm in this fight 110 percent. We're both human so we'll make mistakes. Both of us have. We'll just have to deal with it and move on, together. It's okay to be a little paranoid; that's what's kept us alive, but we can't be paralyzed with fear or they win."

"And I thought I was the hero," Jeff said, half-joking.

They bought fast food on the way home and worked late into the night.

Jeff left at 10 p.m. to contact Stephan back in France. They had arranged for weekly touchpoints for the next four weeks. Jeff had a list of phone numbers to call Stephan at. He found a pay phone a few miles away from their home.

Jeff called four times. No one answered. He was concerned, but their contact time had passed. He knew Stephan would not even try to show up late, so he went home. He would try again in a week using the next number on the list. He hoped Stephan was all right.

DEAD ENDS

The next day, Jeff woke up early again to drive the story packages Amber had produced to different post offices for delivery to reporters all over the world. Amber was prolific. She knew what she was doing and laid the groundwork for the bigger story.

As Jeff drove, he thought about the analysis going on in Virginia. He hoped Alon could put an entire team on researching the organic acid. Jeff was no expert on this type of chemical, and no matter how hard he tried, he just couldn't think of anything so valuable that an alien race would spend trillions to get it in this way. He had the best expert he knew analyzing the sample, so he turned his thoughts to other matters.

The aliens had to have a ship of some kind at the L2 Lagrange point. How else would there be regular traffic to and from this point in space? Maybe they even had a base of some type. Jeff started to wonder if there was some way to detect whatever the aliens had stationed at the L2 Lagrange point. Who in the world could he work with to find a way to discover what was hidden there?

✳ ✳ ✳

As 2 p.m. approached, Jeff was waiting for Mike's call.

At thirty seconds past two, the phone rang. Jeff picked it up on the third ring and said, "It looks like another rainy day." He then looked at his watch and started timing the call.

"Rain is good and bad," Mike replied. Then he continued, "I have some news."

"Great! Let's have it."

"Our former assistant director was assigned to a special project in the FBI as its leader. He has no direct reports but controls all assignments for the entire agency."

"He can put anyone he wants on to anything that crosses the FBI Director's desk?" Jeff asked.

"Yep," Mike replied. "Someday when we have the time, I'll tell you how I found that out."

"Sounds like I really do not want to know."

"Yep!"

"What happened with the sample?"

"Alon has a small team he trusts working on this, and frankly, they don't know what it's used for. In humans, organic acid tests are used to identify nutritional deficiencies, but that's the product of an ailment. It's not really used to do something. Technically, this acid is a Lewis acid, which means it can form a covalent bond with an electron pair. This type of chemical reaction cannot be recreated synthetically. It is naturally occurring in a living host. If the host is extinct, the acid is lost forever. Their best guess is it's a catalyst for some other chemical reaction," Mike said.

Jeff winced when Mike said Alon's name. "No names. If this is the best they could do, I'd have to call it a dead end."

"I hear you!" Mike said. "But I don't want them making things up. This is their honest answer. He did mention that they went to a lot of trouble to make this with a human host."

"What do you mean?"

"The process to make this acid used advanced chemical engineering techniques. More advanced than anything he has ever seen before."

"All right, good work!" Jeff encouraged Mike. "This call is over," and Jeff hung up.

The disappointment on the research team's findings completely drained Jeff. This was the ace. Their physical proof that would hopefully lead to the alien's motives. Now it was a dead end. Jeff walked over to a nearby park and sat for twenty minutes trying to think of a path forward. After his initial despair, his thoughts came back to the L2 Lagrange point. If they could reveal what was there to the world, the shock of it alone would wake people up. They would start asking questions and find Amber's stories.

He needed to talk to Amber, so he drove back to Virginia. As he drove into the driveway, Amber opened the door and smiled. He sat there a moment looking at her and immediately felt a lot better.

Jeff went inside and said, "The lab analysis was not very helpful."

"Really?" Amber said while noticing Jeff's mood.

"Yes," Jeff said as he sat down heavily at their table. "They could confirm that the liquid is an organic acid derived from protein chains that only exist in humans."

"Well, that confirms our story that the liquid came from that horrible manufacturing facility," Amber said.

"Yes, but they have no idea what it's used for," Jeff said with a heavy sigh. "Apparently, in humans, organic acids are used in tests to find nutritional deficiencies. Mike said the technical term is 'Lewis Acid.' These acids are created by living organisms. They cannot be reproduced artificially. They used advanced chemical engineering techniques our lab had never seen before."

"Interesting!"

"What do you mean?"

"I don't know much about chemistry, but they went to a lot of trouble to make a custom recipe that works on humans to create an acid that can only be created in a living host. They must be pretty desperate to get this acid. Think of the effort it took for them to find us, determine they could use us, and engineer this custom recipe."

"Not to mention the cost of factories, the bribes, and finding the fanatics to work with them. They must have spent years working on this."

"Maybe decades."

"Did you deliver the documents all right?" Amber asked.

"Yes," Jeff said. "Everything is going according to plan except our lab findings. A small team is going to keep working on it, but it didn't sound promising. I was trying to think of anything else—any other angle that would expose these aliens and what they're doing. All I could come up with was somehow uncovering what's at the L2 Lagrange point. They must have a ship or a base of some kind there."

"Before we go there, I have some news I need to share," Amber said. "There's a holding company owned by various legal entities with a subsidiary doing work here in the United States in Silicon Valley. This company makes custom electronics used in different military applications for communications and robotic control systems." Amber noticed Jeff's eyes. He was losing focus on the discussion, so she jumped to the point. "Anyway, this company shipped robotic control modules to Burkina Faso. I found this out through customs documents."

"We have a link between a US company and the building of the manufacturing facility in Africa?" Jeff asked.

"Yes," Amber said. "But more importantly, this same company is shipping these same parts to over 200 other locations around the world."

Jeff sat up in his chair and said, "Do you think this means they're building more sites like the one we saw all over the world?"

"I wasn't sure, so I cross-referenced other companies shipping to the same location in Africa against these same companies shipping the same materials to the same 200-plus locations around the world. I found over seventy-five companies that matched. I'm 90 percent sure they're building over 200 more facilities like this one, but...."

"But?" Jeff asked.

"But the quantity of materials being shipped are bigger," Amber said with dread in her voice. "About five times bigger."

"Jeez," Jeff said.

"When you look at all this, there must be thousands of people helping them," Amber said. "How could aliens motivate so many people to help them exterminate the human race?"

"I was pondering that same question today," Jeff said. "The doctor in the Burkina Faso facility was one of them, in fact. He didn't seem to be under any type of alien control. He seemed to be a fanatic. His focus was on medical research, at any cost."

"I was wondering the same thing about the people at the mining facility. The leaders, the truck drivers, the soldiers, and the guards at the factory were all working for the aliens. Only, their goal was killing non-Muslims. Two factions with completely different goals were working at the same facility to serve their own purposes while also meeting the aliens' goal," Jeff said.

"Maybe the aliens are not working directly with people?" Amber hypothesized. "Maybe they use some surrogate, a middleman, to find people passionate about something and align them to their cause?"

"That would mean they have a network of these middlemen and know a hell of a lot about the human race. They would have to be here for decades to pull this off," Jeff said.

"You said that material off the coast of Canada was there for up to 100 years," Amber reminded Jeff.

"Any ideas on how long we have until those new sites come online?" Jeff asked.

"My best guess is three to six months," Amber said.

"Then we have three months to expose these criminals and the aliens," Jeff said with conviction. "So little time. Are any of these new sites in the United States?"

"I could only find data on international shipments. There are no official records for shipments within the country," Amber said. "We can go to California and see what we can find out at the company."

"We could, but it would take time to travel, stake out, and recruit spies," Jeff said. "We only have three months, so we need to be careful how we spend our time. If I were still an agent, I could go to the Department of Commerce and figure this out."

After a few moments of thought, Jeff added, "I can ask Mike to do it the next time I talk to him. I'll need company names and your cross-reference data."

"You got it," Amber said. "You were also saying something about the Lagrange point?"

"Yes. There must be a ship or a base at the L2 Lagrange point," Jeff said. "If we can prove something is there, it will motivate people to fight back."

"You sent my stories today on the space traffic from Africa and back," Amber said. "You also delivered my updates on why the 'bomb' damage in DC could not be from a car bomb. I can document more on the sites being constructed, and I really want to figure out who owns this company in Silicon Valley. Its name is XBC. I cannot find anything that spells out what XBC means. The company is privately held so there's not a lot of official data out there."

"Okay, you do that. I'll follow up with Mike on this company," Jeff said. "I'm also going to try to find a way to detect something at the L2 Lagrange point. I'll try finding a university professor tomorrow. They always like to talk to people."

Amber and Jeff agreed on a plan and worked late into the night, again.

✳ ✳ ✳

The next day, they again woke early. Jeff was driving more than 150 miles a day delivering the stories Amber was writing, while Amber did research and wrote more stories. Today, however, Jeff couldn't help but think they were not doing enough. Not risking enough to make a difference. They had ninety days to make a difference. He hoped he could find someone to talk to at the University of Virginia's Physics Department.

Jeff arrived at the Charlottesville post office at 1:45 p.m. He went to mail the batch of stories from this post office, then waited for Mike's call.

At twenty seconds past 2 p.m., the phone rang. Jeff picked it up on the third ring and said, "It looks like another rainy day." He then looked at his watch and started timing the call.

"Rain is good and bad," Mike replied. Then he continued, "I don't have any new news."

"I understand," Jeff said. "I have a new request for you."

"Shoot," Mike said.

"I need you to check on some companies through the Commerce Department. I want to know if they're shipping a specific list of materials to any locations in the US."

"Sure. That's easy enough," Mike said. "I'll probably have it tomorrow."

"Excellent," Jeff said, and he shared the public website where the data was located.

"If there is nothing else?" Jeff said and waited ten seconds to give Mike time to respond. "This call is over," and Jeff hung up.

Jeff then looked up directions to the University of Virginia. He knew it was one of the oldest universities in Virginia, having been founded by Thomas Jefferson near Monticello. As he drove onto the campus, its history was evident by the buildings' architecture—neo-classical if he remembered right.

Jeff wandered around, asking students for directions until he found the Physics Department. He started checking offices until he found a professor in his office. Louis Berg, PhD was the name on the door.

"Professor Berg?" Jeff asked as he stepped into the office.

The man behind the only desk was in his fifties with black but graying hair and glasses. "Yes. I'm Louis Berg. You're not one of my students, are you?"

"No, sir," Jeff said as he entered the room. "Do you have a few minutes to talk? I was in the neighborhood and just dropped by without an appointment."

"Okay. What's this about?"

"I'm writing a book," Jeff said. "A science fiction book, in fact, and I want to detect a cloaked ship sitting at the L2 Lagrange point. If you had to detect it, what would you do?"

Professor Berg sat back in his chair, smiled, and said, "Well, that is an interesting question. If a ship were cloaked, it wouldn't interact with any form of electromagnetics. Visible light, radar, x-rays, etc., would all detect nothing, right?"

"Yes, of course," Jeff said as if he knew what he was saying.

"The trick is to detect it without an electromagnetic interaction. Or to find a flaw in the cloaking technology at some frequency or wavelength. Or to track something else that is not cloaked and is headed to the location of the cloaked object. Then define the location of where it disappears. Or track some byproduct of the cloaking technology. Or assuming there is some form of metal on the ship, fly something to the L2 Lagrange point and let magnetism or gravity attract it to the ship," Professor Berg said as he laughed and smiled, obviously happy with his reasoning. "I am a big science fiction reader, so I always laugh when they talk about cloaked ships. The expense of cloaking is too high when there are so many ways to defeat the technology. Now stealth is another matter. Stealth technology bends or absorbs electromagnetics and is a much better choice if you want to hide something as long as it's not moving."

"That's very enlightening, Professor. You must have thought about this a lot."

"Yes, I have," the professor said. "Will you be putting my name in your book? What's the name of it and your name? I would love to buy it when it comes out. Can you tell me more about it?"

Jeff had not expected this response, so he had to make things up on the fly. "I'm in the early stages of creating this book. I have very little actually written and no title yet. My name is Jeff Simpson. I may publish under a different name, though; I don't know yet."

"Very well, Jeff," Professor Berg said. "Drop me a note if you ever publish it. I have a lot of papers to grade. Was there anything else?"

"Yes, sir," Jeff said. "If I wanted to build a prototype detector, who could do it? Who would you work with to do it?"

The professor eyed Jeff thoughtfully and said, "If I had this objective, I would work with the scientists and engineers at the University of Hawaii. Their astronomical program is strong, and they have many countries working projects to build detection systems on top of Mauna Kea. It's the best place on Earth to see the stars."

"Why is that, Professor?" Jeff asked.

"The volcano is almost fourteen thousand feet high. It sits above the clouds. It's surrounded by empty ocean, so there are no light sources to pollute starlight. It's a beautiful location, and the night sky is exceptionally clear."

"I guess that makes sense," Jeff said before shaking the professor's hand. "Thank you so much for your time, Professor. You've given me a lot to think about."

The professor smiled and went back to grading papers.

As Jeff left the building, he felt like he had just won the lottery. So many ideas. He needed to get back to the car and write them down quickly.

As Jeff thought about it, the last two ideas were really interesting. They could send something to the L2 Lagrange point and let it find the aliens by using gravity or magnetism. They could also send something that tracks the space traffic going to and from the alien ship right to the ship's location.

Jeff started up the car and drove home as fast as he could without drawing attention.

Amber greeted him at the door, very excited. "I tracked down the owner of the US subsidiary," she stated.

"Which one?" Jeff asked.

"XBC is privately-owned by a company named XZT. And guess who is on the board of XZT?"

"Who?" Jeff asked.

"Your old boss, Zachariah James. XZT is into industrial chemicals, pumps, plumbing, and all kinds of boring things like bolts and hardware. This holding company owns several smaller businesses. At least three of them ship to the same locations. They all use the same shipping company. The shipping company also has a holding company that does a lot shipping with mines and specialty steel plants. The mining companies work with a specific set of distributors. There is an entire web of companies all privately held and all getting very rich."

"How rich?" Jeff asked.

"Easily in the billions," Amber said.

"Let's back up to XZT," Jeff said. "Is anyone else interesting in their management chain?"

"There's an ex-general and an ex-congressman who is now a lobbyist for weapons manufacturers."

"Wonderful. Military experience and political influence."

Amber handed him a sheet of paper.

"I created a map of the flow of materials between countries. Red is raw materials flowing to processing locations and green is finished products flowing to final destinations. You can see over 220 locations around the world and the number seems to be growing."

"It looks like metals out of Africa flow to steel plants in South America," Jeff said.

"That's right," Amber said.

"What are these red lines to Europe?" Jeff asked.

"Precious metals and gems," Amber said. "Most of it from a dollar-volume perspective is diamonds and gold flowing to Switzerland and

Belgium, but just about everything is heading in that direction: silver, platinum, titanium, palladium, you name it."

"All of this is used in the construction of the sites you've found?" Jeff asked.

"Oh, heavens no," Amber said. "The commercial value of all this is easily in the tens of billions each year. The sites I've found are a fraction of this, but don't you see what they've done?"

Jeff looked perplexed so Amber said, "They've built a commercial empire capable of building the materials they need and generating a huge positive cash flow. Some of these companies are more than forty years old. In the last decade, they must have made more than a trillion dollars between them."

Jeff whistled and said, "That kind of money can buy a lot of influence."

"Exactly," Amber said. "And there's one more thing. Your ex-boss, Zachariah James, is on the board of two more of these holding companies as a security advisor, not just XZT."

Jeff sat down and looked again at the paper Amber had handed him before saying, "The bastard is in it for the money. I should go kill him right now."

"Jeff," Amber said, alarmed.

"I won't, but I should. Mike thinks he killed half of my old team."

"I didn't know that. I'm so sorry, Jeff."

Jeff was angry. He took a deep breath to calm himself and said, "He'll pay for what he's done, but we have bigger fish to fry. I have some news as well."

"Really, what?" Amber asked. She was happy to change the topic.

"I met with a physics professor at the University of Virginia today," Jeff said. "He had a wealth of information, including two really good ideas for how we can detect the alien ship in space at the L2 Lagrange point."

"Wow, that's great!" Amber said.

"To find a way to design it, he recommended meeting with people at the University of Hawaii. It seems to be a center for people working on space research ideas and technology," Jeff said.

"Hawaii?" Amber asked. "Why Hawaii?"

"The top of a volcano in the middle of the Pacific Ocean seems to be the best place in the world to look at the stars," Jeff said.

"Hawaii!" Amber said. "Are we going there?"

"Maybe," Jeff said. "I need to figure out a few more things before we decide. I'm starving. Let's finish our discussion over dinner."

Jeff and Amber sent out for Chinese food and worked late into the night again.

ON THE ROAD AGAIN

In the morning, after Jeff left, Amber decided to try to contact her best friend Margo. She tried Margo's cell and office number, but both went to voicemail with an old greeting on them. Concerned, Amber called a mutual friend at the *Washington Post.*

"Hi, Sally. This is Amber."

"Amber? Amber van Hosteen? I thought you were dead! Where have you been?"

Amber winced. She immediately knew she had made a mistake calling Sally, but it was too late to stop now. "Hi, Sally. I'm fine. I was away on a story. It's important that we keep this call between us, okay?"

"Are you in danger? What's going on?"

"It's really best if I don't share anything with you. I was trying to speak with Margo, but I can't reach her. Is she on vacation or something?"

"Oh, Amber, you don't know?"

"Know what?"

"Margo is dead."

"Oh my God! No!"

"She was strangled in her apartment a little over a week ago."

Amber burst into tears and couldn't speak for a moment.

"They never found her killer," Sally continued. "The funeral was two days ago."

"I'm sorry. I have to go. Please don't tell anyone that I called you," Amber said between sobs.

"I understand. Goodbye."

Amber hung up and cried for her friend, not thinking what her call might trigger.

* * *

At 2 p.m., Jeff pulled over to wait for Mike's call. At ten seconds past two, the phone rang. Jeff picked it up on the third ring and said, "It looks like another rainy day." He then looked at his watch and started timing the call.

Mike replied, "Rain is good and bad." Then he continued, "The Africa situation will hit the news today or tomorrow. Six different sources in six different news agencies said they are carrying the story, but nothing on the space angle."

"That's the best news I've had all day," Jeff said. "What about the companies I asked you about?"

"I started to follow up on those companies, but then all my access was revoked to those records," Mike said.

"Where are you now?" Jeff asked urgently.

"I'm in a visitor's office at the Commerce Department."

"Drop everything and get out of there," Jeff said in a commanding voice. "Execute your escape plan. I know you have one. I made you do a plan."

"What? Why?" Mike asked.

"You've been compromised," Jeff said. "You've got to run, right now. Do not go home. Do not contact your friends or family. This call is over, and there will not be another one." Jeff hung up.

Jeff drove home quickly, but he still followed protocol to ensure he had no one following him. He burst into the house. All he found was a startled Amber. She had been crying.

"What's wrong?" Jeff asked.

"Margo's dead. Someone strangled her."

"How do you know?"

"I tried to call her. When I couldn't get through, I called an old friend at the *Post*. She told me."

"How long ago was this?"

"About an hour."

"Pack up," Jeff said. "We need to leave now."

"Why? I used the secure phone."

"Where's the phone?"

"Here," Amber said as she handed the cell phone to Jeff. He pulled the battery and the sim card. "Amber, they probably killed Margo while trying to get to you. When that failed, they put trackers on her phone numbers."

"No!"

"I'm sorry about your friend, but we need to run right now," Jeff said as he started grabbing their things and putting them into bags.

"I got my friend killed, and now they might be on their way here?"

"Yes. Let's go."

Amber helped pack. They were out the door in under five minutes.

As they drove, Jeff said, "I talked to Mike today. He was compromised."

"Will he be all right?"

"He will be if he does what I told him to do," Jeff said. "For once, I hope he does." Jeff remembered little about Mike's escape plan. It involved a distant relative by marriage in the Ozark Mountains. He hoped Mike would stick to the plan.

"Where are we going now?" Amber asked.

"Hawaii."

"All right," Amber said slowly. She was still thinking about her friend.

Jeff decided to try to get her mind off it.

"I have a plan worked out to get us near the West Coast. We start by taking highway 66 to 81 to 64 to Charleston, West Virginia. From there, we charter small planes to Las Vegas through Dallas. We can book a commercial flight from there to Kona, Hawaii."

"First Vegas, then Hawaii," said Amber. "That can't be all bad. Can I gamble?"

"Casinos have video surveillance. We catch people all the time who make the mistake of going gambling."

"Really?" Amber asked.

"All the time."

"In all the excitement, I forgot to mention: The Africa situation is getting press coverage by at least six major news agencies soon."

"Finally, something is happening."

"The first one is not running until tomorrow. We'll have plenty of chances to get newspapers and check websites on the way to Vegas."

✳   ✳   ✳

The drive to Charleston was uneventful. They spent the night in a small B&B and chartered a flight to Dallas. Before they left Dallas, Jeff mailed a package with clothes and money to Kona, Hawaii. That way, when they boarded a commercial airliner to Hawaii, they would not have to explain $50,000 in cash.

When they reached the airport, Jeff spotted a middle-aged couple getting out of a taxi. He walked over and handed them the keys to their car, along with the pink slip he had never signed, saying, "We're leaving this town for work and never coming back. Take this and enjoy your new car. It's right over there." The couple was silent, not knowing what to say or do as Jeff walked away.

"That was nice," Amber told Jeff.

"They looked deserving, and now we have no loose ends from Virginia leading to our escape route."

In Dallas, they took a taxi to another B&B. In the morning, they returned to the airport for a chartered flight to Las Vegas, Nevada.

During their travels, they could read newspaper after newspaper.

"Jeff, these are my stories," Amber said at one point. "The *New York Post* ran my personal interest story on one of the fallen generals. The *Times* ran a story on the Burkina Faso disappearances. The *Wall Street Journal* ran a story on UN lack of involvement and the impact on markets. *The National Enquirer* even ran a story on the possibility of space aliens on Earth."

"The data is out there now. The trail of breadcrumbs is set," Jeff said.

Amber and Jeff felt very good about the impact they'd had in such a short time. Amber felt vindicated. She knew she could get her career back on track once the world knew what she had done and how she had done it. They just needed a few more pieces of the puzzle to drop into place. Thousands of hungry reporters were out there always looking for stories. Several were bound to make the connections.

Once in Vegas, they rented a private, air-conditioned room near the University of Las Vegas for two days. It had its own bath and shower, plus a desk. The sliding glass door led out to the backyard with a pool. Amber couldn't help but wonder if the young man who took their money wasn't the son of the real property owners. Maybe he was renting out a guest room while his parents were out of town. Either way, it was a nice room that fit their needs.

They were both tired from traveling, and Amber was still having a hard time with Margo's death, so Jeff listened as Amber talked about her lost friend. After a quick dinner of more Chinese takeout, they went to bed early.

✳ ✳ ✳

The next day, Amber slept in late while Jeff found a library where he could rent a computer and get their travel plans set. When Jeff returned, Amber had just woken up.

"I got you a breakfast burrito," Jeff said. "I also booked two tickets to Hawaii for early tomorrow morning. Our plane stops in LA, then direct to Kona, Hawaii."

"We get to stay here one more day? Yeah!" Amber said. She walked out to the pool, lay down in the sun, and ate her burrito. Jeff followed her, pulled a chair over, and sat down next to her.

"How are you feeling?"

"Fine."

"I mean about Margo. Are you okay?"

She took a deep breath and said, "No. I killed my best friend."

"That's the wrong way to look at it. You didn't kill anyone. The people we are hunting did. Remember, they killed half of my team; thousands were dying in Africa, and more than 200 of those death factories will go online in less than ninety days. We're making progress, but we're not done. You are not done!"

Amber looked at Jeff and said, "You're right. They're killing thousands, and they intend to kill millions. I just need to relax today. Give me one day."

"All right," Jeff said as he headed inside. He hated the hot sun in Vegas.

They rested most of the day. Jeff went out to get food and more newspapers. Seeing her work in print was the only thing that seemed to cheer up Amber.

✶ ✶ ✶

The next day, they got up early and went to McCarran International Airport in Las Vegas where they caught their flight to LA and Hawaii without incident.

The highlight of the trip was the approach to the big island. The volcanos were huge. The island was either lush green or dark black. The captain spotted a pair of whales, a mother with its calf. The whales' outline from above was crystal clear in the deep blue water below. As they landed, all they could see was dark-black volcanic rock.

They took a taxi to Kona where they had already rented a guest house on the shoreline. Once they were settled, Amber went exploring the shops for local papers and maps, while Jeff went to buy a car.

Jeff pulled into the driveway with a blue 2010 Toyota Camry.

Amber came out to see what Jeff had bought and said, "You sure like ugly four doors."

"Ferraris were all sold out," Jeff said sarcastically. "Besides, we want to blend into the crowds, not stand out."

"Good job!" Amber said. "There's no way we're standing out in this."

"Did you find out anything interesting in the island papers?" Jeff asked as they entered the small guest house.

"There are about ten local papers with sizable circulations," Amber said. "Most focus on local news for one island. There's a business journal on Pacific businesses and a small one focusing on UFOs. None of our stories are in the local newspapers."

"It's only Sunday," Jeff said as they both sat down on a couch facing picture windows. "The big news agencies release their stories on Friday and Saturday. We may see things trickle down to here next week."

"I can't get over this view," Amber said. "This place is incredible."

"Yeah, no white sand beaches, but the ocean hitting the lava rock is pretty," Jeff agreed.

"There's a white sand beach just down the road," Amber said. "We can walk to it in ten minutes."

"We really can't do anything today. The post office is closed, and I can't talk to anyone at the University of Hawaii," Jeff said. "We could go for a swim, grab dinner, and get a good night's sleep."

"That sounds wonderful," Amber said. "I bought a new bathing suit while you were out finding a grandma to buy a car from."

"She did look a little like Betty Ford," Jeff quipped.

The guesthouse they rented had towels and boogie boards, so they decided to go to the beach first. It was a beautiful white sand beach about 100 meters across in a small bay surrounded by black lava rock all around. Four-foot waves crashed into the shore, perfect for boogie boards. After about an hour of swimming and riding the waves, Amber sat at the water line where the waves washed over her feet. She was staring out into the Pacific Ocean.

Jeff had just made a spectacular wipeout that tumbled him head over heels. He decided he'd had enough for today and sat down next to Amber. He noticed her mood and asked, "What are you thinking about?"

Amber looked at Jeff as she said, "I was thinking about what we've done so far. About how many people have died since we left Africa. I don't think news stories will be enough without the alien story coming out."

"Hopefully, the scientists at the University of Hawaii will give us what we need."

MAUNA KEA MYSTERY

The next day, Jeff and Amber were at the post office at 8 a.m. to pick up the package he had sent from Texas. He was relieved to see it had not been opened or tampered with. He took the box to his car and opened it in the trunk with the trunk lid open. Everything was the way he had placed it when he had packed the box. He checked further for bugs or tracking devices. Satisfied everything was in order, he resealed the box and closed the trunk lid.

Now they were off to the University of Hawaii's Astronomy Department. They were surprised to find the university was in Hilo, on the other side of the island, and the main observatories were halfway between. Jeff decided to take Highway 11 to 190 to 200, a two-hour drive.

The drive was beautiful. They started out driving in a lush tropical region overlooking the Pacific Ocean. They dropped close to sea level, driving through dark-black lava fields. Then they started to climb and entered a grassy highland flanked by volcanoes on each side.

Amber began reading some interesting facts about Hawaii as they drove. "Hawaii has ten of the fourteen microclimates that exist in the entire world. There are eight of them on this one island."

"We must have seen two or three of them already," Jeff said as they climbed Highway 200 between the Mauna Loa and Mauna Kea volcanoes.

"Mauna Kea is the best place on Earth to observe space. It's almost fourteen thousand feet above sea level. Its peak is higher than most clouds," Amber continued. "It's one of the few places on Earth where you can drive from sea level to over thirteen thousand feet in less than two hours. They have a mandatory stop at a visitor's center to get acclimated to the altitude."

"Let's hope these scientists in Hilo are as good as Professor Berg said they were," Jeff said.

"Who are we meeting with when we get there?" Amber asked.

"I don't know," Jeff replied.

"You don't have an appointment?" Amber asked.

"No," Jeff answered. "I usually just ask around and find the right people."

"I assumed you had the name of the professor we were going to meet. We should do some research before we walk in there," Amber said.

"We might have to wait around a little, but we should be fine," Jeff said.

Amber just shook her head and kept reading quietly.

After entering Hilo, they found the university close to the highway, which changed to little more than just another city street. They entered the lush green campus and parked near the Imiloa Astronomy Center.

Jeff started looking around the building to find where the professors had their offices. Amber stopped him and asked a student in the hall, "Do you know how I can find professor office hours?"

"Sure," the student replied. "The main desk is around the corner and has office hours posted on a bulletin board."

"Thank you," Amber said with a smile.

"Well, of course, he would tell you," Jeff said.

Amber rolled her eyes as she led him to the bulletin board.

"Professor Crowd has office hours in twenty-five minutes," Amber said. "I read this university has a commerce degree program. I'll head over to the library and the Commerce Department to continue research on the companies I told you about while you talk to this professor."

"Sounds good," Jeff said.

"We can meet for lunch and decide on next steps," Amber said.

"Okay. We'll meet at the library and then decide where to go eat."

Jeff walked the halls while he waited for the professor. He could find information on the professor's degrees and what he was working on. It looked like the Physics and Astronomy Departments shared the same professors. Many of them worked with graduate students on projects that sounded impressive.

Professor Richard Crowd came down the hall wearing a colorful Hawaiian shirt with two students in tow. Jeff walked up to the door as Professor Crowd was unlocking it. "Hello, Professor. My name is Jeff Simpson. I was wondering if I could get about twenty minutes of your time."

The professor seemed surprised, but said, "Yes. I just need to finish something with these two students first, Mr. Simpson."

They entered the small office as Jeff waited outside. The professor seemed to be going over some classroom assignment with his students. The details made no sense to Jeff, so he just waited for the students to leave.

As the students left the office, Jeff entered and reintroduced himself. "Hello, Professor Crowd."

"You're not a salesman, are you?" the professor asked.

Jeff laughed and said, "No, sir. I'm Jeff Simpson. I want to share with you a problem I have and get your opinion on how to solve it."

The professor relaxed a little and said, "All right, let's hear it."

"I'm trying to find a way to detect a cloaked object at the L2 Lagrange point," Jeff said.

This piqued the Professor's interest. "We already found something there two weeks ago," he replied.

"Really," Jeff said as he sat down in a chair opposite the professor's desk. "What was it?"

"We have no idea," the professor replied. "Why exactly are you here—Mr. Simpson, was it?"

"I was going to give you a story about being a science fiction writer, but the truth is I'm from the US Government."

"Really! We reported this to NASA. Did they send you here?"

"Indirectly, yes. Can you tell me more about how you discovered it?"

"We were getting strange readings from our two-meter telescope. We couldn't figure out what was interfering with our instruments. After about a day of trying everything, one of our students suggested an anomaly in space affecting our readings. Sure enough, we found something out there. We can work around it now."

"Is the anomaly stationary? Do you know its location?" Jeff asked.

"Yes, and yes. It's staying in a specific location in space. We have the three-dimensional coordinates."

"I have a story you might find hard to believe, Professor Crowd," Jeff said in a serious tone. "Hearing it may cause you some personal risk. Before I continue, I need to know if you want me to continue."

"Wait," Professor Crowd said as he got up. "We should go to a conference room. I want to bring in my astrophysics partner, Dr. Foyt, on this discussion."

Professor Crowd grabbed three cans of soda from a small refrigerator in his office and hurried down the hall. He stopped at a door with the name Dr. Robert Foyt on it and poked his head in, saying, "Bob, I have someone here about that NASA report. Can you join us in our conference room?"

A voice from the room answered, "Sure. I'll meet you there in a minute."

Jeff and Professor Crowd headed down to the end of the hall where Crowd opened the conference room door to find a lot of students hotly debating some topic. "Sorry, guys; I need my room back," Crowd said. "I can give you one minute to wrap up."

Some complaining mixed in with the main discussion as the meeting spilled out into the hall. The students hastily pulled large sheets of paper off the walls and rolled them up, each student carrying two or three. They kept arguing in a small cluster all the way down the hall as they filtered into another room.

"Do they always work like that?" Jeff asked.

"They're working out a topic for a report I assigned them," Crowd said, smiling. "I encourage discussion and debate. At the end of the day, the person in charge will decide, but it will be an informed decision with all available facts and points of view. Most of the biggest scientific breakthroughs happened because someone challenged the points of view we hold most dear."

"Then you're going to love what I'm about to say, Professor."

"We shall see, and call me Rich," Crowd replied.

As if on cue, the other professor entered the room and shook Jeff's hand. "Hi," he said. "I'm Dr. Robert Foyt. Are you from NASA?"

"No, Dr. Foyt," Jeff said as he stood and shook the professor's hand. "As I was just telling Rich, I'm not from NASA. I belong to another agency in our government which I'm not at liberty to share."

"Do you know Professor Crowd?" Dr. Foyt asked.

"Let's drop the formality, Bob," Rich said. "I think this is going to be an interesting discussion and it may take a while."

"All right," Bob said. "If you insist." Dr. Foyt did not seem to like the idea of being informal, but he went along with it.

"The story I'm about to tell you," Jeff began once they were all seated, "is highly classified and could put you both at some personal risk. Do you want me to continue?"

Both men said, "Yes" simultaneously and without hesitation.

"Very well," Jeff continued. "I'm here seeking information on the anomaly located at Earth's L2 Lagrange point because of telemetry data gathered by the French military on ballistic launch vehicles traveling from Africa to that point in space."

"Preposterous!" Bob said. "No country in Africa can launch something into space, let alone do it multiple times."

"You're right," Jeff said. "The Africans lack the capability, but someone else has the capability and runs launches from Burkina Faso every two to three days. I saw one with my own eyes. I contacted the French government to confirm the launch I saw. That's when I learned that launches are happening on a regular basis, every three days."

The two professors were silent for a moment. Then Rich said, "The United States can't run that many launches from Cape Canaveral. In two months, Burkina Faso will have almost as many space launches as we've had in the whole history of our space program."

"This sounds insane," Bob said. "However, if we assume for a moment that it's true, I can see your interest in the data we reported to NASA."

"It's imperative that we determine what's located at that point in space," Jeff said.

"Wait, it isn't ours?" Bob said.

"No," Jeff replied.

"Then whose is it," Bob asked. "The Russians? Chinese?"

"We don't know," Jeff replied. "But I doubt it's Russian or Chinese in origin."

"What?" Rich said. "If we didn't do it and they didn't do it, who did?"

"That is why I am here, gentlemen!" Jeff said. "We need to find out what is hidden in that anomaly."

After a long silence, Bob said, "I still find this all hard to believe. I know you said you saw something."

"Let me start there," Jeff said. "I was no more than three hundred yards from the launch point."

"Were you in some kind of bunker?" Rich asked.

"No," Jeff answered. "There was a building between the launch location and me. There was no flame. There was no heat. Instead of sound, I heard, or rather felt, a deep rumbling in my chest. There was a soft yellow light that grew brighter as the vehicle moved away from us. It was nothing like the videos you see of a rocket launching. It was doing over 100 miles per hour instantly. It had to be over 1,000 miles per hour when we lost sight of it."

Rich looked at Bob and said, "Gravity drive?"

Bob nodded his head and said, "An extremely efficient gravity drive system with almost no wasted energy."

"Did you look at the launch site after the vehicle was gone?" Rich asked.

"No," Jeff answered. "We had to leave in a hurry. We were not invited guests."

"Pity," Rich said. "If it was a gravity drive, you might have seen debris floating in the air for a short time until the gravity distortion field dissipated. That would have confirmed it was a gravity drive."

"What else can you share with us?" Bob asked. "Every small detail could be very helpful."

"I couldn't see the vehicle," Jeff said. "There was just a faint silhouette hidden in a soft yellow light. The light didn't hurt my eyes. It glowed like a firefly. You can't really see the body of a firefly at a distance, only the light shining from it. The light was beautiful."

The two professors looked at each other. Then Bob said, "That is all very interesting, but we need more details."

"Like what?" Jeff asked.

"Was the rumbling in your chest constant or was it beating like a drum?" Rich asked.

"It was beating like a drum," Jeff said.

"A gravity pulse wave," Bob said excitedly. "Did you see or feel anything else?"

"No," Jeff said. "Professors, I really need to change this conversation. It is imperative we determine what is at the L2 Lagrange point."

"Jeff, you are possibly the first human in history to experience a gravity pulse drive," Bob said. "This is history in the making."

"This entire conversation is classified," Jeff said. "We need to keep this between us."

"What do you want with us then?" Bob asked.

"I need to know how you detected that anomaly and how to discover what is located there."

"Well, the first part is easy enough," Bob said. "We were looking for electromagnetic wave shifts in distant stars to discover if those stars have planets orbiting them. We had very strange anomalies in our data when looking through that point in space. Certain wavelengths of electromagnetic spectrum shifted in unexpected ways while other wavelengths did not. We saw it as distortion in our readings."

"What wavelengths were distorted?" Jeff asked.

"Lower X-rays were fine, but as the X-ray spectrum approached visible light, it became distorted," Bob explained. "The distortion continued up the spectrum all the way into microwaves."

"Is there some way to disrupt or remove the distortion so we can see what is really there?" Jeff asked.

"Not without turning off the source of the distortion," Bob said. "Or removing power from the source. I'm still having a hard time believing this is some alien technology. What proof do you have?"

"You're the experts," Jeff replied. "Do you know of anyone on Earth who has this gravity pulse technology or anything close to it?"

The two professors looked at each other and shook their heads no.

"Either way, I'd like to find a way to expose what's up there," Jeff said. After giving them a minute to process their thoughts, he continued. "Is there any way to work around this distortion field? You said X-rays still pass through it."

"We could use X-rays, but we would need to put something on the other side to collect the X-rays," Rich said. "If we could put something in space, I would just send it to the coordinates we already know and use gravity or magnetism to attach something to the object. We could then use any number of ways to detect the size, shape, and composition of that object."

"Who could build a device like that?" Jeff asked.

"NASA, the Russians, the Chinese, and maybe the European Space Agency," said Bob.

"I will need a government agency if I want to put anything into space?" Jeff asked.

"Yes," Bob said. "Unless you can create your own company, but even then, you would not get very far without government support. Telemetry and logistics require satellite infrastructure."

Jeff nodded and said, "I understand."

"We can give you a full package of information on the anomaly," Rich offered. "We can even work out a design for the type of payload you would need to deliver, but we can't build what you need."

"How long will that take?" Jeff asked.

"A day or two at most," Rich said. "We can put some graduate students on it right away."

"Then I'll be back at the end of the day tomorrow for that package of information," Jeff said. "Please keep this conversation to yourselves. The panic this information could cause could result in the death of billions."

"We understand," Rich said.

"We won't tell our students anything they don't need to know," Bob said.

"Thank you, gentlemen," Jeff replied. "I thank you and your country thanks you."

Jeff shook hands with both professors and left the building. He wondered if he should share more information with them, but being a good spy, he only shared what he needed to so he could get what he needed from them. No amount of new information would get Jeff anything more than what the professors were already willing to share.

Jeff decided to go find Amber and get some lunch. He found her in the library at a computer with a stack of printouts next to her.

"How's it going?" he asked.

Amber never looked up as she said, "I'm going to need a few more hours here."

"No problem," Jeff said. "We can take a break and grab some lunch or keep working. We can come back tomorrow too. I can share some good news when you're ready for it."

Amber looked up then and said, "Maybe I could use some lunch. Just give me a minute and we can go." She collected her stack of documents and organized them before they left.

As they were walking out to the car, Jeff continued, "The professors here have already found an anomaly at the L2 Lagrange point."

"You're kidding me!" Amber exclaimed. "That's wonderful. What is it?"

"They only found an anomaly," Jeff said. "They don't know what it is. They think I was sent by the government. I played along. They'll have a complete package of information for me at the end of the day tomorrow—coordinates, size, even details on how to detect more data on what's there. They just can't build or launch anything we need to detect more information."

"That is good and bad," Amber said thoughtfully. "Any idea who can build it?"

"I have a 'frenemy' in Russia who just might do it," Jeff said.

"A 'frenemy'?" Amber asked.

"A Russian spy who worked with me as many times as against me," Jeff said. "He's a true Russian patriot. I assume they're having as bad a time as we are. Maybe worse."

"Why not work through NASA?" Amber asked. "You can play the government card again. Messing around with the Russians could backfire."

"Russia is still an authoritarian society," Jeff explained. "Anyone in a position of power says go do something and that thing gets done, eventually. We are a democracy, but space projects are highly political. Nothing will get approved without a committee and review by Congress. I don't see how we could get anything done in less than a year. Even then, the wrong people may see it and shoot it down."

"Do you even know how to get in touch with this person?" Amber asked.

"I think so," Jeff said. "Getting there could be an entirely different problem, but I have some ideas there too."

They grabbed lunch and worked until the library closed. Jeff did his own research on what the scientists shared with him, while Amber triangulated shipping data and corporate financial structures.

They ate an early dinner in Hilo and talked as they took the long drive home.

"This one Silicon Valley company builds a key component that you think is associated with a certain phase of construction?" Jeff asked.

"I think so," Amber replied. "They build electronic components that seem to be shipped after certain machinery and plumbing parts. By looking for other shipments to the same place, I see four waves of materials being delivered so far. The first is basic foundation-building stuff like rebars, bolts, and cement hardeners. They must get the cement locally. Then they deliver the metal frame and all the related hardware for the walls and roof. There are tons of it. Then they deliver piping, pumps, wiring, and storage vats. The ones farthest along then get electronics—millions of dollars' worth of electronics."

"How many are at each stage?" Jeff asked.

"About fifty are getting electronics now," Amber explained. "Over three hundred have received the foundation material."

"Damn," Jeff said. "We need to move faster."

"One more thing," Amber said in a somber tone. "Remember how I said these new sites are bigger?"

"Yeah."

"I think they're more than five times bigger," Amber said. "I don't think I've found all the sites yet. I only know for sure when they ship the electronics. Everything else comes from multiple manufacturers. Only one component comes from a single company."

"What was the name again?" Jeff asked. "XBC?"

"Right," Amber said.

"Everything you've found will be critical for catching the people involved in this scheme," Jeff said. "If we had the government behind us, I would just raid that company and make the people there give up their contacts, but we don't. Heck, from what we've seen so far, those people may not even know what they're part of."

"It's so frustrating," Amber said.

"We need to get everything you've documented and put it in a few places, some for safekeeping and some for sharing with the right people when the time comes," Jeff said. "For sharing, we can encrypt it and put it out on some websites. For storing, we should give it to a few people around the world so no one person has everything in one place."

"I can take photocopies of the ledgers and highlight the shipping data relationships," Amber said. "Then I can document how to read it all. I can probably get it done tomorrow with a little help."

"You got it!" Jeff said. "Oh, but tonight, I need to try to contact Stephan again. I'll need to find a pay phone on the way home."

Jeff found a pay phone at a shopping center just off Highway 11 in Kona. He dropped off Amber and headed back to the pay phone while Amber went straight to work documenting the company information.

At 10 p.m., he dialed the contact number Stephan had given him. Someone answered on the third ring, but it wasn't Stephan. It sounded like Dureau.

"Hello," the stranger said.

"Spring is a beautiful time of year," Jeff said as he looked at his watch to start timing the call.

"But spring cannot compare with autumn," the stranger answered.

"Dureau?" Jeff asked.

"Yes, my friend. It is Dureau."

"What happened to Stephan?"

After a brief pause, Dureau said, "He is no longer with us."

"Because of me?"

"No, because he read the situation wrong and walked into a trap," Dureau said. "I killed the man who killed him, but I was not there to protect his back. Tell me you made progress."

"We have," Jeff said. "Did you see Burkina Faso in the papers?"

"Yes," Dureau said. "That was you?"

"Yes," Jeff answered. "We also have the coordinates of an anomaly at the L2 Lagrange point."

"I hope you blow it to hell!" Dureau said.

"I can't do anything like that from here yet," Jeff said. "It sounds like things are going badly in France."

"They are," Dureau said. "I have to go soon."

"Give me a new number for next week," Jeff said. "I may have some actions we need to coordinate."

"Do you know city two?"

"Yes."

"Very good," Dureau said. "Then call 555 1212, this time, city two. Stay alive, my friend." Then Dureau hung up.

Jeff walked back to his car and sat for a few minutes thinking about the friend he had lost. Stephan had been a mentor to Jeff in many ways. He knew the politics in Europe and had taught Jeff how to navigate that part of the world safely. Jeff bowed his head in a silent prayer for his friend and drove home.

Amber greeted him at the door and asked, "Did you reach Stephan?"

"No. I did reach Dureau."

"Really, how is he?" Amber asked. Then she noticed Jeff's stance. "What's wrong?"

"Stephan is dead. Dureau is my contact now."

Tears welled up in Amber's eyes immediately. "I'm so sorry about your friend, Jeff," she said as she hugged him.

Jeff was usually in control of his emotions, but for some reason, he just let go. He tightly hugged Amber and cried as he kissed the top of her head. He choked out, "He was a good man."

After a while, they went to the small kitchen where they sat and talked about their journey so far—the people they had met, the things they had seen, but not the bad things. They found a half-full bottle of rum in a cabinet and cans of Pepsi in the refrigerator that a previous renter must have left. Jeff's glass had alcohol. Amber's did not. They made toasts to Stephan and to lost friends, and then they went to bed.

They had no idea that today's contacts had put everything they had worked for at risk.

ROLL OF THE DICE

The next morning, Jeff and Amber rose early and got ready for the long drive to Hilo. They left by 7 a.m. and arrived at the university a little after 9 a.m.

They went to work immediately documenting the company structures, transactions, and conclusions.

After a few hours, Amber pulled Jeff to a quiet corner of the room and said, "I found something you are not going to believe."

"What?"

"The companies I'm tracking were created after World War II in the late 1940s."

"Wow! Do you think the people in control of these businesses have been working for the aliens since then?"

"Jeff, these companies were formed by people who ran major arms companies in Germany and Japan."

"What do you mean?"

"Executives from those companies formed these companies."

"Are you implying that the aliens were involved with Germany and Japan during World War II?"

"I'm definitely saying they were influential people at that time. What if the aliens were trying to take over the world through military force by using Germany and Japan? When that failed, they reset their plans and helped humans develop the technology to build these factories."

"That would mean we stumbled upon the end game of a seventy-year-old plan. Are there any other facts that build a stronger link to this theory?"

"I don't know, but I can research it."

"Let's focus on the data we have first. We don't want to spread ourselves too thin. This angle is important, but without proof that the aliens exist at all, it's too easy for the government to deny."

As 5 p.m. approached, they were nearly done correlating the information into packages. They would make copies and deliver them in physical and electronic form.

Jeff walked over to meet the professors and gather the information they had on the anomaly. He was tired from a long day working on documents.

As he entered the astronomy building and approached Professor Crowd's office, he knew he had made a mistake. It was too quiet. Suddenly, military police with .45 caliber pistols drawn crowded both ends of the hall. There must have been five men at either end of the narrow hallway. Jeff just stopped walking and put his hands in the air. After an MP handcuffed Jeff's hands behind his back, another knocked on Professor Crowd's office door.

An officer stepped out to look at Jeff and said, "Mr. Simpson, if that is your name, I am Lieutenant James Crawford. You are under arrest for treason and espionage."

"Is that all?" Jeff asked.

The officer smiled and said, "We will talk some more at the base. Your friend from the library will be joining us."

Jeff cursed himself for not paying attention. Now he and Amber were caught with all their data. He could see at least forty military police. He was sure there were probably ten more he could not see.

The MPs herded Jeff to a black SUV. He looked over to see Professor Foyt hand a package of information over to Lieutenant Crawford. He then saw Amber coming out of the library with handcuffs on and all their work in the arms of a female MP.

That was the last thing Jeff saw as they put a black hood over his head. As they started driving, Jeff was memorizing the left and right turns to try to track his direction, but then he thought, *If I ever get out in the open, I just have to look at the volcanoes to know where I am*. Instead, he focused his thoughts on how he would escape. They had put Amber in a separate SUV from him.

They drove for about an hour before stopping at what Jeff assumed was the gate of a military base. He could not smell salt in the air, so it must be an Army base.

The SUV started to move again but more slowly. After it stopped the second time, Jeff was escorted through three doorways with the black hood still over his head. When he sat down in a chair and the hood was finally removed, he was surprised to see Amber sitting next to him.

Lieutenant James Crawford was sitting across a table from them with his hands clasped together in front of him. Their documents were sitting on the table to his left. The room was big enough for the table, which could seat up to eight people, but there were only three chairs. A big MP stood near the solid-looking metal door. A big mirror was on the wall behind Lieutenant Crawford. The rest of the room's walls were bare.

"I'm sorry we had to take you in that way," Lieutenant Crawford said. "I had to put on a show for the brass. They were in one of the other SUVs. Assigning fifty men to capture the two of you seemed excessive, but I wasn't given an opportunity to argue the point. I'm not going to arrest you."

Lieutenant Crawford nodded to the MP who unlocked the handcuffs on Amber, then Jeff.

Jeff and Amber looked at each other in shock. Could they believe him?

"Where are we?" Amber asked.

"You're in the Army Training Center at Pohakula, Hawaii," Lieutenant Crawford explained. "We're in a valley between the Mauna Loa and Mauna Kea volcanoes."

"Why are we here?" Jeff asked as he took Amber's hand. She was trembling slightly.

"The brass that directed this mission was from the Navy," Lieutenant Crawford explained. "We're the US Army. It's our mission to protect the American people. We failed in that mission a few weeks ago, but we've learned, and we are adapting."

"Are you talking about the coup in Washington, DC?" Amber asked.

"Yes, ma'am," Lieutenant Crawford said. "When the Army made its move, elements of the Air Force and Navy interceded. We did not want to kill our own countrymen, so we stood down. We also realized only a handful of elected officials are involved in this. The real perpetrators are a few very powerful non-elected officials."

"Do you have names?" Amber asked.

"Yes, ma'am," Lieutenant Crawford said. "Before I share more, we need to talk about this." He nodded toward the pile of documents next to him.

Jeff looked at Lieutenant Crawford a few seconds, then decided to roll the dice. He would go all in and share almost everything, assuming he was in the hands of the good guys. If he wasn't, they were dead anyway.

"All right, we will level with you, Lieutenant Crawford," Jeff said. "You may or may not know that I am a senior agent with the CIA. I specialize in espionage, intelligence, counterintelligence, and research. My team gets the hard problems no one else can figure out."

"I knew you were in the CIA," Lieutenant Crawford said. "I know the Navy is sending a plane for you that will arrive in four hours."

"I was ordered to follow Amber van Hosteen," Jeff said as he motioned toward Amber. "I was authorized to use any means necessary to prevent her from gathering the information she was seeking that could expose CIA-front companies. She was traveling to Burkina Faso, following leads on possible corporate and government corruption through a trail of holding companies and subsidiaries."

"'Any means necessary'?" Amber repeated. "You never told me that."

"Things moved so fast I forgot about that part until now," Jeff replied. Returning his attention to Lieutenant Crawford, he continued, "I partnered with French operatives and Burkina Faso border police. What Amber was uncovering was disturbing me. When I reported it to my superiors, they ordered me to return to the US with Amber. When I played for more time, I was fired, and now there's a sizable bounty on my head. At the same time, Amber was fired from News Corp and the French agents were recalled. The firings and the recall were within hours of each other."

"I was aware of most of what you said so far," Lieutenant Crawford said. "Please continue."

"This is where it gets weird," Jeff said. "Amber had discovered an entire village that had disappeared and some other strange activities."

"Strange activities?" Lieutenant Crawford asked.

"A mine receiving materials that a mine would never use. Political bribes. We infiltrated this mine to find a factory that took live humans, ran them through a horribly painful process, and killed them. There were also research professionals walking around in lab coats doing experiments on humans. We captured a senior researcher. He knew what was going on in the factory, but I got the impression that not everyone there knew. He was motivated by his lust for knowledge at any price. It was so insane. We also saw the process up close. I think I'll have nightmares the rest of my life about what we saw. Thousands of people screaming in agony until they died. All to produce some organic acid based on human DNA protein chains."

"How do you know so much about this acid?" Lieutenant Crawford asked.

Jeff was starting to get concerned that Lieutenant Crawford displayed so little emotion and asked so few questions.

"We took a sample with us when we left the facility," Jeff said. "I worked with an old colleague to get it analyzed."

"We got away from the facility cleanly. We were lucky to make it out alive. As we were making our way out, we felt something strange and saw a soft yellow light from the other side of the factory. It was a launch vehicle heading toward outer space at tremendous speeds. It wasn't like anything I had ever seen before. Your friends at the university think it's a gravity pulse drive system."

"They mentioned that," Lieutenant Crawford said.

Jeff was getting more concerned. "They mentioned that" was all Lieutenant Crawford had to say?

"I confirmed this launch with the French military." Jeff twisted the truth a little to keep Dureau and Stephan's names out of the discussion. "They informed me there were many other launches."

"Many other launches?" Lieutenant Crawford asked.

This seemed to surprise Lieutenant Crawford. That was a good sign.

"Yes," Jeff answered. "A new one every two to three days. The vehicles are traveling to the L2 Lagrange point. The same place the two professors at the university detected an anomaly in space. I believe there is a spacecraft or base at this point in space."

"You believe?" Lieutenant Crawford said.

"I was talking to the professors at the university to find a way to prove it."

"Amber published a story on what we found in Africa," Jeff continued. "It was published by over twenty different news agencies and then immediately refuted by government officials all over the world. The coordinated response by leaders around the world was alarming!"

"I agree," Lieutenant Crawford said as he looked at Amber. "So this is Amber. She published those stories."

"Yes," Amber said.

"You have no idea how important those stories were," Lieutenant Crawford said. "The coup happened because of them."

"My stories caused Americans to die?" Amber asked as she covered her mouth with both hands.

"The response to your stories uncovered who was involved in the manipulation of our government," Lieutenant Crawford said. "We underestimated how deep the problem ran; that is what cost lives, not your story."

Now Jeff felt like Lieutenant Crawford was really on their side, so he decided to discuss the Hidden Hand.

"When the story failed, we returned to the US and found out about the coup," Jeff continued. "Amber had a brilliant idea to publish pieces of the story to many news agencies around the world. We put hundreds of breadcrumbs in stories of every kind that are leading back to this trail."

"Play a different game," Amber said softly to Jeff.

"I'm sorry," Lieutenant Crawford said. "I did not understand that."

"I only had the idea because Jeff encouraged me to find another way to share our story," Amber said. "I never would have had that idea without him."

Jeff squeezed her hand and continued, "Which brings us to several big questions. How can the governments in multiple countries be corrupted so completely? How does one of the poorest countries on Earth launch space vessels every few days? The US can't even do that. Who or what is coordinating all this behind the scenes?"

"Do you have answers to any of these questions?" Lieutenant Crawford asked.

"I think I do," Jeff said. "Do you remember when I first started following Amber that she was investigating corporate and government corruption?"

Lieutenant Crawford nodded yes.

"We never stopped that investigation. We believe a network of companies not only built the facility in Africa, but they are building over 300 more facilities around the world, and these facilities are roughly five times bigger," Jeff said, pointing to the pile of envelopes under the papers created by the professors at the University of Hawaii. "Those documents show dates when specific goods were shipped to countries around the world. The same materials were previously shipped to Burkina Faso."

"My God," Lieutenant Crawford said.

"We believe an organization called the Hidden Hand has been building huge companies around the world into a financial empire worth trillions of dollars," Jeff said. "They have been rigging elections, buying companies, controlling trade, manipulating markets, smuggling weapons, and assassinating people around the world. We think they're building these facilities." Jeff embellished a little with his description since he could not prove some of his claims. He was hoping to pull out whoever was behind that mirror on the wall and find out one way or another whether this group was really with them or against them.

"We will need to review these documents in detail to substantiate your claims," Lieutenant Crawford said.

"Go ahead. We have copies. We don't need those," Jeff lied in case he needed leverage to keep him and Amber alive in a few minutes. Amber squeezed his hand and gave him a questioning look.

Then the door slowly opened. A very large general entered the room with two other men behind him. The general must have been at least 6' 5". He was balding and likely in his fifties, but he looked like he was in excellent shape. The other two men were both colonels. One was African American, six feet tall, and in excellent shape. The other was a little shorter, Hispanic, and a little overweight.

A guard brought in a chair for the general. He sat down at the head of the table between Lieutenant Crawford on one side and Jeff with Amber on the other. "I'm Brigadier General Daniel Dawson. Behind me is Colonel Miguel Sanchez and Colonel Jeremy Sampson. I'm in charge of US Army Intelligence. I had to tell you in person that your story is incredible. What the two of you have seen and done—I'm at a loss for words—but I can tell you that I will personally put airstrikes on those facilities before they are ever allowed to open their doors for business."

Jeff knew they had now found who was in charge, and it sounded like these people were on his side after all.

"Thank you, General," Amber said. "What about the facility in Africa?"

"As soon as I heard your story, I ordered a spy satellite to change orbit," General Dawson said. "We should have eyes on that part of the world in the next couple of hours. Now I want to know everything you know about this Hidden Hand organization."

"We're happy to share, General," Jeff said, "but Lieutenant Crawford mentioned a plane coming for us. What do you intend to do about that?"

"I intend to have you on an earlier plane to our base in Okinawa," General Dawson said. "I'm going with you, Jeff. We knew bits and pieces of what you shared, but no one has as complete a story as you just shared with Lieutenant Crawford here. I want you on my team."

"I'll work with you, General, but not for you," Jeff said with conviction.

"Jeff, I took over the Joint Armed Forces Intelligence Network. I own the command codes for the satellites and over ten thousand intelligence personnel. I am the commander of the Army in the Pacific. The head of US Naval Operations in Japan and the Marine Corps in Guam and Korea are my good friends and with me," General Dawson explained. "I can help you more than any other person on this planet. If they come after me, I have 150,000 troops, two naval task forces, and a fleet of nuclear attack submarines. We can take the Air Force bases from that four-star prick in Washington so fast it will make his head spin."

"With all due respect, General," Jeff said, "with all these resources at your command, why do I know more than you do?"

General Dawson sat back in his chair and looked more than a little angry, but he said nothing.

Jeff had to speak fast so he did not lose a potential ally. "It's because I am out in the field, untethered, following my instincts. If I had a military chain of command to deal with, I could not be as effective. Don't get me wrong, I'll take your help, but I need to move quickly."

The big general eyed Jeff for thirty seconds before speaking. He was obviously not used to being refused, but he was an intelligence officer and had to be able to listen to facts before making decisions.

"I suppose we can make that work, Jeff," General Dawson finally agreed. "There are a few rules to this game I need you to live by, however."

"What kinds of rules?" Jeff asked.

"We do not assassinate foreign leaders," General Dawson said.

"I agree with you on that point, General," Jeff said.

"We do not cause harm to the American people or innocent civilians," General Dawson continued.

"I agree," Jeff said without hesitation.

"When I tell you something is absolutely critical to do, you do it!" General Dawson said.

"Like what, General?" Jeff said.

"It could be to do something or not to do something," General Dawson said. "It could be anything really, but it will not be one of the previous two statements. I won't ask you to kill a foreign leader or harm a civilian, American or otherwise."

Jeff thought about this statement. It was a little like reporting to the general under certain circumstances. Jeff decided honesty was the best policy, so he said, "I'll consider it, General, but if I disagree, I won't do it. I'll be able to document why later."

"You have some balls looking me in the eye and saying no," General Dawson said. "I could have you arrested and locked up for the rest of your life."

"You could do that, General, but you would not have my skills in the field," Jeff replied. "I want you to know that I will always be absolutely honest with you. If that means I need to tell you things you do not want to hear, you are going to hear them. I think this is how you make a good intelligence team great. If we can't work this way, then we're only pretending to work together."

The general looked Jeff in the eye for a solid twenty seconds, then looked back at his two colonels. One nodded slightly. The other shrugged his shoulders.

"I've decided to trust you, Jeff," General Dawson said. "I think we can learn a thing or two from one another."

"Thank you, General," Jeff replied with a small smile. "Amber and I have some things back in Kona we'd like to take with us."

"Don't worry about your stuff," General Dawson said. "It's already on its way here. We'll tow your car to the base. Are copies of all your previous work with your stuff?"

"No," Jeff said. "I can give you a website with everything on it and the encryption codes to open the files. Everything we've done so far is there except the documents on the table."

"Very good," General Dawson said. "Now we need to learn more about this Hidden Hand."

"What do you know so far?" Jeff asked.

"Assume nothing," General Dawson replied.

Jeff wondered how close to the truth that answer really was. Over the next hour, Jeff and Amber went over all the data that had led them to discovering the Hidden Hand. Then they covered the Hidden Hand's extensive business and political connections, including Jeff's old boss. Chairs were brought in for the two colonels, who asked a constant stream of questions along the way while Lieutenant Crawford wrote notes on their conversation. A lieutenant entered the room and took the stack of documents off the table, then returned with the originals and a stack of copies. No doubt another copy somewhere was being loaded into military intelligence computers for analysis.

Another soldier entered the room carrying a tray filled with glasses of ice water. He put them down, then whispered something to the general before leaving the room.

"Your stuff just arrived, and our plane is ready to go," General Dawson said. "We can grab something to eat at the officers' mess hall and be on the plane in half an hour. We'll be in Okinawa eight hours after that."

"It's fortunate we're heading west, General," Jeff said. "I'll be setting up a meeting in Hong Kong and eventually need to reach Russia."

"Russia?" General Dawson exclaimed. "I got to tell you, Jeff, Asia is a real shitstorm right now. Coups, assassinations, civil unrest, military factions fighting with each other. It's really bad."

"Sounds like the US," Jeff replied.

"Ouch," Colonel Sampson said.

"That must be telling me more of what I do not want to hear," General Dawson said. "Keep it up. We need it."

"I'm curious about one thing, General. Did the professors turn us in?"

"They did," Lieutenant Crawford said.

After a quick dinner of chicken, mashed potatoes, and peas, they met General Dawson and Colonel Sampson on the runway. Their belongings were all packed in duffel bags piled near the rear cargo ramp. As they grabbed their things and carried them up the ramp, General Dawson finished some final instructions to Colonel Sampson and followed them with one duffel bag on his shoulder.

The Army green cargo plane had long benches on both sides and rollers for pallets down the center. One pallet of boxes and equipment was covered by an Army-green tarp. There was easily room for five more. They sat down and fastened seatbelts as the cargo ramp closed. The plane taxied and took off quickly.

General Dawson said, "I'm going to grab some shuteye. It's an eight-hour flight. The head is up front just through that door and to the right. Feel free to stretch out and get comfortable."

The general grabbed a small cap from his back pocket, tilted it over his eyes, and stretched out his legs. He was asleep in minutes.

"Wow," Amber said. "I've never seen anyone fall asleep so fast."

Jeff could barely hear her over the engine noise. "Let's move a little farther toward the back of the plane so we can talk and not wake up the general."

Amber started to check through the duffel bags to see what was packed and if anything important was missing.

"We're very lucky that things turned out this way," Jeff said. "I have to admit I was scared when the military police rushed into the hallway with guns drawn."

"When they put that hood over my head in the black SUV, I was so scared I peed a little," Amber said.

Jeff laughed.

"Hey! That's not funny," Amber said defensively.

"I'm sorry," Jeff said. "You just surprised me."

"You're surprised," Amber said. "I still haven't been able to change. I found some clean clothes. I'm going to use the bathroom and get changed into something warmer."

"All right," Jeff said. "I'll be here, checking for puddles."

Amber shot him an angry look, then smiled and made her way to the front of the plane around the cargo pallet.

What Jeff hadn't said was that he wasn't scared for himself—he was scared for Amber. He wondered whether there was a way he could convince her not to follow him to Russia. He thought about it as he pulled up a duffel bag for a pillow and laid out on the bench.

When Amber returned, Jeff was asleep. Amber looked first at the general and then at Jeff. She shook her head and said, "Men. You feed them a little food, leave them alone for a minute, and they are fast asleep." She repacked the other two duffel bags and put them up on the bench for pillows, but no matter how hard she tried, she could not sleep. It was a long flight. Who knew what they would find once they landed?

PARTNERS IN CRIME

Amber felt her ears plug before a hard jolt told her they had landed.

General Dawson just sat up, looked around, and adjusted his cap to the normal position on his head. He smiled at Amber and said in a booming voice, easily heard over the sound of the engines, "We're home!"

Jeff almost fell off the bench as he woke up. He sat dazed and groggy for a minute before he looked over at Amber and noticed how tired she looked. "Did you get any sleep?"

"I don't know how anyone could get any sleep on these hard benches," Amber yelled over the engine noise.

"You learn to make do in the military," Jeff said as he smiled at her. "You grab a nap whenever and wherever you can. What time is it?"

"We arrived in Okinawa, Japan at 11:05 a.m., Wednesday," the general said, never looking at his watch.

Time zones never failed to cause Jeff confusion until he adjusted to local time. He tried to figure out what time it was in Hawaii, but he gave up. His mind was too clouded from his recent slumber.

When the cargo ramp lowered, they were greeted by a wall of warm humid air. It was about 80 degrees with greater than 80 percent humidity. At the bottom of the ramp were four MPs, two officers, and two Army-green Jeeps.

"Welcome home, General," one of the officers said with a salute.

"It's good to be back," General Dawson replied, returning the salute as the only three passengers on the plane walked down the ramp. "What's the sitrep?"

"Nothing new beyond the information you found from these two," another officer replied. "We've been digging deep into the data last night and today. We also have photos on the Burkina Faso site."

"What did you find?" General Dawson asked.

"There was some type of facility there, but it's been melted into a giant pool of slag," the first officer explained.

"Covering their tracks," General Dawson said. "That was smart."

"We have more questions for your guests if we could escort them to a briefing room," the second officer said.

"They had a rough flight," General Dawson said. "Find them quarters on base and give them a few hours to eat and rest." Turning to Jeff and Amber, he asked, "Are you folks okay with briefing my intelligence team about two hours from now?"

"Sure," Jeff said.

"We'll need a few things like a toothbrush and something to eat," Amber said.

"Major Jones will find you quarters and show you around the base," General Dawson said. "Everything you need should be at the PX or the mess hall." He turned to Major Jones and said, "Get them a guest pass. Show them around the base and how things work." The general then turned to the other officer and said, "You're with me, Jim. We need to meet with the Japanese today." Two MPs and the other officer peeled off with the general and got into a Jeep on the edge of the runway.

"I'll be happy to show you folks around the base," Major Jones said. "I'm looking forward to talking with you later today. I'm leading one of the intelligence teams here on the base. The data you shared is awesome. I have so many questions, but they can wait until later."

Major Jones showed them the grocery store, also called the PX, and the cafeteria, also called the mess hall. He took them to the front gate where they received badges allowing them access to public areas on the base and to return onto the base when they left. Finally, they met a sergeant who found them accommodations on the base. The room was small like the guest house in Hawaii, but it was clean and had all the basics.

Amber lay down while Jeff explored the base. The immediate difference he noticed between this base and any other military base was the lush green foliage and flowers blooming everywhere. Every unpaved scrap of land was green.

Jeff started walking around the base perimeter and observing the base's security protocols in action. He was impressed. Everywhere there were guards, they were two-man teams. They not only defended the perimeter but had checkpoints to vital areas inside the base. Teams were swapped out every two hours to reduce fatigue and keep guards sharp. The only real flaw Jeff saw was that the entire system was designed against infiltration and anti-personnel defense. Armored vehicles or even a delivery truck could just run right through the fences and most of the light frame buildings.

Next, Jeff decided to check out the mess hall. He was starving. The mess hall was a simple, no-frills cafeteria. It did have wooden tables and benches that were nicer than most of the mess halls he had been in. It served some pre-made dishes, some grab-and-go items like sandwiches or local fruit, and a "make-it-yourself" sandwich bar. Jeff made a simple ham-and-cheese sandwich on white bread with chips, but it hit the spot. He bought two more—another for him and one for Amber. Time flew by until it was almost time for them to meet with Major Jones.

When Jeff returned, Amber had just gotten out of the shower and was half-dressed. "I'll be out in a few minutes."

"I got you some lunch."

"How sweet of you." She sat down and started eating.

"You must be starving," Jeff said. He poured her a glass of water to go with her meal. He noticed she was still tired and said, "I know we need to meet with the Army in ten minutes, but you don't need to rush. I can meet with Major Jones first and you can take your time getting ready."

"Thank you," Amber said. "I've pulled all-nighters before. I don't know why I'm so tired."

"It's jet lag. Your body needs to adjust to this time zone," Jeff said. "I usually have a harder time going East myself. For some people heading West is worse. I like to get out in the sun for at least a few minutes so my body knows it's day time and never go to bed before 9 p.m. at the earliest. I seem to adjust quicker that way, but time zone changes just mess with my head. I almost never get the time right for a few days."

When Jeff saw how hungry Amber was, he cut his second sandwich in half and left the other half for her. She had finished the first sandwich and started on her half.

As Jeff leaned against the wall and waited for a reply, he admired Amber. Tired and starving, she was still beautiful. Her red hair framed a heart-shaped face holding piercing-green, almond-shaped eyes. She was intelligent, worldly, funny, and had a figure with all the right curves.

Amber was halfway through the half-sandwich when she noticed Jeff staring at her. "What is it?" she asked.

Jeff shook himself out of his thoughts and said, "I was just waiting for an answer. Do you want me to go first?"

"For a second there, I thought you were leering at me," Amber said. "Yes. You go ahead first, and I'll catch up. I still remember where the building is."

"Okay," Jeff said with a smile. "Don't forget your badge." He gave Amber one last look, then exited their little house.

Jeff walked over to the building Major Jones was at with a few minutes to spare. It was a big building—the only one he had seen made from concrete that was not an aircraft hangar. He entered a reception area with about ten chairs lined up along two walls. The rest of the room had a polished wood, four-foot-high wall. An MP stood behind a glass screen like a bank teller in a bad neighborhood. There were desks behind him where three more MPs were working. Part of the wooden half-wall had a gate that led to the work area and a door leading into the rest of the building. This must be a high security building, Jeff noted.

The MP noticed Jeff enter and said, "Can I help you, sir?"

"Yes," Jeff said. "I have an appointment with Major Jones."

"Wasn't there a woman accompanying you for this appointment, sir?" the MP asked.

"Yes," Jeff said. "She'll be here later. I can start the appointment with Major Jones at his convenience."

"All right," the MP said. "Have a seat and I'll let Major Jones know you're here." He then called someone.

Major Jones came through the door seconds after the MP hung up the phone.

"Jeff Smith!" Major Jones said as he hit a button that opened the wooden gate to the door Major Jones had just come through. "I'm glad you made it here on time." The Major looked around the room and said, "Where's Amber?"

"She was tired from the trip so she'll be here a little later," Jeff explained.

"All right," Major Jones said. "We can get started; come in." Major Jones led Jeff into a maze of corridors. The many doors off the corridors either had military personnel names or the names of places in Japan. Jeff guessed the places were conference rooms. Every door had a set of numbers that followed a pattern. Even though their path was confusing, Jeff knew from the door numbers right where he was and could figure out how to get back to the exit.

They stopped at a room named Kyoto. As they entered, Jeff was impressed. About twenty chairs were around a long black table with microphones for each seat built into the table. An overhead projector with a large screen was at the opposite end of the room from the entrance. There were counters along both walls with drawers. There was even a glass door to a half-sized refrigerator under the counter. Glasses with several pitchers of ice water were on one counter, along with fruit and cookies. Two other officers were already in the room: a captain and a lieutenant.

Everyone else was eating a cookie, so Jeff grabbed one and sat down. He joked, "So this is how the Army spends $100 billion a year." No one laughed. Tough crowd.

Major Jones was standing at the back of the room by the door they had entered from. "This is the best room in the building," he said. "They're not all like this. We pulled out all the stops for you, Jeff. I'd like this to be an open conversation and to get some tough questions answered."

"I'm happy to help any way I can, Major," Jeff said.

"Great!" Major Jones said. "Let's start with introductions. On my left is Captain Yee. He leads my Pacific and East Asia Intelligence unit. Next to him is Lieutenant Tam, a member of Captain Yee's team."

As Jeff assessed the room, he noted that Captain Yee and Lieutenant Tam were both female with East-Asian ancestry. He would have to assess their skills by the questions they asked since he'd had no time to research them in advance and now lacked the CIA support staff he'd once had.

"Pleased to meet you," Jeff said.

"We want to start with the copious quantity of information created by you and Amber," Major Jones said. "The volume of information alone is quite impressive."

"Thank you," Jeff said. "Most of the credit there goes to Amber."

"Indeed. First, we need to understand whether a few things were true or a means to an end," Major Jones said.

"A means to an end?" Jeff asked.

"A fabrication to direct people to the right conclusion even though the thing in question was not real," Captain Yee clarified.

"We were never using misinformation or disinformation," Jeff said. "If anything, we were using a counter-disinformation strategy."

"Interesting," Captain Yee said. "We were trying to understand why the original stories were broken up into so many smaller stories with pieces of the original."

"You were running a counter-disinformation operation to get the pieces past the censors," Lieutenant Tam said, "so that once those pieces came together, no one could easily refute them."

"That's correct," Jeff said.

"Fascinating," Major Jones said. "Now on to my first questions. This material found in the Pacific Ocean off the coast of the Queen Charlotte Islands—was it, in fact, real nanite technology?"

"That information was Class 12 classified, need to know," Jeff said. "We never published it in any of our stories."

"No," Major Jones said. "But there was a detailed report from you to CIA Assistant Director Zachariah James."

"That is true."

"Were you Class 12?" Captain Yee asked.

"I was Class 14," Jeff replied. "Not that it matters anymore."

The Major looked at Jeff for a moment, then said, "No one in this room is Class 14, including me."

Jeff could feel that now everyone in the room had a much higher respect for him than before. He said, "My team would get the hard problems no one could solve. That included research, intelligence, and counterintelligence. I had a great staff. Now a large percentage of them are likely dead."

"I'm sorry, Jeff," Major Jones said sincerely.

"Since I get to decide on who needs to know, I'll let you know," Jeff continued. "This material is real. A sample is in an Army research center ten stories under the Virginia countryside."

"I've never heard of this facility," Major Jones said.

"It's also Class 12 need to know," Jeff replied.

"All the information about being perfect spheres and resting in a default state is true?" Major Jones asked.

"That's the result of an analysis by one of the best research teams in the country," Jeff answered.

"Fascinating," Major Jones said.

"My second question is about the vehicle launched from Burkina Faso," Major Jones said. "Was that real?"

"Yes, it was," Jeff said. "I asked the French military to verify the launch. They not only verified it; they said there were launches every two to three days from the same location. The destination was Earth's L2 Lagrange point."

"And you believe there's an alien presence at that location in space?" Captain Yee asked.

"I believe there's a vessel or a base at that location in space," Jeff said. "I also think whoever is located there is running a covert operation designed to kill millions of people here on Earth."

"I cannot help but notice that you didn't say anything about aliens," Lieutenant Tam said.

"While there's a lot of evidence that infers an alien entity, I cannot directly prove it," Jeff said. "There are no alien bodies. No one has seen one. No one has even talked to one."

"We may have someone who talked to one," Lieutenant Tam said.

"Really?" Jeff asked.

"Yes—" Lieutenant Tam began.

"Lieutenant Tam," Captain Yee interrupted, as if to stop her from saying something she shouldn't.

"Jeff was a Class 14 Agent in the CIA," Major Jones said. "I think he has information we need to know, and we have information he does not know. Together, we may be able to piece together what is really going on in the world. General Dawson has cleared us to work with him. I'm going to allow sharing all our intelligence on this matter. Please continue, Lieutenant Tam."

"We were working with a little-known agency in the Chinese government," Lieutenant Tam said. "We captured an agent who was working for an organization that could be loosely translated as the Hidden Hand. When we tried to move him to Beijing, the plane we used exploded, killing all passengers."

"A bomb?" Jeff asked.

"We found no evidence of an explosive device," Lieutenant Tam replied. "Our best guess is that the fuel tanks just exploded for some unknown reason. This agent had multiple cells working for him within the Chinese government. He was manipulating markets, smuggling weapons, supporting human trafficking, and authorizing construction permits."

"Did you cross-reference the permits with any of the sites in China that Amber detailed in our documents?" Jeff asked.

"Yes," Lieutenant Tam said. "Some were an obvious match. Others will require more research to see if there are relationships."

"Someone killed that agent to hide something," Jeff commented. "Do we know what?"

"We thought he was the top of the pyramid until his odd death caused us to investigate further," Lieutenant Tam said. "There's a Chinese industrialist whose name I will not share here. He's probably one of the richest men in the world, though we don't have records on his wealth."

"Interesting. Does his influence go beyond China?" Jeff asked.

"Financially, yes. Politically, not that we can find now," Lieutenant Tam replied.

"That could be the way they work," Jeff said. "An ultra-rich industrialist with a group of senior agents working toward a set of goals set by a central entity."

Lieutenant Tam looked at Captain Yee, who nodded. Then Lieutenant Tam said, "There's something more. This man has holding companies that own property near major population centers. Each one has a major construction project in-flight. The companies are also parking large numbers of heavy cargo trucks at these facilities. We have only inspected five so far, but we could not figure out what they were doing. We thought they were military sites building manufacturing plants for a new weapons system. When we read your documents, they sounded like the facility described in Africa. We haven't cross-referenced these sites with your list in detail yet, but a quick review showed overlaps."

"If your estimates are right, two hundred of these factories could depopulate China in one hundred days," Captain Yee said. "The agent we captured had purchased permits for over 200 sites."

"Maybe that's their goal," Jeff said.

"What goal?" Major Jones asked.

"To depopulate large areas of the Earth quickly," Jeff said. "Burkina Faso may have only been a test run. The liquid it produced could have been a production sample before replicating the process at more locations. If they could do it quickly enough, they could avoid a coordinated response."

The room was silent as the enormity of Jeff's comment sunk in. Jeff was taken aback himself by what he had said.

The political situation in the United States and France then started to make sense. Jeff thought out loud, "And if they could cause political unrest in the more advanced nations, they could buy enough time to execute their plan without a coordinated military response."

"What do you mean, Jeff?" Major Jones asked.

"Think about the deep divisions in our own country's leadership right now," Jeff explained. "General Dawson said he has this part of the world under his direct control."

"That may be an overstatement, Jeff," Major Jones said. "The Air Force bases are not being friendly right now, and the Department of the Navy wants the General's stars."

Jeff knew that wanting the General's stars meant wanting to strip him of his rank and dishonorably discharge him, but it was also a metaphor for killing a general because no general would willingly give up his stars without a fight.

"The general said he would take the Air Force bases quickly if needed," Jeff said.

"It's true that no Air Force base can survive on its own without Army or Marine ground support," Major Jones said.

"Regardless," Jeff said, "just look at the division in our own military out here in the Pacific. How can we coordinate an assault on foreign soil if we don't even trust each other?"

"I see your point," Major Jones said.

"My next question is about what you and Amber saw inside the facility in Burkina Faso," Major Jones said. "You saw thousands of people placed in glass enclosures breathing poisonous gas and being injected with chemicals?"

"Yes," Jeff said. "It was one of the most horrific experiences of my life. A thousand muffled cries in agony make a sound I never want to hear again as long as I live."

If there had been any doubts in the minds of the people in this room that Jeff and Amber had seen the nightmare they described in their documentation, they were convinced now by the look on Jeff's face.

"You actually have a sample of this liquid they were extracting?" Major Jones asked.

"Yes," Jeff confirmed. "I actually have three samples. Only one is in the United States." Jeff realized he had missed his chance to ask Dureau the status of the sample he had taken to Spain and the one Stephan had taken to France. He hoped Dureau could make their next phone call.

"Where are the others?" Major Jones asked.

"I'll let you know when I find out myself," Jeff said. He hadn't lied, but it was an extension of the truth. Jeff never put all his eggs in one basket. Years of espionage had taught him always to hold something in reserve.

"Where is the sample in the US?" Major Jones asked.

"It's in the same place as the nanite material sample," Jeff said. "I'm not sure it should be retrieved until the political situation in Washington gets resolved."

"I agree," Major Jones said.

There was a knock at the door. Major Jones opened the door to find an MP had escorted Amber to the room. "Welcome, Amber," Major Jones said with a warm smile. "I have been so looking forward to meeting you."

"Thank you," Amber replied as she looked round the room of officers. She immediately started to assess the room and the people in it as the major made introductions. She noted everyone was an officer except herself and Jeff. Two of the officers were women. She noted their ranks, ethnicities, uniforms, insignias, height, weight, age, hair color, eye color, and every detail, including their shoes.

"Let's take a ten-minute break now," Major Jones said. "We can go to the bathroom, get something to eat or drink, or check our email, but be back here in ten minutes or less. Jeff, you can catch Amber up on our conversation so far."

"Sure," Jeff said.

"Oh, and if you need to use the restroom, an MP will need to escort you," Major Jones added before he left the room.

"So what did I miss?" Amber asked.

"Mainly, Major Jones and his team wanted to verify that certain parts of our story were true," Jeff explained.

"Like what?" Amber asked.

Jeff listed off the discussion points so far. "The nanite material we found in the Pacific. The vehicle that launched into space from Burkina Faso. The facility and what we saw inside. Did we really see what we said we saw? Did we really have a sample from the facility? Where was the sample?"

"Basically everything!" Amber said.

"Yeah," Jeff said with a laugh. "Basically everything!"

"Well," Amber said. "I think I'll get myself some fruit and a soda to stay awake. You want anything?"

"Another cookie," Jeff said.

"You are so bad," Amber said as she slapped his wrist and smiled. Then she got up to get them snacks.

Just as Amber returned from the other side of the table, Major Jones reentered the room. He stood at the end of the room near the door and said, "All right, everyone, now that you have all had a break, we should be good for the next few hours. I'll give each officer in the room a chance to ask their questions. We should try to stick to common topics at a given time, then move on."

The next three hours was an intense question-and-answer session. Every aspect of Jeff and Amber's journey was picked apart, analyzed, and discussed. It was clear to Jeff that Lieutenant Tam had field experience as an agent. Captain Yee seemed to have a deep understanding of Chinese and Korean politics.

As the meeting wrapped up, Jeff pulled Major Jones to the side and asked, "Major Jones, I had made an agreement with the general about our…relationship."

"Yes," Major Jones said. "I'm aware of the agreement."

"I need to contact a Russian agent," Jeff said.

"Russia has been difficult to communicate with recently," Major Jones said.

"All I need is a phone and some privacy," Jeff said. "Can I use a phone for long distance calls here somewhere?"

"You can use my office phone," Major Jones said. "Follow me." Jeff gave Amber a hand signal that he was leaving and followed Major Jones out of the room.

Lieutenant Tam escorted Amber out of the building and walked with Amber to her small house on the base. It was still warm as the sun started to set over the hills to the West. Lieutenant Tam asked, "How long have you known Jeff?"

"We've been adversaries for over a year," Amber replied. "I only really got to know him after he rescued me from a small village in Burkina Faso. We've been running and hiding ever since."

"He rescued you?" Lieutenant Tam asked.

"Yes," Amber replied. "I was investigating the disappearance of an entire village in the mountains. After looking over the unoccupied village, I moved on to surveillance of the mining facility. I went back to the village to spend the night since it was close and empty. The next morning, armed bandits woke me. They were stealing from the village. I was trapped until Jeff and his friends came and saved me."

"That's quite a story," Lieutenant Tam said. "The work you did to document your journey and write those stories is amazing considering the stress you must have been under. We could provide you logistical support and a steady stream of intelligence to analyze and write about if you're interested?"

Amber realized this was not girl talk after work. Lieutenant Tam was offering her a job. "That's an interesting offer, but I'm jet-lagged and not ready to make any decisions. Could we talk about it tomorrow, Lieutenant?"

"Of course," Lieutenant Tam replied with a smile. "Until tomorrow then." Then Lieutenant Tam turned away and walked down the street.

Amber walked up to the porch of their little house and watched Lieutenant Tam walking away. She thought about Lieutenant Tam's offer. Having a safe place to live and a support network for her work would be wonderful, but Jeff was planning to meet with the Russians. He said it would be dangerous. She hadn't thought about what came next. They had been running from place to place and country to country for almost a month now. Amber didn't even consider staying put for a while.

Meanwhile, Major Jones had led Jeff to his office. It was a little small with a small desk, a bookshelf, and a counter on one wall with storage cabinets beneath. The major said, "Just dial 9 to get an outside line. I'll be back in ten minutes or so. Please stay here until I return. You'll need an escort to leave the building."

"Thank you, Major," Jeff said as the major left the room. Jeff had memorized the contact number for a Russian spy he had worked with in North Africa. They had partnered to prevent stolen plutonium from reaching Libya. Neither of their agencies ever knew they had a partnership. They had agreed to help one another again if a need arose that served both their national interests.

Jeff dialed the number and checked his watch to time the call. A woman answered on the third ring. She said, "*Zdravstvuj*," an informal form of "hello" in Russian.

Jeff replied, "Spring in Siberia is beautiful."

The woman hesitated for a moment, then said in a lowered voice in English with a heavy Russian accent, "It is still cold as the grave."

"And twice as deep," Jeff replied.

"Why do you call?" the woman asked.

"I am a friend of Sergei," Jeff replied. "I would like to speak with him."

"Sergei is hard to reach," the woman replied.

"I can give you a number where he can call me at 8 a.m. or 4 p.m. Vladivostok time," Jeff said. Then he gave the woman the number of a cell phone he had just purchased on the base.

"I try to give to Sergei," the woman said. "He may call. He may no."

"Thank you," Jeff said and hung up.

Sergei Sokolov was a little like Jeff Smith in Russia—he had a very common first and last name. Sergei was a very senior agent in the Russian Federation.

If Jeff were going to meet Sergei, he would need the Army's help getting to him. That would likely mean revealing his fake identity. That is, assuming the Army had not already found it when it grabbed his and Amber's things in Hawaii.

Jeff was thinking about next steps when Major Jones returned. He sat on the edge of his desk and looked at Jeff, sitting in his chair. Jeff was about to get up and move when he said, "Jeff, I spoke with the general. I know you have an agreement to move on."

"I do," Jeff said in a firm voice. "Is there a problem?"

"No," Major Jones said. "Honestly, I would prefer having you work for us, but I lost that argument. I was thinking more about Amber."

"What about Amber?" Jeff asked.

"You two have been through a lot together," Major Jones said. "She has been amazing considering everything you've been through."

"But?" Jeff said.

"But," Major Jones said, "she is not a field agent. You are good at what you do, but you've been lucky."

"And?" Jeff said.

"And," Major Jones said, "that young lady has some excellent talents I could really use right now. I can put her to work doing what she does best and keep her safe here in Japan. I can work up a full alias, a cover story, the whole nine yards."

"You should probably talk to Amber about that," Jeff said.

"Lieutenant Tam already has," Major Jones said. "Amber said she needed to think about it."

"Then why are you talking to me?" Jeff said.

"I know you two are close," Major Jones said. When Jeff gave a questioning look, he continued, "I noticed it in the interrogation video with Lieutenant Crawford in Hawaii. Don't let your feelings for this girl get her killed. I promise you, man to man, that I will keep her as safe as my own family."

Jeff looked down at the desk to think. He was angry at Major Jones for prying into their personal lives, but finding Amber a safe place to live with the work she loved was a win-win. It was, at least, as safe as anyone could be—lately, it felt like everything had been thrown into a blender, then switched on high.

Jeff finally looked up at the major and said, "Thank you for this kind offer, Major Jones. I appreciate it, but at the end of the day, it's Amber's decision. I can't make her mind up for her. Lord knows I've tried, but it has never worked so far."

The major gave an odd smile and said, "I'm sure you're tired and would like to get back to your house. Think about my offer. We can talk some more tomorrow."

The major escorted Jeff out of the building without another word until they reached the reception area where the MPs were stationed. He said, "Think about what I said. Goodnight."

Jeff exited the building and walked straight to his temporary home. The sun had set and it was getting dark fast. He saw Amber in the distance, on the porch pacing. She saw Jeff and walked to greet him.

"Hi," Amber said with a smile.

"Hi," Jeff said. "Why were you out on the porch?"

"This jet lag is pretty bad," Amber said. "If I go inside, I'll probably fall asleep. I have something I wanted to talk to you about."

"Is it Lieutenant Tam's offer?" Jeff asked as they started to stroll down the street.

"You already know about that?" Amber asked. "Did they offer you a job too?"

"No," Jeff replied. "He was actually worried about you."

"About me," Amber said.

"Yes. He started by saying he wanted me to work for him, but the general agreed to let me go my own way," Jeff explained. "Then he pointed out that even a well-trained operative in Russia was in danger every moment. The Russians don't just arrest spies." Jeff embellished the major's words with a few of his own thoughts.

"Then why are you going?" Amber asked.

"Because my instincts tell me it's the right next move," Jeff said.

"I can't talk you out of it?" Amber asked with hope in her voice.

"No," Jeff replied. "I've already started the ball rolling. I should make contact sometime tomorrow. I'll probably have to leave in a hurry once I know where I'm going."

Amber did not reply.

"The major promised to keep you as safe as his own family," Jeff said. "He offered to create an alias and a cover story. He also said he really needs your skills."

Jeff stopped and took both of Amber's hands in his. He looked her in the eye and said, "We've been through a lot together, but I think the major's offer is the right move for right now. At the end of the day, it's your life and your decision. I'm only sharing my opinion."

"This whole situation sucks." They both laughed, then Amber continued, "Right from the beginning, it was nothing but dirt and death. You've kept me alive this past month. You're an incredible man, Jeff Smith."

"I'm very good at what I do, Amber," Jeff replied. "I will expose what is hiding out there in space and come back. I promise."

Amber pulled her hands away and said, "I'm going for a walk to think this through. Good night."

"Good night," Jeff replied. He fell asleep on the couch before Amber returned.

TRAVEL PLANS

The next day, Jeff woke early and quietly left without waking Amber. He went for a walk and waited for Sergei to call.

He checked his watch. At 8:20, the phone rang. Jeff answered on the third ring. He said, "Spring in Siberia is beautiful."

A male voice replied in English with a heavy Russian accent, "It is still cold as the grave."

"And twice as deep," Jeff replied.

"Why do you call, Mr. Smith?" the man asked.

Since the caller used Jeff's name, he assumed it was Sergei and that Sergei thought it was safe to use names. It had been a few years since Jeff had spoken to him, and he could not remember the voice exactly. He decided to play along.

"Strange things have been happening in both of our countries lately," Jeff said.

"Things are always strange in your country," Sergei said.

"I think I know why," Jeff said. "Are you interested?"

The silence lasted twenty seconds before Sergei asked, "How soon can you be in Hong Kong?"

"A day or two," Jeff replied.

"There are pay phones at the exit door of the international terminal," Sergei said. "Go to the phone furthest from the door and wait for a call there."

"That's it?" Jeff said.

"Two days," Sergei said. "No more." Then he hung up.

If Sergei was in league with the Hidden Hand, this trip would be the perfect assassination setup. Jeff always weighed the risks versus the rewards of every operation he was involved in and found ways to reduce his risk. If he was going to reduce the risk here, he was going to need help. He decided that including the major in his operational plan was the best way to reduce the risk.

Jeff was hungry, so he stopped by the mess hall and ate a big breakfast of steak, eggs, and orange juice since he might not have another good meal for days. He looked around the room and noticed Lieutenant Tam sitting alone in a corner. She tried to pretend she wasn't watching him, but Jeff knew a spy watching a target when he saw it.

He decided to walk over to her and let her know he had spotted her. He deposited his dirty tray on the dirty dishes conveyor belt, refilled his orange juice, and walked over to Lieutenant Tam, who looked a little irritated. "Mind if I join you?" he asked her.

"No," Lieutenant Tam said. "I'm not staying long, but you're welcome to join me."

"Thanks," Jeff said as he sat down. He decided to get right to the point. "You're following me. Who's following Amber?"

"I decided to follow you on my own," Lieutenant Tam said.

Jeff knew the first rule of the spy business. If you are caught, deny everything and blame it all on yourself. He saw right through it, but he decided to play along to see where this would go. "So, you don't trust me?"

Lieutenant Tam looked Jeff in the eye and said, "I don't trust anyone."

"Good," Jeff said. "You shouldn't."

They looked at each other for a moment. The Jeff continued, "I know you're a field agent. You might be the major's best. So what do you not like about me?"

Lieutenant Tam looked at her food, which she had not touched, and smiled. "Your story is too fantastic." She looked up at Jeff. "Your mission is unclear. You drop out of the back roads of Africa with piles of documentation on a fairy tale and everyone just believes you."

"You don't believe me?" Jeff asked.

"I'm not sure," Lieutenant Tam said in a leery voice as she studied Jeff's face. "Who called you this morning?"

"An old acquaintance," Jeff said.

"An old acquaintance with the number to a cellphone you just bought on a secure military base?" Lieutenant Tam asked.

"The major probably already told you I'm planning on leaving soon," Jeff said. "I called my contact from his phone last night."

"And the return call is on an unsecure cell phone," Lieutenant Tam said.

"Unsecure and untapped," Jeff said. "Old habits die hard when they keep you alive."

Lieutenant Tam just looked at Jeff. He got the feeling that a snake had coiled and was ready to strike.

"I was planning on visiting the major right now," Jeff said. "Care to join me?"

She stood and said, "That's a good idea. Let's go."

Jeff finished his orange juice and turned to go. When he noticed Lieutenant Tam was leaving her food tray on the table, he said, "Police your tray, Lieutenant. Your mother doesn't work here."

Anger flashed across her dark eyes. Jeff could sense the snake coiling again. Then she relaxed and picked up her tray. They deposited their dishes and walked through the busy morning streets of the base to the same building as the day before. Jeff was pushing her buttons on purpose to see how she handled herself. He guessed the major was going to have her accompany him if he asked for help on this mission. He wanted to get a sense of who he was working with.

Lieutenant Tam was silent until they entered the building. Her badge opened the wooden gate to the guard station, and she ordered the MP on duty to give Jeff a visitor badge. After the MP opened the door to the rest of the building, Lieutenant Tam guided Jeff through the maze of corridors. As Jeff followed her, he noticed the Lieutenant moved gracefully, like a cat ready to leap at any moment. She was small, about 5' 4". Her dark hair was hidden in her cap. Her face was pleasant to look at, but he never saw warmth in her smile. She seemed to study the world around her like it was all one big science experiment. Not bad qualities for an agent.

They stopped at a conference room door labeled Ohu. Lieutenant Tam opened the door and asked Jeff to wait in the room while she retrieved Major Jones. The room was small with an oval table, four chairs, and a white board. No leather chairs, gloss black finishes, or projector screens here. The furniture was all plastic and Formica, and not very comfortable. He was starting to get bored, so he picked up a marker and drew a fair rendering of the Chinese coastline and the major islands in the South China Sea. He was just adding capital city names when the major entered the room, followed by Lieutenant Tam.

"Good morning, Major Jones," Jeff said as he motioned to the whiteboard. "I was just entertaining myself while I waited."

"Not a bad map," the major commented. "Lieutenant Tam tells me you have a mission in the works."

Jeff became serious and said, "I've contacted a Russian Agent I've worked with before. He should be able to help me with my goal."

"What goal is that, Jeff?" Major Jones asked.

"Detecting whatever is located at the L2 Lagrange point," Jeff said. "I believe by detecting what is there, we can alert leaders around the globe to the danger they face. Furthermore, I believe it will complicate any plans to kill large numbers of people. Amber estimated that those factories could start up in as little as three months."

"Why involve the Russians?" Major Jones asked.

"Because space funding in the US is political, and it could take years to launch a detection device," Jeff explained. "The Russians do not have that problem. If I can convince the right player to order it, we can have something launched in weeks."

"This sounds like you're gambling with your life, Jeff, on very long odds," Major Jones said in a worried voice. Lieutenant Tam just studied Jeff in silence.

"Never tell me the odds," Jeff replied. "I only need the objective. This brings me to a request. I need to meet this agent in Hong Kong in less than two days."

"That should be easy enough," Major Jones said. "We could get you there any number of ways."

"I also need a partner," Jeff said. "The meeting setup smells like a trap. I need someone to watch my back."

Lieutenant Tam sat up straight and said to Major Jones, "Sir, I volunteer."

"I don't like this one bit," Major Jones said. "Two top assets walking into a likely trap, all to find an unknown third party who would violate his country's chain of command to launch a probe into outer space. I do not like it at all."

"I believe this mission is our best chance to break the stranglehold on Earth's governments," Jeff explained. "I grant you the risk is high, but the reward is avoiding the largest loss of human life in our history. I can mitigate risks, Major. I can manipulate governments, but I would have a better chance if I'm not alone."

"Sir," Lieutenant Tam said to Major Jones. "You know I'm not convinced that this story is true. I want to take this mission to either confirm or deny the truth. I'm the best person for this mission."

"I don't have many people left, Lieutenant Tam," Major Jones said in an angry voice. He sat back, took a deep breath, then continued, "I've lost some good agents on hasty missions with poor planning. This feels like another one."

"I only have two days and the clock is ticking," Jeff said. "Every minute that goes by, the world is that much closer to these factories going online. I need an answer."

"I don't know," Major Jones said.

"Tick! Tock!" Jeff said.

"There is no plan," Major Jones said.

"Tick! Tock!"

"I don't want to lose another agent to a poorly planned mission," Major Jones said.

"Lieutenant Tam and I can make our plan en route," Jeff replied. "Tick! Tock!"

Major Jones was getting angry. He just looked at Jeff.

Jeff broke the silence by saying, "Very well, Major. I'm going either way, and I don't have time to waste. You said it would be easy to get there. I'd like to arrange transportation now."

"There's a diplomatic flight going out tonight to Hong Kong, then moving on to Thailand," Lieutenant Tam said. "We can join that flight as part of its security detail. When the diplomats leave the airport, we can peel off and go to your meeting. The Chinese will be following us, though, so we'll need to lose them first."

"Works for me, but I don't think the major has made a decision yet," Jeff said to Lieutenant Tam as he looked back at the major. "Tick! Tock!"

"Jesus, would you stop doing that," the major said as he stood up and headed for the door. He opened the door and turned to Jeff. "If you get her killed, don't come back." He then turned to Lieutenant Tam and said, "Against my better judgment, I'm authorizing this op. You can take anything you need. Come back to us, Jessica." He then left the room.

"So, you have a first name—Jessica," Jeff said with a smile.

"My friends call me Jessica. You can call me Lieutenant," Lieutenant Jessica Tam said in a cold voice. "Wait here while I grab an ops planner and get us on the diplomatic security team."

✳ ✳ ✳

The next four hours were a series of meetings with various people planning the details of their mission and contingencies.

Jeff was impressed with the lieutenant's knowledge of Hong Kong, China, and operational planning. She left no detail unresolved. Her knowledge would be valuable and complementary since Jeff primarily worked in Europe, Africa, and Russia.

By 1 p.m., Jeff was starving, so they broke for lunch and Jeff went to find Amber. He needed to share that he was leaving at 7 p.m.

Jeff found Amber in their little house doing some research in several books. She looked up and smiled when he came in. "I missed you this morning."

"I had to make a contact and didn't want to wake you," Jeff explained. "There's no easy way to say this. I have to leave at 7 p.m."

Amber looked down at the table covered in papers and books. "It's decided then. You're leaving without me."

"I thought we decided last night," Jeff said.

"I guess I wasn't expecting things to happen so soon," Amber said as she looked up with a forced smile.

"The second to last thing in the world I want to do is leave you."

"What's the last thing?" Amber asked.

Jeff looked Amber in the eyes and said, "To get you killed." After a moment of silence, he continued, "This mission will be dangerous. I'll be tightrope walking on razor blades. Pointy end up."

Amber smiled and said, "I get your point. How many missions have you been on that were as dangerous as this one?"

Jeff thought about it. "I'd say this could make the top ten."

Amber was startled for a moment. "You had ten other missions as bad as this one?"

"Ten missions worse than this one," Jeff corrected.

"You made it through those," Amber said, her voice filled with hope. "That means the odds are pretty good that I'll see you again."

Jeff smiled and said, "I guess they are. Do you want to grab some lunch with me?"

"Yes, I do," Amber said.

They left their cozy house and walked over to the mess hall. They made their own sandwiches. Jeff made a simple ham and cheese on white bread, while Amber made a turkey and avocado on rye bread with lettuce, tomato, dill pickle, and sprouts. Jeff was feeling a little sandwich envy when he sat down and saw Amber's creation, but it didn't bother him enough to change anything.

They had a great time eating and talking about nothing in particular, like any couple who were best friends stepping out for a quick bite to eat. As Amber was explaining some new data she had come across, Jeff zoned out a little and thought to himself, *This might be our last meal together. I'm really going to miss her.*

He tuned in as she finished and said, "That's amazing."

"I know," Amber said. "The military seems to be able to get information I didn't even know existed."

"You accepted Major Jones' offer then?" Jeff asked.

"I told him I would give it a trial run," Amber said as she finished her sandwich. "He was in a strange mood, like he was distracted or something."

"That was probably my fault," Jeff said. "I asked for a partner on this mission, and he was not happy when Lieutenant Tam volunteered."

"Oh," Amber said with an edge to her voice. "Lieutenant Tam is going?"

"Yes," Jeff explained. "She's a good agent. Her skills complement mine. We should make a good team. There were a few things I didn't like about the meeting with my contact. Having some backup will even the odds if things go wrong. Is something wrong?"

"I noticed she couldn't stop staring at you in our meeting yesterday," Amber said.

"She was sizing me up," Jeff said. "She doesn't believe our story. She's cold and analytical, and she definitely has a deadly grace like a stalking cat." Jeff noticed Amber getting more agitated and asked, "You're not concerned about me going on a mission with her, are you?"

"No," Amber said.

Jeff laughed. "I think that woman hates me."

Jeff looked at his watch and said, "I need to report in to a briefing. I'll be leaving the base soon to join a diplomatic mission that was already leaving the country tonight. I'd be surprised if this took more than two weeks, one way or the other."

"Take care of yourself, Jeff," Amber said with a forced smile.

They got up and Jeff cleared the trays from the table, depositing them in the dirty dishes alcove. They walked out of the mess hall and went their separate ways.

Amber looked back over her shoulder and wondered, *Will I ever see him again?*

THE RUSSIAN CONNECTION

Jeff met Lieutenant Tam at the now familiar entrance to Major Jones' office complex. Instead of going inside, she led him to a black GMC SUV and they got into the back seats. The driver and front passenger were both MPs.

"This is your cover story," Lieutenant Tam said as she handed Jeff a large envelope. "Your name is Jeff McDonald." Inside was a passport and cover story.

"Did I grow up on a farm? E I E I O."

The MPs both laughed.

Lieutenant Tam just gave Jeff an icy stare and said, "I am now Jessica Kim. We are both ex-military and come from different parts of the country. We do not know each other. Driver take us to the runway."

They took a military transport from Okinawa to Narita International Airport, east of Tokyo. Duffel bags were packed and waiting for them on the plane. They changed and practiced their personas on the way to Narita.

When they landed, they were ushered to a police building where they were cleared through security and taken to the diplomatic party waiting in a private terminal. They met the Japanese security police officer in charge.

A small, handsome-looking Japanese man walked up to them and said, "Hello, Jessica." He then turned to Jeff and said, "I am Lieutenant

Hoshi Nakamura, your commanding officer. You are part of the security staff for Japanese diplomats traveling to China tonight. I see you are already suited up. Here is your 9 MM Beretta pistol, bayonet, and Uzi submachine gun. I know your true purpose. No one else on this plane does. Jessica has vouched for you. Do not disappoint me."

Jeff started to speak when Lieutenant Tam cut him off and said with a small bow gesture, "Thank you, Hoshi. You honor me."

They quickly slipped into character and awaited their departure.

At 6:20 p.m., the diplomats started entering the building from sleek white limousines. At 6:40, they started to board the plane. As Jeff observed his charges, he noticed that the twelve people boarding the plane were diplomats, some with family members. No one on the plane was under fifty outside of the security detail.

The plane wasn't large, but it was luxurious. The diplomats and their guests sat up front in large reclining chairs that also swiveled side to side to make conversation easier. A wall with a small door separated an economy section in the back of the plane from the rest. The ten-person security detail sat in the economy section.

Jeff and Jessica sat separately and kept to themselves. Jeff slept most of the seven-hour journey.

Lieutenant Nakamura woke Jeff when he announced they would be landing soon.

After landing, Jeff and Jessica remained on the plane along with two others. The remaining six security team members accompanied the diplomats and their guests without their Uzis to a high-end hotel in Hong Kong. An armored car sat behind the diplomat's plane, keeping an eye on their armed guests. The security guards patrolled outside the aircraft one at a time on regular shifts.

Jeff and Jessica suited up as Chinese firefighters. They started a small electrical fire in the back of the aircraft. When the firefighters came in to put out the flames, they stepped out of the bathrooms and walked off the plane to a cargo vehicle that was pulling trailers. It had stopped to lend aid. They jumped into the cargo trailers and waited. Twenty minutes later, the cargo vehicle entered the terminal and deposited them inside. Once inside the terminal building, they shed the firefighting gear and a friendly cargo handler guided them to an exit door. From there, they grabbed separate taxis to a restaurant near their safe house.

They were in the safe house by 10 p.m., right on schedule. Once they had a chance to rest and eat microwaved frozen dinners, they went over their plans for the next day and turned in early.

The next morning, they rose early and took separate taxis back to the airport. Jessica took a position near the terminal building that made it look like she was waiting for a ride. She wore a black leather jacket that hid a small radio receiver with a cord to an earpiece hidden under her long sable hair. Once Jeff spotted her, he made his way to the pay phones. It was a busy morning and all three phones were occupied. Jeff waited patiently for the elderly woman on the phone to finish her animated conversation in Chinese. He felt a little sorry for whoever was on the other end of that call.

When the woman finished, Jeff stepped up and took the handset off the hook while he held his finger on the switch hook to allow a new call to come in. This made it look like he was busy listening on a call, so no one would come up and want to use the phone before he received his call. Jeff was wearing a long beige trench coat with a radio transmitter under his left arm and a wire that led to his left hand. By holding the phone in his left hand, Jessica could hear everything Jeff heard.

Jeff checked his watch and started tracking the time. Five minutes after he arrived, the phone rang. Jeff let the phone ring three times before picking it up. "Hello."

"Welcome to Hong Kong, Jeff," said the voice he associated with Sergei in a thick Russian accent. "You've made it in time. Now follow these instructions and do not be late. Take a bus to the Hong Kong University Visitors Center. It is a brick building with a brick courtyard. There is a phone booth across the courtyard from the building. You have thirty-five minutes."

The phone call ended with a click.

Jeff ran to find the bus station and the right bus to the university. Jessica would likely take a taxi and beat Jeff there. She could then set up her surveillance location and be ready when he arrived. When he finally made it to the bus station, Jeff found the bus routes were simple and easy to understand. Route 3 would take him straight to Hong Kong University. It was about thirty minutes away and the next bus left in two minutes. It was a tight timeline, but he could make it, so he bought a day pass.

When he boarded the bus, he sat near the back where he could exit quickly while keeping an eye on the passengers. He spotted two men who could be working for Sergei. One was bigger than the average Asian on the bus. His hair was cut short and he seemed a little nervous. The other was Caucasian. His dark hair and complexion could be Russian or Eastern European. He wore a heavy gray coat that could be hiding something, along with jeans and boots that would not look out of place on a military uniform.

After a few stops, a woman got on. She sat with the big Asian man; they obviously knew each other, which explained his nervousness. They got off together at the next stop. That left the European in the gray coat. Ordinarily, Jeff would employ counter-surveillance techniques to verify his tail, but he simply did not have the time, so he sat calmly and pretended everything was fine until he reached his destination.

Jeff arrived with only minutes to spare, and he still needed to find the phone. He was glad to see signs in Chinese and English. He was breathing heavily as he ran up a small hill to reach the courtyard. He heard a phone start ringing and ran to it.

Jeff could not reach the phone before the fourth ring. Out of breath, he picked up the phone in his left hand and said, "Hello."

"You sound out of breath, Jeff," Sergei said. "This next part is easier. Walk down Hill Road toward the ocean. Take a left on Shing Said Road and take a seat on the first benches you come to in Belcher Bay Park."

The call ended with a loud click.

Jeff started walking downhill and found Hill Road. He looked around, but he did not see the European or Jessica. He quickly reached a dead end and turned left onto Shing Said Road. He noted the wharves and older buildings off to his right. He seemed to be entering the worst part of town. As he approached the park, he noticed some drug addicts and a few others who seemed too physically fit to be sitting in a park at midmorning on a workday.

When a van pulled up and the physically fit men stood up, he knew his transportation had arrived.

Two Chinese men pulled him into the van. They put a hood over his head, took his coat, patted him down, and took his pistol when they found it in an ankle holster. They tied his hands behind his back with rope and sat him down in the back of the van. All of this happened quickly and without a word.

After a few minutes of twisting and turning, the van came to a stop and the horrible metallic squeal of a large door opening that had not been lubed in ages signaled they had reached their destination. When the horrible noise stopped, the van pulled forward and the squeal resumed. Jeff took a deep breath and got ready to face his fate.

He was ushered from the van to what he assumed was a room just off the main warehouse. He heard a door close and was pushed roughly into a chair. He sat there for close to five minutes before the door opened again and heavy footsteps approached him on a concrete floor.

When the hood was finally removed from his head, it took a few seconds for his eyes to adjust. The blurry figure in front of him resolved into a big, burly Russian he had never seen before. The man was at least 6' 4" and close to 300 pounds. His face had a prominent nose, but a small mouth. His beady little eyes stared at Jeff from under a straw-colored mop of hair. A two-way radio, which looked like a toy in his huge hand, crackled to life in Russian. From the Russian that Jeff knew, it sounded like the man on the other end of the radio asked, "Is it him?"

The big man replied, "Da." ("Yes" in Russian.) Then the big man just stood near the door Jeff assumed he had been brought in by. The room was long, about forty by fifteen feet. The walls were unfinished drywall that looked old. There was a wood-framed door and a window with cheap white blinds covered in dust. Jeff could make out a warehouse through the blinds but little more. He sat in a chair that was the only furniture in the room. The single bare bulb above him was the only light in the room.

Jeff then heard a second door open behind him. He decided not to try to look. He would let this mystery person come into view if he wanted to.

The mystery person stood there until the door closed. At least one other person entered the room with him. "Jeff Smith!" the mystery person said with the same thick Russian-accented voice Jeff had heard on the phone when he talked to Sergei. "I must be extra careful these days. There are a few old acquaintances who dropped by and tried to kill me. How do I know you are not another one?"

"You don't," Jeff said in a level, matter-of-fact voice. "But I'm here because I need your help, Sergei, not to kill you."

"How do I know that for sure?" Sergei asked.

"For one thing, I never call a mark to let him know I'm coming!" Jeff said.

"That could be a ploy," Sergei said.

"I'm not that stupid," Jeff replied.

"You impressed me with your skills in the past, Mr. Smith," Sergei said. "Forgive me if I do not trust you."

"Then let me get to the point, Sergei," Jeff said. "I know what's behind the political mess in both of our countries. We need to move quickly if we want to prevent even more loss of life."

Sergei said something in Russian that Jeff did not understand. Everyone in the room left except Sergei. He then walked in front of Jeff. Jeff's memory of Sergei came back to him. He was a mid-sized man, about 5' 10", but well-muscled for his size. He had short black hair and a handsome face with a thin, well-manicured mustache. He wore all black, a black shirt, black vest, black pants, a black belt, and black shoes. It made him look like the bad guy in a cheap movie.

"So, you want to save the world again, Mr. Smith?" Sergei asked with a wry smile.

"This time the stakes could not be higher," Jeff said.

"Are millions of American lives at stake?" Sergei asked.

"Billions of human lives are at stake," Jeff replied.

Sergei seemed surprised for an instant, but he recovered quickly and hid it. He said, "How does this affect my government?"

"I believe agents inside both our governments are working to disrupt the chain of command and fragment our ability to defend ourselves," Jeff said. "They all report to a common organization, but many of them do not seem to know it."

"What is the name of this mysterious organization?" Sergei asked.

"The Hidden Hand," Jeff said. He watched Sergei for any signs. Surprise, confirmation, curiosity, but the Russian had the best poker face Jeff had ever seen. The two men looked at each other in silence for a few moments, and then Sergei seemed to decide and lowered his facade.

"I discovered a cell of the Hidden Hand in the Russian military four weeks ago," Sergei said. "I killed them all in a bloody firefight. I took a company of elite troops to their corrupt military base. Less than 50 percent survived. That is when my life became more dangerous than usual."

"Were you able to find out anything more about their organization?" Jeff asked.

"Only afterward did I discover I had not killed the organization's leader," Sergei said. "Only an underling. I have been searching for the leader ever since."

"How close are you to finding the leader?" Jeff asked.

"I will say no more on the subject until you tell me a lot more than the name of an organization I already knew about," Sergei said.

"This is going to be hard to believe, Sergei, but hear me out before you decide either way, okay?" Jeff asked.

"I am here to listen and to learn," Sergei said.

Jeff remembered Sergei to be mentally sharp, quick-tempered, and decisive. Jeff had to make sure he did not get a bullet in the head before Sergei heard the punch line, so he needed to be succinct and add the part about aliens later.

"Sergei," Jeff began, "the Hidden Hand is a multi-headed beast. We have documentation linking it to companies with billions in assets and the organization overall earned at least $1 trillion US over the last ten years."

"You say you have this documented?" Sergei asked.

"Yes," Jeff replied. "In detail. We have also linked leaders in my own government as board members for these companies or their subsidiaries—powerful men who have taken control of parts of my government. They are manipulating events, suppressing the news, and the people who try to expose them are disappearing."

"I have found similar things in my own country," Sergei said. "Continue!"

"We've noticed patterns in the flow of goods between these companies and to various sites around the world," Jeff said. "They're building large facilities at these sites. Hundreds of them."

"What are these facilities for?" Sergei asked.

"I was inside one of them in Africa," Jeff explained as he looked away from Sergei with a distant stare. "The things I saw there will haunt me for the rest of my life." He then looked back at Sergei.

"We have heard of things happening in Africa," Sergei said.

"The country is Burkina Faso," Jeff said. "Thousands of people are being taken and killed through a tortuous process that produces an organic acid. The acid is loaded on a vessel and launched into space where that vessel disappears at the Earth's L2 Lagrange point!"

Sergei looked at Jeff like he was insane and said, "The L2 what? A spaceship? I suppose there are little green aliens running this facility, too?"

"I was in that factory, Sergei," Jeff said with deadly seriousness. "I saw that ship launch from Burkina Faso with my own eyes. The French military confirmed that launch and others that were happening every two to three days."

"The Soviet Union's space program couldn't have launched that many vessels into space that fast," Sergei said. "How is one of the poorest countries on Earth able to do that?"

"Obviously, it didn't!" Jeff said with certainty in his voice. "The question is who is?"

"You are trying to tell me," Sergei summarized, "that the Hidden Hand is a multinational organization that owns companies making billions of dollars, that manipulates governments around the globe, and is building factories to process human beings to ship an organic acid to outer space? To the L what point?"

"Yes," Jeff said. "The L2 Lagrange point is a place in space where the gravity of Earth and the sun are equalized so it is very easy for something to remain in a stationary orbit relative to the Earth for long periods of time. Scientists at the University of Hawaii confirmed an anomaly is located there. It was interfering with their observations of distant star systems."

"My God," Sergei said. He stared at the concrete floor in front of Jeff's feet as he said, "How many of these factories are in Russia?"

"None that I can tell," Jeff answered. "They are in China, Southeast Asia, India, Muslim countries, Africa, South America, but none in Europe, the US, Canada, Australia, or Russia. We don't know why."

"More advanced countries would be harder to control," Sergei said. "Most of the Earth's population is in those other countries."

"You don't seem surprised by anything I'm saying," Jeff said as he studied Sergei.

Sergei looked up and said, "Spaceships and the L2 thing is a big surprise, but it all kind of makes sense to me now."

"What do you mean?" Jeff asked.

"It is no coincidence I am in Hong Kong," Sergei said. "Our reconnaissance satellites discovered those huge facilities under construction all over China. We wanted to find out what they were going to be used for. We thought it might be a weapons system, but the design was all wrong. If I believe your story for a second, then if I wanted to kill a lot of people, wouldn't I go after the biggest population centers on the planet? The countries you named would have 80 percent of the population. If I could keep the more advanced countries busy with other agendas, I could swoop in, take what I need, and leave before any organized resistance could muster. The planning and coordination to do that would be amazing."

"I have a plan to stop them," Jeff said.

"How?" Sergei asked.

"Plan B is to bomb the facilities before they open," Jeff said.

"You want Russia to bomb Chinese factories?" Sergei said. "That would start World War III and kill us all."

"That is why it's Plan B," Jeff said with a smile. "Plan A is to launch a detection device to the L2 Lagrange point to expose whatever is there. Once we can prove aliens are stationed in Earth's orbit, the whole house of cards should crumble on the Hidden Hand. We have enough data on their financials and who has been doing what to catch most of them. We can get the corrupt officials out of our governments and hunt down the rest."

"Why do you think this will work?" Sergei asked.

"Most of the people we have found working for the Hand do not know who they are working for or the bigger picture," Jeff explained. "I believe that once people know the impact of what they're doing, they'll stop doing it. The organization will fall apart from the bottom up. Once we arrest the people at the top, all we'll need to hunt down are the middle layers. Most of them are probably criminals of some sort."

"It could work, but launching a detection device into space," Sergei said, "that will take some doing. Why not use NASA?"

"Politics," Jeff said. "It would be too easy for the hand to stop any funding for the project. In Russia, we just need the right person to buy in."

"Times have changed," Sergei said. "Russia is broke. We cannot afford to launch things into space. The space agency is trying to partner with the Americans to get anything done."

"Then I came here for nothing," Jeff said.

"Maybe," Sergei said. "Maybe not."

"What do you mean?" Jeff asked.

Sergei went behind Jeff and untied his hands. "You may have the right idea but the wrong agency."

"What is the right agency?" Jeff asked.

"The Russian military," Sergei said. "It has as many rockets as the US. I know someone there who might be able to help, but we need to travel to Vladivostok."

"We!" Jeff said. "I've convinced you?"

"You've convinced me you believe it," Sergei said. "I am not so sure. I need to see this documentation and confirm some of your story."

"Like what?" Jeff asked.

"The anomaly at the L2 thing. The corporations, the facilities at other countries, and any details on what these facilities do—that was my mission here," Sergei explained. "You'll be helping me complete it."

"I can do that," Jeff said.

"Was the woman who followed you here a friend?" Sergei asked.

"Yes," Jeff said with concern. "You didn't hurt her, did you?"

"She is watching our building," Sergei said. "Why don't you go get her and I will bring you both to our communications room. Boris will accompany you."

Sergei banged on the wall two times with his fist. The big blonde Russian came in immediately. He and Sergei exchanged some words in Russian; then Boris waved for Jeff to follow him as he left the room. They walked through a large warehouse with brick walls and a corrugated metal roof. Inside were a lot of wooden crates with Chinese writing on them, a white van, and the single-story office complex Jeff had come out of. Jeff saw six men with automatic weapons who held them like they knew how to use them. Jeff and Boris walked twenty yards to a large steel door. Boris opened a small door embedded in the larger one. As Jeff exited and looked around, he saw Lieutenant Tam move from behind some bushes near the road. Jeff walked halfway up the driveway and motioned her to come over.

She did not move at first, so Jeff yelled, "It's safe! They've already spotted you!"

The lieutenant cautiously stalked out from behind the bushes and hid the weapon she had drawn. Jeff walked up to her and said, "The contact was a success. Sergei is here, and he's willing to help, but he wants to confirm some of what I've shared. I'll need your help connecting with the website we set up."

"Major Jones did not authorize any information sharing with foreign nationals," Jessica said. "I'll need authorization."

"I'm authorized to lead this op on the general's authority," Jeff reminded Jessica. "I don't need additional authorization to share anything I brought with me to Okinawa."

Lieutenant Jessica Tam looked warily at Jeff and then at the building. "I'm still going to inform my chain of command."

"I'm fine with that," Jeff said as he offered his arm to Lieutenant Tam and said, "Shall we?" She looked at his arm like it was a viper and walked toward the door being held open by Boris. She eyed Boris up and down before entering through the door. Jeff followed, and Boris closed the door. Jeff introduced them, saying, "Jessica, Boris; Boris, Jessica." Jessica seemed mildly irritated while her attention was focused on assessing the threats in the room.

Boris led them to a different office door, which led to a corridor with many doors. He picked one and led them into a large room packed with electronic communications and surveillance equipment. It had a square table at the end of the room with several chairs and a whiteboard on the wall. Boris went to Sergei, who was busy talking to someone operating the equipment and said something in Russian. Sergei looked up, smiled, and walked over.

"And who is this charming creature?" Sergei asked as he offered his hand to Jessica.

"Sergei, may I introduce Lieutenant Jessica Tam from US Army Intelligence," Jeff said. "Jessica, this is Sergei Sokolov, our contact."

"I'm very pleased to meet you, Jessica," Sergei said as he took Jessica's hand and kissed it.

"As am I, Sergei," she replied with a big smile.

Jeff was taken aback by Jessica's warm smile. It was the first he had seen the entire time he had known her. She and Sergei seemed to have some chemistry.

Jeff cleared his throat and said, "Jessica can give you access to the data you requested, Sergei."

"Excellent!" Sergei said. "Let me introduce you to my technical support, Jessica." Sergei offered his arm to Jessica. She slipped her arm through his, still smiling, and snuggled close to Sergei as he led her to his colleague.

Jeff was left standing there as if he did not exist. He shook his head and followed them to the equipment console. He looked over his shoulder to see Boris laughing near the door.

After ten minutes of talking and typing, the files started downloading to Sergei's network. Jeff began explaining how the files were organized and where Sergei could find the information he was looking for. Sergei was impressed with the data's scope and organization.

"Once we have possession of these files, I'll have a team start reviewing them," Sergei said. "There will be questions."

"We will answer anything we know the answer to," Jeff said.

"You mentioned earlier that you were looking for the leader of a cell," Jeff said until Sergei abruptly cut him off.

"Stop!" Sergei said. "Come with me." He led Jeff and Jessica to another room with a table and chairs. Jeff found it interesting that Sergei must not trust his own men in the communications room.

"Forgive me," Sergei said. "This is sensitive information. Very few people in the world know anything of what I am about to share." He looked at Jeff and then Jessica.

Jeff realized Sergei was not sure if Jessica could be trusted with this information. Jeff gave a nod and Sergei continued.

"We assaulted the military base harboring a Hidden Hand cell," Sergei explained. "It was bloody, and they fought to the last man. No one was left alive who did not work for me. They burned large sections of the base to destroy any information they had. Our forensic teams found very little, but a string of emails in an unencrypted personal computer referred to a general. The Russian military is organized like other European powers. A colonel reports to a general. Generals report to higher generals, but in Russia, the highest general reports to no one and is a member of the inner circle with the president. This base was run by a colonel. His commanding officer is a general I know well whose name I will not share. I shared this correspondence with this general. The warning he gave me made me think it was his commanding officer who led the cell. When I researched this lead, I realized it was the defense minister, not the general, who was 'calling all the shots' as you Americans say it. None of the generals I've talked to like this minister, and most are afraid of him. The ones who are not afraid are angry."

"Is the general in charge of the Strategic Missile Troops afraid or angry with this defense minister?" Jeff asked.

Sergei smiled and said, "Angry."

"I think we have a path forward," Jeff stated.

"Nothing can happen until I verify this story. I must be convinced before we start talking to generals," Sergei said.

"Of course," Jeff said in a relaxed voice. He was doing a good job of hiding the excitement he was feeling inside. This crazy idea had a chance to work. He looked over at Jessica and saw her studying him again. He could not read what she was thinking, which made him uncomfortable.

Sergei continued, "Jeff and I will be traveling to Vladivostok. You are welcome to join us, Jessica, or to return to your hotel."

"I wouldn't miss this for the world," Jessica replied in a sweet voice Jeff had never before heard coming from those lips. He could not tell whether she really liked Sergei or she was just working him. Time would tell.

The Russians were well organized. Once the decision was made to leave for Vladivostok, their entire operation was packed for travel, and trucks started to leave the warehouse in less than one hour.

As the trucks were leaving the warehouse, two white Toyota Haice vans pulled up outside. Sergei hurried a hand-picked group of men, plus Jeff and Jessica into the vans. One van would have a driver, with Boris riding shotgun, and then Jessica, Jeff, Sergei, and two other men. Five men got into the other van. Everyone carried a bag or suitcase except Jeff, Jessica, and Sergei.

They drove in silence until they reached an old wharf a few minutes away. Sergei herded everyone into three small wooden boats with little 7 horsepower outboard motors. They crept away from the dock to a Syrian cargo freighter in the harbor named *Hafez*. She looked about 120 feet long and well maintained. As the small wooden boats pulled alongside, a metal stairway was lowered down the ship's side. They quickly climbed seven switch-backed flights of stairs and were ushered down a stairway into the cargo hold of the ship. They passed by large wooden crates, each marked with words written in Russian, Arabic, or Chinese. They passed the main cargo hold and entered a dark hallway leading to a large 15' x 20' room. Communications equipment lined one end of the room while a kitchen was at the other end. In the middle were tables and chairs.

Sergei walked over to Jeff and Jessica. He spread his arms wide and said with a smile, "Home sweet home. It will take us a little more than a day to reach Vladivostok Harbor. The data you shared is being downloaded and analyzed. By the time we reach Mother Russia, I should have an assessment of your data."

"Where is the strategic missile forces commander located?" Jeff asked.

"General Ivan Sergeev is in Moscow or one of the many military bases scattered across Russia," Sergei replied. "I have some people working on hunting him down. It is never an easy task, even for his closest aides."

The three of them took a seat at one of the tables. Jeff remarked, "I thought the Ministry of Defense was a powerless organization in Russia. It just seems to be a liaison office designed to work with other countries. It has no real power over the Russian military."

"This is true," Sergei said as he smiled at Jessica.

"Then how is he controlling generals in the Russian military?" Jeff asked.

"He seems to have leverage over everyone in the military," Sergei explained. "I do not know what exactly. They hate the man, but they are afraid of him."

"Maybe this General Sergeev can shed some light on this topic," Jeff said.

"Perhaps," Sergei replied.

Sergei was called away by one of the men working the communications equipment in the back of the room. Everyone was busy around them, so Jeff and Jessica talked about their plans once they reached Vladivostok.

Eventually, everyone had dinner. After dinner, they were assigned bunks for the evening. Jeff and Jessica slept in different rooms. The night was uneventful.

✲   ✲   ✲

The next day, Jeff woke to the sound of horns bellowing. He dressed quickly and went to the main room where he had spent most of the day before. It was empty except for two equipment operators. He decided to backtrack the way they came in and went out onto the main deck. They had reached the harbor of Vladivostok. Jeff could see the city surrounding the large natural bay. The air was humid but still cold— only sixty degrees at best. He saw the naval base off to the portside with at least fifty ships docked there. Jeff moved forward and eventually found Sergei and Jessica talking near the ship's bow. As Jeff approached, he heard Sergei talking about the parks in Vladivostok. They moved past the naval base toward a commercial port.

"There you are," Jeff said, interrupting Sergei. "I was starting to wonder if I got left behind."

"I was just educating Jessica on the places to go in Vladivostok," Sergei said with pride. "And the places not to go," he added in a normal voice. "We will be docking soon. Once in port, you will go to a safe house while I try to reach our general."

"That works for me," Jeff said. He looked at Jessica and Sergei, who were both staring back at him. Starting to feel like the proverbial fifth wheel, he said, "I'll just go back downstairs and get ready to go."

As Jeff left, Sergei renewed his discussion with Jessica about the city. Meanwhile, Jeff went below to grab a shower and a quick meal. He was sitting in the main room with a few of Sergei's men when he felt the ship come to a stop. Sergei popped his head into a doorway and said, "Come, Jeff. We go now."

Sergei led Jeff into the cargo area instead of up to the main deck and stopped at a large crate. Jessica was waiting nearby. He smiled at her and got an icy stare in return. He really wondered what he had done to piss her off.

"I need you both to go into this crate. We will pick you up in a van and drive you to the safe house where you will be unpacked. A duplicate crate will be delivered to a politician with their order intact," Sergei explained.

"You're a government official. You can't just bring us into the country?" Jeff asked.

"Eh," Sergei said as he sought the right words, "things are not, as you say, 'cut and dry.'"

Jeff just raised an eyebrow. Sergei began to get uncomfortable and explained, "We are not one big happy family here in Russia these days. It is best if American CIA and Military Intelligence is not ushered in through the official channels."

Jeff looked at the crate and said, "If I can take ten hours in a coffin, I guess I can handle an hour in a crate."

"Eh," Sergei said as he sought the right words, again, "it could be more than four hours. Things do not move very fast on Russian docks."

"Ladies first," Jeff said to Jessica with a smile and a wave of his arm. He received the same icy stare as she walked into the crate. Jeff followed, and Sergei sealed the crate. The crate was square on the bottom and tall enough for Jeff to stand if he stooped a little. Each wall was big enough for Jeff and Jessica to sit side by side with room to spare.

They both sat cross-legged in the crate and started to wait. Jeff decided to ask Jessica about her attitude. "Did I say or do something to offend you?"

Jessica laughed and replied, "I thought you were romantic with Amber. At first, you were being charming, but I didn't want you to get any ideas. When we met Sergei, I could tell he liked me, so I played along. I told him you made a pass at me and I was angry with you. He was being chivalrous by keeping me at his side the entire trip."

"You two didn't…do something last night?" Jeff asked.

"Sergei is kind and handsome," Jessica said. "What I do with him is my business."

"Fair enough," Jeff said. "Did you learn anything I should know?"

"He thinks highly of you," Jessica said. "He probably would not have believed your story coming from any other American. He is struggling with some of the same things in his agency that you are in yours."

"Did you tell him about my recent status change?" Jeff asked.

"No, of course not," Jessica replied. "That would be bad for both of us."

"What do we do for the next few hours?" Jeff asked.

"I didn't get much sleep," Jessica said. "I'm taking a nap."

Jeff surmised from Jessica's answer that she had done something with Sergei. While Jessica slept, Jeff decided to meditate and collect his thoughts on what needed to happen next. Jeff was too anxious for sleep. His actions over the next few days could mean success or failure for everyone.

It was over an hour before the crate moved an inch. They were then banged around the cargo hold until a sling was attached. Next, a crane lifted them out of the ship and deposited them roughly on a flatbed truck with a bang. The truck must have moved them to a warehouse where a forklift picked up the crate and set it roughly to wait for an hour or so. Then Sergei and another man came near the crate and started arguing in Russian. It was about five minutes of argument until the other man seemed to agree with Sergei and stamped the crate with a thud. Fifteen minutes later, a forklift picked up the crate and deposited it in what Jeff assumed was a delivery truck of some kind with an enclosed cargo bed.

It was another ten minutes of slow driving and waiting until the truck seemed to exit the docks and pick up speed. Thirty minutes later, they stopped and Sergei began to open the crate.

Jessica slept most of the time until Jeff shook her and said, "I think we're here." She stretched like a cat after a nap, and then sat with her knees to her chest, facing the creaking noises as she waited for the crate to open. Jeff crouched down next to her and leaned against the crate's back wall.

One entire wall of the crate opened at once and light from a warehouse flooded it. Jessica got up and walked out immediately. Jeff took a second to let his eyes adjust before also getting up and walking out of the crate. They were in a modern warehouse with concrete walls, concrete floors, and bright lighting. It was empty except for a boxy-looking light blue car called a Lada Riva.

Sergei helped Jessica into the car while two other men "helped" Jeff. They got in and left quickly in the underpowered four-door. They drove through the streets of Vladivostok until they reached a long driveway and pulled off the road. A small house with a view of the harbor sat at the end of the driveway.

The driver got out to open the garage door. Everyone else stayed in the car until it was safely inside the two-car garage with the main door fully closed. They then exited the car and went into the small house. The driver stayed in the car. It was a simple home with very little furniture. Sergei introduced a man already in the house named Alexei Ivanovich. Jeff and Jessica would stay with Alexei until their contact was set up. Sergei would stop by later when time permitted.

They settled in, expecting to wait a few days. Alexei was a good host, but he was also a jailer. They were instructed not to leave the house for any reason.

✳ ✳ ✳

The next day, Sergei showed up and entered the house the same way as the day before. He was excited and spoke quickly in broken English. "I have contacted our friend. He has meeting with defense minister in Drovyanaya in two days."

"That is excellent news, Sergei!" Jeff said. "How do we get there?"

"Have you heard of the Siberian Express?" Sergei asked.

"Yes," Jeff replied.

"You are about to get on board," Sergei said. "Get ready. You leave in twenty minutes. I need to pick up something before we go. I leave you in Alexei's capable hands. *Dasvidaniya*."

Jeff and Jessica were ready in minutes. Alexei seemed surprised he was leaving and took some time to get ready. They went into the garage where another blue four-door Lada Riva waited for them. Alexei drove them up the peninsula to the train station at the northern end of town. Then he had them wait in the car while he bought tickets for them. He carried a lot of paperwork with him, so Sergei must have acquired travel documentation for them. When Alexei returned to the car, he parked in a nearby parking area. He escorted the Americans to a waiting area and asked them not to speak or draw any attention to themselves. They sat and waited for about twenty minutes until Sergei arrived with an entourage of four other men. He quickly ushered them toward the train platform where the train was already parked. They cut the line of passengers and boarded after checking tickets and documentation.

They split up between two private cars. Sergei, Jeff, and Jessica sat down together in the car while Alexei guarded the door.

Sergei sat down and took a deep breath before saying, "Now we have some time together to talk. My staff started to analyze the documentation you shared with us. It is impressive. They will not get through it all in detail for some time, but the initial analysis confirms your story. They could also cross-check it with many references we already had. We need to build our story for the general."

"You know him better than we do," Jeff said. "What is going to grab his attention?"

"The truth," Sergei said. "But we need to start with some facts you provided that are less…controversial."

"Then use that foundation to build the bigger picture," Jessica added.

"Yes," Sergei said with a smile. "Exactly. General Sergeev hates Minister Grachney more than your Senator McCarthy hated communism. Anything that feeds that hatred cannot hurt our story."

"If the defense minister is the one driving unrest in your country, we just need to add those facts into our story," Jeff said.

"Agreed," Sergei said.

The rest of the day was spent working on their story and preparing for the meeting with General Sergeev. They only left their private room to use the restroom. As they worked, Jeff noticed the scene outside their window changing from windswept hills to mountains covered with dense forest. Snow clung to the rugged terrain where the sun was blocked by trees or the mountainside. Since it was only early autumn, it must be cold and getting colder.

When Jeff asked about where they were headed, Sergei explained it was to a military base near Lake Baikal. The lake was more than 400 kilometers long, 25 million years old, 1,700 meters deep, and held 20 percent of the world's fresh water. The region was cold, rugged, and sparsely populated. The base was easily defended and difficult to penetrate.

They worked into the night but felt prepared when they went to sleep. Jeff was ushered to a private room with a big Russian who did not speak English. Sergei and Jessica went to their own room.

The next morning, they woke early and ate in their private room. Everything was ready as they pulled into a train station in the middle of nowhere. Sergei had explained that they would take a bus to the city of Drovyanaya where the military would pick them up.

They had arrived at the train station one day before the defense minister would arrive. The bus to Drovyanaya arrived on time at 9 a.m. local time and picked up a specific list of named passengers. Jeff had not realized that Sergei had a cover name for both him and Jessica. When Sergei handed him his ticket, his cover name was Alexander Ivanov. Sergei and his six-man entourage boarded the bus with Jeff and Jessica. Sergei and Jessica took seats near the front. Jeff had to go farther back to find an open seat. Two of Sergei's men sat immediately behind him while the rest sat farther back. They had a three-hour ride to the Drovyanaya.

The town was small, but the bus station was built to keep travelers warm in sub-zero conditions. Fortunately, it was a balmy 45 degrees. As they exited the bus, a man in a Russian Federation military uniform met Sergei and herded his team toward an old but well-maintained olive-green bus. The bus seated nine people, not counting the driver. It had a sloped front and off-road tires. The interior was Spartan but comfortable. The soldier who led them to the bus sat in the front next to the driver, who was also in the military. They both wore the insignia of the Russian Federation's Strategic Missile Troops.

They exited the small town quickly and drove for twenty minutes to the military base. As they approached, Jeff could see a barbed wire topped chain-link fence that stretched off as far as he could see in either direction over the rolling hills. Trees and vegetation were removed for 100 meters on either side of the fence. The gate had ten guards and an elaborate set of movable barriers. As they approached the gate, the soldier in the passenger seat shared the documents he had gathered from his passengers and got out of the bus to talk with the guards inside the guard house. As they waited, Jeff noticed light-armored vehicles parked near the gate in a parking lot. Five minutes later, the soldier emerged with their travel documents and the bus proceeded through the barriers. An armored car pulled out of the parking area and followed them.

Ten minutes later, they approached a concrete compound that looked like a giant toddler had piled his blocks haphazardly in three piles. Jeff was surprised by how small the compound was. It could barely hold 100 men.

The soldier told Sergei to "wait here" in Russian and walked over to two guards at the front of the biggest building. They talked for about thirty seconds before he signaled Sergei to come. Everyone except the driver piled out of the van and walked toward the entrance. Once inside, four more guards funneled them through a metal detector like in an airport. They surrendered all their weapons and entered a seating area.

After ten minutes of milling around and finally sitting, the double doors opened. An officer with four heavily armed guards entered the room and called out for Sergei. He walked over and talked to the officer for a few minutes. Jeff knew the Russian military ranks and insignias. Sergei was talking to a captain—about the equivalent of a captain in the US military, a senior rank for a meet and greet. Several times during the conversation, Jeff heard his cover name and Jessica's.

After a few more minutes of talking quickly in Russian with his comrades, Sergei turned and said, "We will be escorted to a waiting room to meet General Sergeev. This is Captain Orlov. He is our guide and liaison. My men will wait for me here. The three of us will continue with the captain."

Sergei's men did not seem happy. Sergei shut down the argument with a final sharp statement.

Captain Orlov said, in almost perfect English, "Please follow me." He led them through a set of corridors to huge double doors. When the captain punched a code into a keypad on the wall, the doors opened to a large elevator. Everyone moved in silence into the elevator. After the doors closed, Jeff was thrown off balance. He had expected to go up, but instead, they descended rapidly.

Jeff could not tell how many floors they dropped, but it had to be at least 100 feet, if not significantly more. Sergei was playing with his jacket zipper. Jeff could see why Sergei might be uncomfortable. He was bringing a CIA spy and a US Army Intelligence Officer into a secret facility originally built by the Soviet Union.

When the elevator stopped, they entered a long concrete corridor. They walked past multiple doors until they entered a plush conference room with oversized leather chairs, a highly-polished wood table, thick dark-blue carpets, and wooden panels on the walls.

The captain stood near the front of the room. Two guards flanked the inside of the only door to the room and two remained outside. Sergei and Jessica sat on one side of the table while Jeff sat on the other. They waited in silence. Sergei was starting to sweat.

Seeing Sergei so nervous, Jeff wondered whether he had put his trust in the wrong man. He hadn't come all this way just to face a firing squad. This plan had to work.

THE LION'S DEN

After Jeff, Jessica, and Sergei sat and stared at one another for twenty minutes, three men entered the room and introduced themselves. Army General Ivan Sergeev, General of Strategic Missile Troops for the Russian Federation, was around 5' 10" and thin, with gray hair covering his entire head and deep blue eyes that were sharp and penetrating. Major General Konstantin Petrov, commander of the 53rd Rocket Army, was 5' 7", overweight, and bald except for thin wisps of gray around his ears and the back of his head. He looked more like a banker than a general. Colonel Vladislav Lebedev was commander of the 4th Rocket Division, including the base they were now on. The colonel was six feet and had a full head of sandy blond hair. He looked physically fit and had a commanding presence.

Sergei then spoke. "I am Sergei Sokolov, Near East Director of the Russian Federation's Foreign Intelligence Service."

Sergei was more senior than Jeff. Jessica began studying Sergei with the same look she had given Jeff back in Okinawa. Jeff wished he could read his partner better.

Up until now, the discussion had been all in Russian. Sergei changed to English and continued, "I have a surprise for you. May I introduce Jeff Smith, Special Operations Manager from the American CIA, and Lieutenant Jessica Tam, US Army Intelligence out of Okinawa."

Every Russian in the room immediately looked like he had taken a big bite out of a sour lemon. General Petrov was the first to say, "Are you insane, Sokolov? This is one of our most secure facilities, yet you brought CIA and US Army intelligence operatives here!" The veins in the general's neck were popping out. His face was bright red.

Then General Sergeev said in a calm voice, "In a time not long past, you would have signed the death warrants for yourself and your friends for this action, Sergei. You know this. Why should I not kill you now?"

"I have dire news," Sergei said. "The entire world is in peril, and you, General Sergeev, are the only man who can help avert disaster."

General Petrov stood and pointed at Sergei, saying with venom in his voice, "This man is a fool. I name him a traitor and I will execute him myself." The major general reached for his side arm.

General Sergeev pulled his sidearm with lightning speed and pointed it at General Petrov. "Hold your judgment, Major General. I will listen to what Mr. Sokolov has to say and then pass my judgment. Guards, disarm Major General Petrov."

One of the guards moved immediately to grab the gun from the major general's holster. Once he took possession, he quickly moved back to his previous position.

The colonel then said in Russian, "Guards, you will clear the room now and reinforce the guard in the corridor. Return Major General Petrov's weapon to him when he exits this room." The colonel turned to General Sergeev, who nodded agreement. The guards left immediately, and the room was silent again.

Sergei took a deep breath and continued in English, "The Americans are here because they have gathered proof of a global organization that has corrupted governments and is building huge factories around the world."

"The West has always been corrupt," General Petrov said. "Why should we care?"

"This corruption extends to the Russian Federation," Sergei explained. "I have proof that Defense Minister Pavlov Grachney is working with this organization and subverting the rule of our president."

General Petrov began spitting venom again. "This is preposterous! You are an American puppet and should hang, Sokolov."

Petrov could not have thrown a bigger insult into Sergei's face, but to his credit, Sergei remained calm and continued, "I have confirmed the American story with facts gathered by our own operatives. I was already in China investigating their massive construction projects to determine their purpose when Jeff contacted me."

"Misinformation," Petrov growled. "Don't you think it convenient they show up now?"

Jeff stepped in on queue after Sergei. "These projects are building factories designed to kill thousands of human beings per day and extract an organic compound from them. I have seen the inside of one of these factories in Africa."

"Pure fantasy," Petrov said.

"The slaughter in Burkina Faso is a cover story," Jeff continued. "The real story is that over 100,000 people have been brutally killed in one of these factories. Hundreds more of these factories are being constructed all over the world."

"I have visited five of these sites myself," Sergei added. "Satellite data found the sites, but the data could not tell us what the factories were doing. We thought it was a weapons program, but the site design is all wrong for weapons."

"They are also delivering hundreds of heavy trucks to these sites," Jeff added. "The companies filling these orders are all owned by a handful of very wealthy men. It took close to a month of digging to reveal who was behind the layers of corporations and holding companies."

Sergei added, "One of these men is Pavlov Grachney."

"This fantasy has gone on far enough," General Petrov proclaimed. "I want these men thrown behind bars now!"

General Sergeev raised one finger and silenced the other general. He slowly leaned forward and said to General Petrov, "I knew you were one of Grachney's men, but I had no idea how far you would go to betray your country."

Major General Petrov sat up straight. "How dare you accuse me!"

General Sergeev's calm tone did not match the fierce look in his eyes—like that of an eagle ready to pierce its prey with razor-sharp talons. He said, "I accuse you of treason, of the subversion of my authority, and the misappropriation of Russian military resources."

"I will not stand for this," General Petrov said as he stood and headed for the door.

General Sergeev looked at the colonel, who drew his 9 MM Beretta and said, "Return to your, Chair Major General Petrov. You have not been excused by your commanding officer."

Petrov turned with an evil sneer and said, "Do you really think you can hold me, Sergeev? Your days in the military are already numbered. You should have retired when you were given the chance."

"And who would take my place, Petrov?" General Sergeev asked. "You?"

"Yes, it will be me," Petrov said. "With me in control of our missiles, we will make the Americans fear us again. The Chinese, the French, and the Germans will bow to our will. We will make Russia powerful again. You need to get out of my way."

"Forgive me, Comrade Petrov," General Sergeev said sarcastically. "The Soviet Union no longer exists. True power does not come from fear. It comes from respect, and I have lost all respect for you. Guards!"

Two burly guards who had previously been in the room entered with pistols drawn.

"Major General Petrov is under arrest for treason," General Sergeev said in Russian.

Colonel Lebedev continued, "Place him in solitary confinement. He is to see no one and speak with no one without direct orders from my lips. Understood?"

"*Da*," the two guards said in unison.

General Petrov complained until a pistol was shoved into each of his kidneys and each guard took one of his arms, practically lifting him off the floor.

After the doors closed, General Sergeev asked the colonel in English, "Can the guards be trusted?"

"Yes, General," Colonel Lebedev said. "I have moved anyone loyal to General Petrov off this base."

"Good," General Sergeev said. "Double the guard just in case."

"Yes, General," Colonel Lebedev said as he left the room.

"There is more to this story, General," Jeff said. He needed to get them back on track so he could give this general his ultimate request.

"Please continue," General Sergeev said.

"I saw something as I was exiting the factory in Burkina Faso," Jeff continued. "It was the launch of a space vessel. It was not like anything I had ever seen before."

"How so?" General Sergeev asked.

"The propulsion system did not create huge orange flames or heat," Jeff said. "It was a light-yellow color. It should have incinerated me, but it obviously didn't. Later, I contacted the French military. They confirmed this launch and many more. They also tracked the trajectory of the launch to the L2 Lagrange point in Earth's orbit. Later, I met with scientists from the observatories on Mauna Kea Hawaii. They spotted an anomaly at the L2 Lagrange point that was affecting their research."

The general's eyes narrowed as he studied Jeff like a hawk studies its next meal. The general seemed to be struggling with something.

Sergei stepped into the opening in the conversation and said, "My team has confirmed many of the details in the extensive documentation Jeff has shared with me, but not the space launches."

The general was silent a moment longer, then finally said, "We have spotted those launches and others from Africa. We had no idea where they went. Our systems are designed to track objects in near Earth orbit, not as far out as the L2 Lagrange point."

"General Sergeev," Jeff said in a firm tone, "I believe the entity causing unrest in both our countries and behind the building of these factories all over the world is operating from the L2 Lagrange point orbiting Earth."

"I thought if something was out there, it would be yours," General Sergeev said.

"It is not ours, General," Jeff replied.

"It is not ours," General Sergeev confirmed. "If it is not yours and not ours, whose is it?"

"That is what I would like to find out, General," Jeff said as seriously as he could. "I have plans for a detection device that could be attached to a rocket. It's designed to detect a stealth or cloaked object."

The general sat back and asked, "What do you expect to find?"

"I'm not sure, General," Jeff said honestly. "But I think the best way to make people like Major General Petrov understand they are being duped is to expose whatever is hidden in that anomaly."

"How are they being…'duped' did you say?" General Sergeev asked.

"Major General Petrov believes his actions will make Russia great," Jeff explained. "What he is actually doing is driving political unrest within the world's advanced countries. We are so distracted with internal unrest and distrust of each other that we are not preventing the deaths of billions of people."

"Why do you care who lives or dies in some other country?" General Sergeev asked.

"I saw what they did in Africa," Jeff said with conviction. "I will not let that happen again as long as I live."

"Why come to me, Mr. Smith?" General Sergeev asked. "You have a senior position in the American CIA. Why do you need me?"

"Because the same kind of corruption I saw here today with General Petrov has already happened in Washington," Jeff answered. "Communications channels have been shut down. The media is being censored, and my own boss is one of the people making money from all this."

General Sergeev sat forward and stared at Jeff as if weighing what he had said. He then looked at Sergei and Jessica. He asked Jessica, "US army Intelligence has been uncharacteristically quiet. What do you make of all this, Lieutenant?"

"At first, I was skeptical," Jessica said truthfully. She looked over at Jeff and said, "Now I am here risking my life to bring you this message." She looked back at the general and said, "I believe it."

The general looked back at Jeff and said, "I have decided to help you, Mr. Smith, but your plan to detect something at the L2 Lagrange point is not going to work. I've decided on a more direct approach."

"General?" Jeff said.

"I plan to attack. One thing I know about space, Mr. Smith, is that logistics is the Achilles heel of any space endeavor. If we even damage it, whatever it is, the craft or their operators will need to come to ground to repair or replenish. When they do, we will know the location of their base of operations and crush them."

Jeff liked the idea of attacking and possibly killing whatever was located at that point in space since it had engineered the deaths of millions. He just had this nagging question in his gut that said: *What if these are advanced beings from another world and we attack them? Will this start an interstellar war?*

"How would we attack them, General?" Jeff asked.

Before General Sergeev could answer, the colonel returned with two new guards. "Forgive my interruption, General," he said. "You now have a six-man team assigned as your personal bodyguard. They will protect you at all times."

"Thank you, Colonel," the General said. "Mr. Smith, you asked how I would attack this point in space. That is my task to work on. In the meantime, you are my guests. This is, as you Americans say, 'an offer you cannot refuse.' Sergei, I will hold you personally accountable for their actions. Colonel Lebedev will show you to your rooms. We will meet again tomorrow after I meet with our defense minister."

The general then got up and left the room.

Sergei, Jeff, and Jessica were ushered out of the room and guided down a set of corridors to individual rooms. They were searched and stripped of anything that was not clothing—watches, pens, wallets, everything. When the search was over, they were brought a meal and locked inside. The rooms were comfortable with a bed, a couch, a desk with pen and paper, and a separate bathroom, but they were in prison cells, no matter how comfortable, and many stories underground. At this point, all they could do was wait.

The next morning, Jeff heard a knock on the door and received breakfast. A few hours later, he was escorted from his room by two guards and down a hall where Jessica joined him with two more guards. They were guided down more concrete corridors to large double doors that led into a large operations room. There, large monitors on the walls seemed to be tracking satellites and monitoring the Earth's surface. Twenty people were at large consoles, and at least ten armed guards were in the room. A large curved-glass walled room behind the consoles had a view of the entire operation. The general and another man were having a heated argument in that room.

Sergei walked over to Jeff and Jessica. He nodded to the guards who stood nearby to keep watch over the Americans. "Our new friend with the nice suit is the Defense Minister," Sergei explained to Jeff and Jessica. "They have been arguing about the arrest of General Petrov for over thirty minutes. The general wants you to speak to our minister with your data." Jessica and Jeff looked at each other, then at Sergei.

"This should be interesting," Jeff said.

Sergei waved to catch the general's attention. General Sergeev waved him in. "That is our queue," said Sergei. "This is what we planned for. Don't blow it!"

The glass-walled room was large. The general and the defense minister were in the center of a large open space near a podium that led to theater-style seats and a movie screen. The seats appeared to swivel toward the screen at one end of the room or toward the podium near the entrance.

The defense minister was about 5' 10" with thick dark hair and a dark complexion. He seemed young compared to other Russian politicians, probably in his early forties. The only thing in the room thicker than this man's mustache was his eyebrows. He had two fit young men in their late twenties behind him in nice matching suits with their jackets unbuttoned. They probably had pistols in shoulder holsters.

The general had two guards with machine guns flanking the only door into the room. Four guards were watching Jeff and Jessica while four more were scattered about the room with pistols in their belt holsters. Jeff was looking for cover in case people started shooting. The last thing he would want to do is pick up a gun in this room.

The general and minister were arguing in Russian. Jeff caught something about being a patriot while you are a traitor.

The general changed to English and said, "I have brought here before you your accusers, Minister Grachney. This is Jeff Smith from the American CIA and Lieutenant Jessica Tam from US Army Intelligence."

"Are you insane bringing them into this facility?" Defense Minister Pavlov Grachney asked in a rage. "You will hang for treason, Sergeev." Grachney looked at Jeff with hatred in his eyes as a sneer formed on his lips. He pointed at Jeff and said, "You must kill him immediately!"

"I may hang," General Sergeev said in a calm, even tone, "or I may not, but I will bring you to justice for what you have done."

"What have I done, Sergeev?" the minister asked.

"You have subverted the chain of command," Jeff said. "You issued orders directly to military units without passing through the proper channels. A capital offense in time of war."

"I deny these charges, and we are not at war," Grachney said in disgust. "You would ruin your career over this filthy lie, Sergeev?"

"I have shared with Sergei Sokolov detailed accounts of orders intercepted by US listening stations from Defense Minister Pavlov Grachney to Major General Konstantin Petrov and other senior Russian military commanders to redeploy troops and capture Russian Federation properties without presidential approval or informing the proper chain of command."

"The Russian Federation's Foreign Intelligence Service confirmed these messages," Sergei said.

The defense minister was surprised for a second and then became arrogant. "I do not need your permission. I have powerful allies who will bring about a new world order with Mother Russia in its rightful place as leader of this new world. You can hide behind fools and rules or see the writing on the wall, Sergeev. Join me or die with the rest of the fools who oppose us."

"You are hardly in a position to threaten me, Defense Minister," General Sergeev said in a deadly calm voice.

The minister smiled and said, "Oh, but you are mistaken, Sergeev." He pulled a slip of paper out of his vest pocket and continued, "Call this radio frequency. You will find I have a full tank battalion five miles north of this facility. If I do not contact them by 2 p.m. today, they have been instructed to attack this facility and kill everyone in it."

Jeff knew that despite the incredible firepower this base controlled, it was also very vulnerable to an assault by superior ground forces, like a battalion of main battle tanks. It seemed the minister had them in checkmate. Jeff glanced at the wall clock. It was only 11 a.m. They still had time to do something.

The general nodded to Colonel Lebedev. The colonel walked over and took the note from Minister Grachney. He walked out of the room to a communications console. Everyone watched through the glass wall in silence as the operator contacted someone and handed the headset to the colonel. After a few minutes, the colonel returned.

"General," Colonel Lebedev said formally, "I have contacted the commander of the 23rd Armored Battalion of the Russian Army. He is preparing to assault this facility at 2 p.m. today unless Minister Grachney personally orders him to stand down."

"Just as I said, General," the minister said with a self-satisfied smile. "Now release General Petrov, kill these Americans, and escort me to the surface."

Jeff felt dread in the pit of his stomach. Had he really gotten this far only to fall victim to a political gambit by a power-hungry maniac? He noticed Jessica had become a coiled snake, once again ready to strike. He signaled her to hold. Her frown seemed to signal agreement.

The general studied the grinning maniac for a few seconds with his hawk-like stare. Then he said, "I will drop a nuke on this facility before I turn Russia's strategic weapons over to the likes of you. Arrest them!"

Grachney's smile slid from his face and turned to shock. His face went pale. Grachney's guards hesitated, not knowing what to do next. The general's guards moved in with practiced discipline and disarmed Minister Grachney's bodyguards.

"Colonel," the general continued, "lock up his guards and bring the minister with me. I want to show him what we have been working on. Sergei, you may bring your friends."

The colonel worked with his guards to execute the general's orders. Sergei, Jeff, Jessica, and the minister, with one guard holding him by the arm, moved from the glass-walled room to the operations center.

"Mr. Smith, your idea of exposing whatever lies in wait for us at the L2 Lagrange point was a good idea. The colonel's staff and I have been working on it all night," General Sergeev said. "Our plan is simple."

The general walked over to a desk lamp and turned the light 90 degrees toward him. "Let us say this light is the sun." He picked up an apple off a desk and held it up toward the light, about two feet away in his left hand. "And this apple is the Earth." He took a pencil from his chest pocket with his right hand and pointed it at a point on the other side of the apple, away from the light. "The L2 Lagrange point is here where the gravity of the Earth and sun equalize to create a stable orbit far from Earth; it costs very little energy to maintain orbit there. If something is hiding there, I intend to fire a 10-kiloton warhead to this location and explode it. If the anomaly your scientists found contains anything, we should be able to see it once the blast wave clears the area. If nothing else, the electromagnetic pulse should destabilize any cloaking technology or the heat from the blast should radiate from the hull of any ship."

"General Sergeev," Grachney said, "you cannot launch a missile. The Americans will see it as an attack."

"I have a US Army Intelligence officer who will tell them it is not," General Sergeev replied as he extended a hand toward Jessica. Jessica nodded in agreement with the general.

Jeff noticed that the defense minister had finally started using General Sergeev's title when he addressed him. Calling him only by his last name was very disrespectful. Perhaps he was rethinking his next move. Jeff started to feel the knot in his stomach relax a little.

"We will also be launching this missile from a satellite, not from the ground," General Sergeev said.

"Orbital nuclear weapons are a violation of at least three treaties," Jeff said.

"I am aware of this," the general said. "We only have three. It would take too long to reset a ground-based ICBM to the new attack profile, and it would set off alarms around the world." He held up the apple again. "A space-based missile can launch here, on the opposite side of the Earth where no one located at the L2 Lagrange point could see it. We fire the engines until they come around the Earth, then stop. As the rocket continues around the Earth, once it is out of sight, we fire the engines again and continue four times expending the main fuel tanks. We then break orbit on the fourth pass and fly on momentum along a ballistic trajectory 1.5 million kilometers to intersect the L2 Lagrange point. As we get close, we turn on active radar and ping the target location while also using infrared and high-energy signals to locate targets."

"I do not know what these Americans have told you, General Sergeev," the minister said. "I beg you to reconsider. You are exposing our most secret weapons to attack ghosts."

"Someone or something has taken advantage of you, Minister Grachney," General Sergeev said. "I mean to expose and attack the perpetrators now while we still can."

"Fine, I will call off the attack while you chase this fairy tale," the minister said. "Once you find there is nothing there, you will surrender me and General Petrov to the Army. Agreed?"

"Agreed," the General said. "Colonel, engage Mira 6 and 7."

The operator at the launch console looked back at the colonel with confusion on his face. In Russian, he said, "Sir, there is no Mira 6 and 7."

The colonel approached the console and began typing in commands overriding the security lockouts that hid the secret missiles even from their own operations staff. "There," the colonel said as he pointed at the console. "Mira 5, 6, and 7 are now accessible. Run these flight coordinates for 6 and 7 only."

The general had connected Russian Strategic Missile and Space Warfare assets from across the Russian Federation. At one time, the base they stood in had controlled more than 1,400 land-based ICBMs. Now only 430 were active, but they were advanced MIRV designs. Each missile could target warheads to multiple destinations at the same time as well as deploy decoys to thwart anti-missile defense systems. Even though the ground-based communications systems sending telemetry and programs to their satellites were operated by other agencies, General Sergeev could override their operators and send his stealth messages at will.

Jeff turned to Sergei and said, "How could those get into space without anyone knowing about it?"

"Americans think their technology is superior, so they laugh when our communication satellites are ten times bigger than yours," Sergei said. "Now you know why they are so much bigger."

"Everything is ready, General," Colonel Lebedev said in English. "We hit our launch window in ninety minutes."

"Excellent," General Sergeev said. "We have time for lunch. We can eat in the observation room, Colonel."

"Yes, General," the colonel replied.

Guards brought in long folding tables that were set up in the open space by the podium. An all-you-can-eat buffet of soup, salad, and self-made sandwiches was spread out on the counter on one side of the room. Tea, water, and coffee with cups and glasses were placed on the other side.

Everyone ate a healthy portion of food like nothing was wrong in the world.

A SHOT IN THE DARK

Jeff could hardly believe it as he sat down to eat right before the Russians fired an illegal nuclear weapon, possibly at an alien race. He was so nervous that he felt his blood pressure must be over 175. He picked at his food until the general said, "You have not heard everything our American friends have to share, Minister."

"I can hardly wait," the defense minister said, his voice thick with sarcasm.

The general, not seeming to notice, said, "Jeff, why don't you share the story of the factories with our defense minister?"

"Certainly," Jeff said. The general seemed to be trying to win over the defense minister. Lunch may have been part of his approach. Clever. Jeff needed to be succinct, so he got right to the point. "My team tracked through a series of shell companies and holding companies to a financial conglomerate making billions of dollars every year. They were creating and shipping specialized materials to over 275 locations around the world."

"The West is good at making money," the minister said. "So what?"

"These sites are building factories designed to slaughter thousands of people every day," Jeff said.

The minister looked at him and said, "More fairy tales?"

"No, Minister Grachney," Sergei said. "We spotted these sites being built in China. I investigated a few. We thought it might be a weapons program, but the design made no sense. When Jeff shared with me the description of the factory he saw in operation in Africa, the design made sense."

The defense minister just looked at Sergei like he was mad.

"I saw the people being brought in on trucks, Minister," Jeff said. "I saw them suffering in pain inside the factory. I saw their dead bodies dropped into huge bins, twenty-five at a time, and carted off like garbage. I'll never forget the sight of it as long as I live."

"Bravo, my American actors," the minister said as he clapped. "You put on an impressive play to get the Russian military to waste its secret weapons on a hoax, to tarnish our reputation in the international community, and turn our people against funding our military." He pointed his fork at Jeff and added, "I see through your little games."

"The missile was my idea, not theirs," the general said.

"I was investigating the sites in China before Jeff ever contacted me," Sergei said.

"There is one more piece of the story I left out," Jeff added. "When I left the factory in Burkina Faso, I saw a vessel launch into space."

"And now there are little green men at the L2 whatever point." Grachney laughed a deep belly laugh. "Now I have heard everything I need to hear."

Jeff continued, "The propulsion system was not like anything I had ever seen before. It gave off a yellow light but no flame and no heat. Instead of a rocket engine's roar, there was a deep pulsing that you felt in your chest rather than heard. If it were a modern rocket, I should have been incinerated."

"A pity you weren't," Grachney said.

Jeff ignored the comment and continued, "I was behind a building, but I was no more than 200 yards away. It left the ground at more than 100 miles per hour and disappeared in seconds, not two minutes like a NASA launch in Florida."

The colonel and general became very interested in the new information Jeff shared. "How many seconds?" the colonel asked.

Jeff thought about it and said, "Ten to twelve. No more. I confirmed the launch with the French military. They shared that there were regular launches from that part of Africa."

"Those launches do not continue," the colonel stated.

"No," Jeff agreed. "And the factory was turned into a giant slag pit somehow."

"How convenient," Grachney said.

"Open your eyes, Pavlov," the general said in a stern voice like a father scolding an unruly child. "Who are these mysterious powerful friends of yours? Have you even met them? What if that is all an illusion? What if they are using you to facilitate the slaughter of millions? Maybe even billions."

The minister had a great poker face. He studied the general for a few moments and said, "We have an agreement, general. We shall see what your missiles tell us."

"Yes, we will, Minister Grachney," the general said. "It will take about a day for the missiles to reach their targets. Will you talk with your tank commander and give us one day?"

"Of course. We can do it now," the minister said.

Colonel Lebedev escorted Minister Grachney to the communications console and connected him with the tank battalion's commander. Grachney gave them until 5 p.m. the next day to release him.

Jeff, Jessica, Sergei, and the defense minister with his guards stood behind the consoles as the colonel's team worked on the launch process. General Sergeev briefly pulled Jeff, Jessica, and Sergei into the glass-walled room to talk about the message Jessica would share with her superiors. They decided not to share the entire story yet for fear it could tip off whoever was at the L2 Lagrange point. Instead, they would call the launch a Russian satellite malfunction. If the Russians could not gain control over the satellite, they would angle it out into space away from Earth.

The geek in Jeff was excited to watch these twenty people prepare and launch their payload from the satellite. They did a countdown just like NASA, only it was the colonel's voice over the silent room rather than a loudspeaker to the entire base.

The launch went smoothly. The main engine of Mira 6 burned for five minutes before shutting down. Jessica was then escorted to the communication console to call her base and report that the rocket was a Russian satellite malfunction. She called Captain Yee directly to report that she was in Russia. She was working with the Russian Foreign

Intelligence Service and Russian military. She and Jeff were fine. She then shared the satellite malfunction information and ended the call.

General Sergeev also called multiple Russian Federation officials to inform them of the satellite malfunction and a cascading failure that might affect other satellites. The Russian Federation government was now aware and could manage official communications with the West and China.

The group's plan was now put into action. They would burn the main engine three more times about every hour as the missile moved behind the Earth relative to the L2 Lagrange point.

On the fourth burn, they would angle the missile out of near-Earth orbit to the L2 Lagrange point 1.5 million kilometers away. About twenty hours after the last burn, they would detonate at the L2 Lagrange point near whatever they could find. If they found nothing, they would make a guess based on the data from the scientists at the University of Hawaii.

After a tense hour, the second burn was ordered, and to Jeff's surprise, Mira 7 was launched. As the general came walking over with a smile on his face, Jeff asked, "General Sergeev, may I ask why we are launching another missile?"

"The first missile will detect targets," General Sergeev said. "The second will attack a target with a 10-kiloton warhead. My last missile, Mira 5, has a 1-megaton warhead. We will hold this in reserve for now."

"The second missile will follow an hour behind?" Jeff asked.

"Yes," General Sergeev confirmed. "Plenty of time for us to analyze targets and deliver the targeting information to Mira 7."

"What if the cloak is restored before the missile gets there, General?" Jeff asked.

"Any object in space must follow some basic rules of physics," General Sergeev explained. "If we see them for even a few minutes, we will know where to target them."

Jeff thought the general might be overly confident, but he shook his head in agreement and said no more.

The colonel called the general over to discuss something. The defense minister went to the glass-walled room to sit down and write something. The rest of the observers watched and waited. Burn two and three of the first missile and burn one and two of the second went smoothly.

Jeff could feel the excitement in the room as the fourth burn approached. The colonel counted down from twenty to zero. His staff members executed their jobs flawlessly. Every step was well-orchestrated. Every process ran as expected. After the burn, the room started to build with excited voices as the colonel called for replies from each station.

After the last station reported, the colonel said, "General, Mira 6 is on track to target." The entire room broke out into cheers, handshaking, and backslapping. Sergei hugged Jessica, and Jeff even had a hand slap him on the back.

"Mira 6 has reached the calculated velocity and is on track to detonate at the L2 Lagrange point in twenty hours," General Sergeev said with a big smile. He was proud of his team.

Even the colonel cracked a smile before he calmed down the room and started the third burn of Mira 7.

The general walked over to his guests and said, "This is the first time they have ever launched anything into space beyond Earth orbit. Now they manage two missiles at the same time."

"It is quite an accomplishment, General Sergeev," Jessica said. "Your team are professionals, and the discipline of their training shows in their performance."

The general gave a slight bow to Jessica and said, "Thank you. That is the only compliment I think I have ever received from an American military officer."

"Hopefully, it is the first of many more to come, General Sergeev," Jessica said with a smile.

The general gave Jessica the eagle stare for a moment before smiling and walking away. Jeff was so caught up in his plans that he hadn't realized what Jessica had so astutely observed. This was likely the closest the United States and Russia had worked together toward a common military goal since World War II. Historians might view this as a major breakthrough in the relationship between East and West. These actions could save a billion Chinese lives.

Jeff turned to Sergei and Jessica and said with a smile, "This could be the start of a beautiful friendship."

Sergei turned to Jessica and said, "Yes, it could."

Sergei had obviously missed Jeff's point, and Jessica stared at him again. Jeff decided to be quiet and wait for Mira 7's final burn.

After Mira 7 was on its way to the L2 Lagrange point, there was another round of cheers, handshakes, and congratulations all around. The general brought everyone into the glass-walled room except two men who kept an eye on everything. A glass of vodka on ice was poured for everyone in the room—even the Americans and the defense minister.

General Sergeev stepped up on the podium and raised his voice over the milling crowd to say, "Today, we executed two precision-timed space launches with less than twenty-four-hours' notice. History will not just remember your skill and dedication to duty. You will be honored as heroes! We are a free and independent Russia. To Mother Russia!"

The crowd responded as one, "To Mother Russia!" Then they drank their glasses of vodka in one gulp and cheered.

The excitement in the room was contagious. Jeff wished he could speak Russian well enough to mingle, but he could barely understand half the words people spoke in the loud room. The general must have shared at least some of what they were doing with the colonel's staff. He wondered how much?

General Sergeev walked up to Jeff, who was standing alone, and said in English, "I see you are trying to talk with people, but your Russian is not so good."

"I've never had an ear for languages," Jeff admitted. "I usually rely on someone in my team for communications."

Not knowing what he should talk about, Jeff decided to talk about the weather. "I understand it is getting very cold above us right now."

"I grew up in Siberia, Mr. Smith," the General said. "Only the coldest winters here can compare. We live in a beautiful country, but it can be harsh."

"How did you end up here, General?" Jeff asked.

"I always excelled at math and science in school, but I lacked the political connections to go to university. My father convinced me to join the army and work to get a military education. At first, I was assigned to guard duties, but eventually, my commanding officer saw I was smart. He never had to tell me anything twice. He eventually appointed me to officer training. He was a good mentor and friend."

"Where is he now?" Jeff asked.

"He moved back to Belorussia and retired. Tell me, Jeff, how did you meet Sergei Sokolov?"

"A criminal organization in Russia stole fissionable material," Jeff explained. "My organization found out about it and discovered that the criminals were planning on selling the material to Libya. They were moving the material through Egypt. I offered Sergei information and logistical support for his help with the recovery. I promised him that his men would walk away with the material if he helped me."

"Why wouldn't you want to take the material for your country to analyze?"

"Honestly, General, we already know everything about how you create and manage your nuclear materials," Jeff said, "including how you track the material by value instead of by weight. I believe we have an agreement to try to change that?"

The general ignored the last part and said, "You must have upheld your part of the bargain?"

"I'm glad I did," Jeff said as he raised his glass and clinked it against the general's. They both drank; then the general nodded to Jeff before moving on to a group of his men.

After about forty-five minutes, people started to filter out of the room and guards came over to escort Jeff and Jessica to their rooms. A steaming hot meal of Russian fish soup with rye bread awaited them. Jeff was surprised by how rich and filling the soup was. After a few glasses of vodka and a good meal, since there was nothing better to do, he lay down and went to sleep.

NEW BEGINNING

Jeff was woken the next day by a knock on the door. A guard delivered a breakfast consisting of a hardboiled egg, apple slices, and coffee. Jeff ate and freshened up the best he could. Then he waited until Sergei opened the door. Jessica was behind him in the hallway with two guards.

"It is almost time for what you Americans call 'the main event,'" Sergei said. "We have been summoned to attend."

"I can't wait," Jeff said as he exited the room.

They were escorted to the operations center and asked to remain in the glass-walled room. The defense minister was there with two guards. Two more entered the room with Sergei, Jeff, and Jessica. Two more guards with machine guns stood at either side of the door.

Defense Minister Grachney was pacing the floor like a caged bear. "Ah, the Three Stooges have been brought to entertain me. What nonsense shall we talk about today? Are the spots on Jupiter now floating cities?"

In Russian, Sergei replied, "These people are guests of the Russian Federation and should be treated with respect."

"Respect must be earned," Grachney said. "You have a lot of work to do to earn mine, Sokolov."

After a brief silence, Sergei motioned Jeff and Jessica to move to the glass windows and pointed to the various groups of workers. "Those men over there are working on course and speed calculations. Those are working out the final timing for arming the warheads. That group is working on targeting systems. They plan to switch on active targeting two minutes before the missile impacts. Hopefully, they do not have defenses that can react that quickly."

"How do you know all this, Sergei?" Jessica asked.

"I have more…freedom than you do," Sergei explained. "I have been talking to the colonel and his staff. I am fascinated by their work. To be able to pinpoint something so far away with such accuracy. I am in awe of what they do."

"How long until the first intercept?" Jeff asked.

"Less than two hours," Sergei answered. "You see that clock on the wall on the far right? That is the countdown timer."

The large digital clock showed 1:53:20 as the seconds ticked down. It was hard not to be excited, but it was also incredibly boring to watch the clock tick down.

At twenty minutes to contact, the sounds from the operations center were piped in over speakers in the large glass-walled conference room.

The final targeting information was transmitted at the ten-minute mark and confirmation received with eight minutes and thirty-five seconds to spare. The missile was now self-guided with on-board sensors and guidance data.

The excitement grew as the seconds ticked down to the two-minute mark. Ten seconds later, they received confirmation that active targeting had gone live. They were now sending high energy radio waves toward the anomaly. Sensors were looking for reflected radar waves to find a target. The missile was also looking for infrared or ultraviolet energy signatures.

At one minute, thirty seconds an operator on the flight tracking console said in Russian, "The missile detected something and is veering off our default target by 10,000 kilometers. I have the coordinates. It has detected anomalies and is interpreting them as targets."

At forty seconds, the operator said, "The missile is detecting multiple targets in a tight formation. Six targets."

At thirty-seven seconds, "Eight targets!"

Minister Grachney stood up and walked over to the window with a look of disbelief on his face.

At twenty-two seconds, the operator's voice was filled with excitement. "Ten targets!"

At ten seconds, "The missile selected the largest target, Colonel. I have lost contact."

At 1.5 million kilometers, radio communications, even at the speed of light, take a few seconds to reach their destination. Add network delays from the receiving dish somewhere in the world and computer processing time and the missile data coming from the operator was already ten seconds old when he spoke his first words.

"Now we wait for an explosion," the general said to the colonel as they looked at each other.

The wall clock hit zero and kept counting. Everyone was tense. As the wall clock counted off the seconds, everyone stared at it in anticipation. Was the missile destroyed? Would the warhead detonate, or would the missile just keep going into the vast void of space at over 100,000 kilometers per hour?

As the wall clock hit eleven-plus seconds, another excited operator called out, "We have detonation! We have detonation!"

Colonel Lebedev walked over to the console to see the reading. He looked up at the general and said in Russian, "Confirmed 10-kiloton nuclear detonation, General." Sergei repeated it in English for Jeff and Jessica.

General Sergeev said, "Optics? Sensors?"

The optics operator replied first. "The blast wave has not yet cleared."

The sensors operator replied next. "We can only see the blast wave. It will take thirty seconds to clear."

Sergei continued to translate.

As the wall clock ticked second by second, it felt like time was slowing to a standstill. Each second was agony to watch.

When the clock hit forty-five-plus seconds, the sensor operator said, "I am getting a contact. We found something. I am trying to resolve the detail."

At fifty-five-plus seconds, the optics operator said, "We have spotted multiple contacts. Currently, three contacts."

"Are they moving?" General Sergeev asked.

"No, General," the optics operator replied.

"I want targeting information fed to Mira 7 now," General Sergeev ordered.

Defense Minister Grachney said in English, "May God have mercy on us all." He stood and stared in shock.

The operations center was a beehive of activity as more data was collected and processed. Over the next half hour, the number of contacts grew to twelve—one large vessel, two slightly smaller, two about half the size of the second largest, and seven much smaller objects that could also be vessels. The twelve contacts remained stationary as the second missile homed in on them.

The final targeting information was transmitted at the ten-minute mark, and confirmation was received with eight minutes and twenty seconds to spare. The missile was now self-guided with on-board sensors and guidance data.

The excitement grew again as the seconds ticked down to the two-minute mark. Ten seconds later, they received confirmation that passive targeting went live. Mira 7 was locked on the largest vessel and closing fast. The missile had no need for active sensors since it was receiving good data and not being jammed or attacked.

At the one-minute, thirty-seconds mark, General Sergeev asked, "Is there any movement?"

"No signs of movement, General," the sensor operator replied.

At the one-minute mark, the sensor operator urgently called out, "We have movement. We have movement."

"Remain calm," Colonel Lebedev said. "What is moving?"

"All the smaller contacts are moving away from the larger ones, Colonel," the sensor operator reported. "They are moving very fast."

"Have the large contacts moved?" General Sergeev asked.

"No, sir," the sensor operator replied. "Wait! The next two largest vessels have moved between the largest and our missile, General."

At thirty seconds, the flight operator called out, "The missile is under attack. It has deployed countermeasures."

The missiles carried five dummy warheads designed to attract anti-missile defenses. They deployed in different directions while the original warhead stayed on track to its destination. The five dummy warheads were giving off signals exactly like the original warhead while the original went silent.

At negative-ten seconds, the flight operator called out, "I have lost contact with the missile."

Time slowed down again as the seconds ticked down to zero. Tension was thick in the air as every eye not looking at a console stared at the wall clock.

At eight-plus seconds, the optical operator called out, "We have detonation!" The room instantly erupted in cheering.

The colonel was trying to quiet everyone. They eventually heard the sensor operator confirm the detonation at eleven-plus seconds.

At fifteen-plus seconds, the general called out over the noise, "I need damage assessments!" The room quieted down as everyone went to work.

The sensor operator replied, "I should have data in twenty seconds."

At twenty-five-plus seconds, the sensor operator called out, "The small contacts are returning to the large contacts!"

At forty-plus seconds, the optics operator called out, "The large vessel is venting gases! A debris cloud is surrounding the vessel."

At fifty-five-plus seconds, the sensor operator called out, "The large vessel's hull is radioactive. Spectrum analysis is consistent with atmosphere escaping into space. Debris of the same type as the vessel's hull alloys is floating around the vessel. One of the second largest vessels is also damaged and venting atmosphere. There are other small objects around the second damaged ship. It could be cargo or...."

"Take over, Colonel," General Sergeev said to Colonel Lebedev. He walked over to the glass-walled room and walked straight to the defense minister.

"Minister Grachney," the general said, looking down at the defense minister, who was sitting with his hands on his head. "We had a deal, did we not?"

"Yes, we do," the defense minister said in a defeated voice as he looked up to the general. "How can I have been such a fool? I have never met my benefactors. We always met through proxies or over phone calls."

As he sat down, General Sergeev said in a reconciliatory tone, "You are only a fool, Pavlov, if you take this new information and do nothing differently. Now is the time for decisive action to unify our country and mend old wounds. We have not beaten them yet, but we will—together."

The defense minister looked at the old warrior with renewed respect and seemed to draw strength from their conversation. "I have a lot of people to talk to, General Sergeev. May I have your permission to start with General Petrov?"

The general looked over to the guards assigned to the defense minister and said, "Escort Defense Minister Grachney to visit General Petrov. Once they have finished talking, escort them here."

After crisp salutes, the guards escorted the defense minister from the room.

The general walked over to Sergei and his American guests and said, "If there was nothing in that anomaly, I probably would only live long enough to see you three shot. I would follow soon after."

"I am glad it did not turn out that way, General," Sergei said.

"This is only the beginning, General," Jeff said. "We need to ferret out everyone working for the owners of those ships. We haven't won yet."

"No, but I am recording the optical and sensor data," the general said with a smile. "With your eyewitness testimony, the fog will be lifted from the world's eyes. The shroud of secrecy and deceit will be burned away by the truth."

Sergei stood straight, and with tears forming in his eyes, he said, "General Sergeev, you have made me even more proud to be Russian! I will make sure this secret is told. The shroud will burn."

General Sergeev gave Sergei a smile and said, "Kiss me and I will put you behind bars." He then turned and left the room to talk to Colonel Lebedev.

"Do you think he meant that?" Jessica asked.

Sergei laughed and said, "It is an old Russian joke in Siberia. Didn't we just save the world?"

"I think we did," Jessica replied with a smile to Sergei.

"Then we must celebrate," Sergei said as he opened a cabinet and pulled out an unopened bottle of vodka. "I may have hidden this yesterday." He grabbed water glasses that were set out on one of the counters near the sink and ice from a bucket near the glasses. He poured two-ounce shots straight over ice and handed out the glasses.

"To a beautiful friendship," Jessica said, copying Jeff's quote from the other day, but she only had eyes for Sergei.

Sergei raised his glass and said, "To lifting the fog from the world's eye and burning the shroud of secrecy."

Jeff thought a quote by Churchill would be most appropriate, "My friends, 'This is not the end, or the beginning. Not the beginning of the end but the end of the beginning.' We still have much work to do, but the future is now in our hands." He motioned to the large display screen tracking the twelve objects in space and added, "Not theirs!"

Jessica gave him that odd stare again while Sergei said, "I never liked Churchill's speeches, but I will still drink to yours."

All three raised their glasses and downed their drinks in one shot. Then their day became even more exciting.

ULTIMATUM

The speaker was still sharing the conversation from the operations center. It was a dull background noise of people working and talking in small groups.

Suddenly, the sensor operator called out, "The fleet is moving, General!"

"Where?" asked General Sergeev.

"Triangulating now," the sensor operator replied as his team worked feverishly. "The moon, General."

General Sergeev had a brief discussion with Colonel Lebedev. He then walked to the front of the room and said in a loud voice in Russian, "We have taken the first step in the liberation of our country, and likely the world, from oppression and deceit. We now need to take the right next steps. I will start by communicating to these ships that I intend to turn them to ash if they do not surrender or leave our planet's orbit. This could lead to attacks upon us. I am placing this base on alert and sending away all non-essential personnel. This message will be sent in twenty minutes."

Sergei translated in the glass-walled room.

The communications console operator called out in Russian, "General, there is a priority call to Defense Minister Grachney from his office in Moscow!"

The general nodded to the colonel, who assigned a guard to retrieve the defense minister. A few minutes later, Defense Minister Grachney and General Petrov entered the operations room. The colonel gave the defense minister a headset and put one on himself. The minister and the colonel argued a moment in Russian; then the minister put on the headset.

The recording of the conversation they later listened to was almost surreal. The defense minister's mysterious benefactor never gave him a name, number, location, or any identifying information. When the minister pressed for something to call the man by, the man just said "benefactor." The male Russian voice was prim and proper, almost aristocratic. He used formal language constructs, which in Russia were primarily used for important interactions like business meetings, courtroom sessions, government interactions, and a boy asking a girl's father for her hand in marriage.

The minister's benefactor was not pleased by the attack in space. He wanted to know who had ordered it and why he was not informed before such an action had been taken.

Defense Minister Grachney's reply was epic. "You and I have worked together for more than five years. You have helped me with my career. You have made me rich and powerful, but we have never met. You say that you want to help me make Russia a leading world power again— that together we would make the West fear us again. But you had other plans, didn't you?"

When his words were met with silence, Grachney continued, "You were playing me for a fool. You were using me and my country to destroy our entire species." Venom was dripping from the minister's voice. His hatred grew with every word. "You are a monster, and I am your puppet no longer. Army General Ivan Sergeev is authorized to use every asset to turn your ships to ash. Surrender your ships or leave our space now!"

Grachney's benefactor took his time to reply. "Defense Minister Grachney, your actions have limited our options. We will comply in one Earth day."

Minister Grachney looked back at General Sergeev. The general had a grim look on his face as he shook his head no. He raised one finger. Grachney said, "You have one hour to comply. If you have not left Earth's orbit or landed your ships at a place of my choosing, you will be fired upon. The moon is part of Earth's orbit. Your time starts now."

The communications console operator then said, "Communication has been terminated."

General Sergeev said in a stern voice, "Prepare Mira 5 for launch."

"We said we would give them one hour, General," Minister Grachney said to General Sergeev.

"It will take ninety minutes to launch and gain escape velocity," General Sergeev explained. "It will take another hour for the missile to reach the moon. Their ships are fast. I do not want my last missile destroyed before it is launched."

"General Petrov!" General Sergeev said as he moved in front of General Petrov. "Do you have anything to say?"

"Army General Ivan Sergeev, I am a loyal officer of the Russian Federation," General Petrov said while standing at attention. "I was wrong to question you or your authority. I was misled into thinking that a revolution was about to start—a new age for our people. I was wrong, and I will suffer the consequences for my actions."

"General Petrov," General Sergeev said in an almost kind voice, like a father talking to his son, "it is a new age for our people. We are the first in our world to discover there is intelligent life beyond our tiny planet. That life is malevolent toward us. It has tried and failed to subvert our government. It has tried and failed to take billions of human lives all over our world. If ever there was a new age for our people, for the people of the world, it is now."

There was silence in the room as the gravity of General Sergeev's words settled on the minds of everyone who heard him.

"I will need intelligent officers to lead our countrymen in the years to come, General Petrov," General Sergeev said. "I know who brought that tank brigade here." General Petrov smiled briefly. "I know whose cunning brought them to our doorstep undetected. Can you apply these skills in service to me once again?"

General Petrov stood tall and tried to suck in his ample belly as he said loud and clear, "I can, sir!"

General Sergeev put his right hand on General Petrov's left shoulder and said, "Thank you. Be at ease." General Petrov was visibly relieved, probably because he could have been facing a firing squad today. He watched General Sergeev with a respect he had never previously shown.

General Sergeev then moved on to Defense Minister Grachney and said, "We should go to the conference room and talk." The general led the defense minister toward the conference room with two guards close behind. As they reached the room, the general said to the guards, "Remain outside the room." He then entered the room and said in a booming voice, "Clear the room. Sergei, you and your American allies can remain."

Jeff made a mental note of the term "American allies." This could mean the beginning of a very big change for East-West relations.

Everyone sat down at the table except the general. He stood with his hands behind his back and said in formal Russian, while Sergei translated, "Defense Minister Pavlov Grachney, under the articles of the Russian Federation, it is my duty to place you under arrest for treason. I have no choice in this matter, but you do!"

"What choice do I have, General?" Minister Grachney said in English.

The conversation smoothly changed to English as the general explained, "General Petrov was not the only man to work for you. If you expose the others, it could make all the difference in your trial."

The defense minister thought silently for a moment and then said, "I understand, General. I am the main contact with my *benefactor*. I have ten agents who work for me. Each of them has ten operatives. Each of those ten also has ten, and so on, in a cell structure much like the KGB of old. I know my agents and know of their operatives. The rest is a black box to me."

"So you do not know how deep the structure goes or how many people in total are involved?" Jeff asked.

"No," Minister Grachney replied.

"Do you know any other people in your position with direct contact with the benefactor?" Jeff asked.

"I know of two," the minister said. "One in the United States and one in Britain, but I do not know any names."

"We need a coordinated intervention in the command and control structure," Jessica said. "If we can move quickly enough, we can disrupt these organizations and capture most of their senior members."

"The agent in the United States—how can we find him?" Jeff asked.

"He is very powerful," Grachney said. "He controls an empire of corporations and politicians, but he only works through proxies. I can give you company names and politicians' names, no more."

"Write them down and we will follow up on them," Jessica said.

"Excuse me, General," said Colonel Lebedev, entering the room. "We have an optimal firing solution if we launch in the next fifteen minutes."

"I will leave these matters to you, Sergei," the general replied. "I must return to the launch." He and the colonel left the room.

The team in the glass-walled room exchanged information and made plans. They stopped long enough to see Mira 5 launch her 1-Megaton warhead into space, then kept working.

They stopped again ninety minutes later as Mira 5 left Earth's orbit on its way to the moon. The twelve alien space vessels were fast. They had already entered the moon's orbit and were slowing down.

Activity in the operations center was still being shared inside the room. Sergei started to translate as their attention shifted to the excited voices from the main room.

The optics console operator was quickly going over what the optics team was seeing as the alien vessels approached the Earth's moon. "Five smaller vessels are towing the largest vessel. Here are images captured as the fleet circled our moon the first time."

The damage to their largest vessel was easy to spot on the images. There was a large hole in the hull. Debris captured by the gravity of the vessel was circling it. A glow of radioactive particles trailed the vessel. Several spots on the hull glowed red.

The sensors console operator reported next. "Electromagnetic telescopic sensors are picking up lethal levels of radiation in the alpha, beta, and gamma range. There is an unknown form of electromagnetic radiation connecting the five towing vessels to the big vessel being towed. We can see the signature, but we have never seen anything like it before. Similar but different levels of electromagnetic radiation are moving between the vessels and surrounding each vessel. Each has a different reading, but none are like anything we have ever seen."

"Projected trajectory?" General Sergeev asked.

The flight operations console operator replied, "All twelve contacts are slowing down. We do not know their final trajectory because it is changing very rapidly."

"Take your best guess, Lieutenant," General Sergeev said.

"My best guess?" the operator said as he looked at Colonel Lebedev. The colonel nodded encouragement. The operator answered, "My best guess is that they are slowing to land their damaged vessel on the dark side of the moon, General. From there, they can run a rescue mission, a salvage mission, or begin repairs. I have no way of knowing which they will do. On the dark side of the moon, we will have no way to see them and targeting them will be more difficult."

The general seemed impressed with this analysis. He thought for a moment before saying, "Colonel, I need targeting solutions for any object on the surface or in orbit of Earth's moon. If there is a base on our moon, destroying it is our top priority. Otherwise, I want to take out at least one of the two next largest vessels. You have fifty minutes. Understood?"

"Yes, General," Colonel Lebedev said as he came briefly to attention. He then moved to the flight operations team and started talking through their options.

The team in the glass-walled room huddled around a table. Jessica asked Sergei, "Does he really think there is an alien base on the moon?"

Minister Grachney replied, "General Sergeev is thinking through all the possible outcomes. He is a clever man. I underestimated him."

The communications console operator suddenly became excited. "Colonel Lebedev! Colonel! I have reports of multiple launches from all over the Earth."

"What kinds of launches?" the colonel asked.

"From where?" General Sergeev asked.

He was talking to someone on his headset and relayed information as he got it. "The United Kingdom. Multiples in Africa. Multiples from South America, Pakistan, India, China, and Southeast Asia. The profile is not a standard missile launch."

"Flight operations, detect and track these new contacts," Colonel Lebedev ordered.

After a stressful few minutes, the flight operations lead said, "We are tracking twelve targets leaving Earth's orbit. Trajectory will place them in lunar orbit in ten minutes."

"Ten minutes?" Jessica said. "It's taking our rocket an hour to reach the moon."

"Are they attempting to intercept Mira 5?" General Sergeev asked.

"No, sir," the flight operations lead replied. "They will never be within 50,000 kilometers of Mira 5 until she enters orbit."

The colonel and general both looked relieved after hearing that news.

"They are pulling out," Defense Minister Grachney said. "They are leaving. They recalled all their assets and they are going to leave. The attacks are working."

"They could be regrouping before attacking us," Jeff said.

"I don't think so," Jessica replied. "Why would an enemy reveal its hidden locations and fly all the way out to the moon just to turn around and come back? We could pick a few off as they reentered the Earth's atmosphere and use atmospheric fighters to defend ourselves. We are not as fast as they are, but we have numbers."

"We shall have to wait and see," Sergei said.

It was impossible to do anything else but nervously watch the wall clock counting down the mission timer and listen to the activity in the operations center. The alien fleet had slowed to the point that it was stationary in orbit on the dark side of the moon. The radiation signature of the damaged vessel appeared to have dropped to the moon's surface.

At negative-ten minutes, two sets of targeting parameters were sent to Mira 5. One for an orbital target and one for a target on the moon's surface.

The colonel, the general, and the flight operation lead were in a heated debate over which target to select. The conversation was going too fast for Jeff and Jessica to follow until Colonel Lebedev said, "With respect, General, I think we should target an active threat, not the damaged ship."

"By the radiation readings, we know the damaged ship is on the surface now," the flight operations lead said. "If there is a base, they are at its location. Mira 5 can easily target the radiation."

Colonel Lebedev said, "If there were a base, it would have the same stealth technology as the fleet. We would not see the radiation if that vessel was in such a base."

General Sergeev interrupted them and said, "I have made my decision. We will target the ships in orbit. Execute targeting package alpha."

"Yes, General," the lead flight operator said, and his team went to work.

At negative-two minutes, the flight operator said, "Targeting package alpha is confirmed. The missile is tracking twenty targets."

At negative-forty seconds, "Twenty-four targets!"

At negative-ten seconds, "The missile selected one of the largest targets, Colonel. I have lost contact."

Mira 5 was also a MIRV design. The missile cone deployed five decoy warheads, each sending signals identical to the original missile, while the last missile silently delivered its one-megaton warhead to the selected target.

At three-plus seconds, the optics operator called out, "We have detonation, General!"

A round of cheers broke out, but they were quickly silenced by the colonel.

At eight-plus seconds, the sensor operator called out. "Confirmed! We have a one-megaton nuclear detonation over the moon's surface."

The air was thick with tension. Every eye not watching a console was glued to the clock. The silence was excruciating.

At forty-five-plus seconds, the sensor operator called out, "I am picking up secondary detonations! At least I think they are detonations. The energy readings are strange, but the amplitude is equivalent to a five-kiloton explosion." Another round of cheers broke out in the room, but no one tried to stop them this time.

After a full minute of celebrating, the room quieted as the communications operator called out, "There is an urgent call to Defense Minister Grachney from his office in Moscow!"

The general and colonel met the minister at the large glass doors. The minister said, "I know what to do." The three of them walked in silence to the communications console where Colonel Lebedev handed the minister a headset and put one on himself.

The sensor operator called out. "I am picking up more energy discharges. The readings are constant. They seem too smooth to be an explosion. I have never seen anything like this."

The colonel, the general, and a few others crowded around the sensor operator's console to see what she was looking at. After thirty seconds, the energy signal ended.

"This is Defense Minister Grachney," he said.

The aristocratic voice of Minister Grachney's benefactor spoke in formal Russian. "You have continued your attacks on us when we told you we would comply in one Earth day. Why?"

"I told you that you had one hour to comply," the minister said. "You came toward Earth instead of leaving. You landed on our moon. Our attacks will continue if you remain in this solar system."

"We need to recover our wounded," Grachney's benefactor said.

"You have one hour before our strongest missiles reach you," Minister Grachney said. "Be gone by then or die." Then he hung up.

Everyone in the room looked confused by the conversation. Everyone except General Sergeev and General Petrov. They both had smiles on their faces. Their missiles could not be retargeted for days, but the aliens did not know that.

General Sergeev said, "An exceptional ploy, Defense Minister. Well done."

"Thank you, General," the minister replied.

"We must tell the Americans what we have done," General Petrov said.

"We have a plan and are ready to execute it on your orders, General Sergeev," the minister replied.

"Brief me in the conference room," General Sergeev said.

While the General was being briefed, they were interrupted by cheers in the operations room. The aliens were leaving the moon's orbit at high speed. It was later determined that twenty-six vessels were in the alien fleet. Only twenty-two had left orbit. It was proven later that the other four were either abandoned or destroyed.

NEW WORLD ORDER

Once the general was comfortable with the plan, they moved quickly. The two generals and the defense minister left for Moscow the next day where Defense Minister Grachney met with his agents face to face and arrested them.

Major Jones' team and Amber had also been busy determining who was involved in businesses and governments worldwide. They had built a model of the Hidden Hand organization and who could be trusted to counter them. They also had an information package ready to communicate to the world on what was really happening. They posted it on social media first, and then released the official package to nations all over the world. Amber was already in New York where she was leading a covert team under the US press secretary to take back all media channels on the same day.

The Russian pictures of the damaged spacecraft orbiting the moon became the iconic images of that eventful day. The night before the social media package was released, arrests happened all over the United States, Europe, Canada, Russia, China, Japan, and many other countries around the world. The following day, a full media blitz on the aliens, the Hidden Hand, and government corruption brought the world up to speed on what had almost happened. The spotlight was on East-West cooperation and the Russian attacks on the aliens' ships. Anyone with a Russian accent received random hugs and kisses around the world.

Eventually, once the entire story was told, Jeff and Amber became more famous than movie stars.

Some days later, Jeff found Mike at his cabin in the mountains, fishing and happily playing computer games. Alon and his team still had the samples.

After the initial shock and the reforming of governments with new leaders, the people of Earth began to see each other in a new light. They had a common enemy that could return at any time. They eventually learned that these aliens had been influencing humans as far back as World War II. People began to ask: What were the aliens' motives? Why were they here? Why did they want to kill us in their factories? How can we defend ourselves?

Earth's advanced nations built a joint space program to go to the moon and look for any remaining alien presence. What they found were two damaged spaceships and a lot of debris. It would take years to gather the wreckage and analyze the alien technology, but they began immediately.

Within a year, a World Congress was formed to end conflicts, improve the quality of life, and build the technical ability to defend humans from any alien species. Progress was slow. The road was difficult, but it was working.

Not every agent or operative working for the Hidden Hand was captured. Some escaped and were on the run. Some committed suicide once they learned what they had done. Some were never found because no one knew they even existed. Jeff was hired back into the CIA and promoted to assistant director. His job was to find any remaining Hidden Hand cells. The rich power broker in the United States, named Felix Monroe, killed himself, but his henchmen were still at large. It was Jeff's number-one priority to find them.

Amber was hired by the US Commerce Department to rebuild the model for media oversight and ensure the integrity of US news agencies.

Jeff and Amber were now celebrities, Washington insiders, and on the invite list for every public and private party.

One of these parties was a lavish event in New York City. Key people from every G-7 country were there. Jeff and Amber were personally invited by a wealthy businessman who was financing many companies doing alien technology research and development work.

After hors d'oeuvres, cocktails, mingling with the world's elite, a five-course lobster dinner, and more cocktails, everyone was happy to have come to this party. They could now talk face to face with people they had only previously met on the phone. About an hour after dinner, Jeff and Amber were invited to the roof to meet their mysterious host, Abrahim Abdi. When Jeff and Amber walked onto the roof of this impressive building, they found him waiting for them, looking out over New York's skyline.

"Hello," Amber said.

"Hello," replied Abrahim as he turned from the view and walked toward them. "May I call you Jeff and Amber?"

"Yes, of course," Amber replied.

"I was looking forward to meeting you both all day long," Abrahim said with a smile.

As Abrahim approached, Jeff automatically sized up the man. He was a little shorter than Jeff with a heavier build. He looked like a weightlifter. Abrahim wore a fine dark blue suit that probably cost more than Jeff made in a week. He wore polished black shoes and cuff links but no tie.

As Abrahim came to a stop close to them, Amber asked with a smile, "Why did you want to see us tonight, Abrahim?"

"I wanted to share a story with you," Abrahim said as he walked over to the edge of the roof. Jeff and Amber followed. "My tale begins with an orphan found wandering the streets of Cairo. That orphan was selling fruit when he saw an expensive car stop nearby. The boy walked up to the rich man getting out of the car and gave him his best sales pitch. It was a lie, of course."

Jeff and Amber laughed politely.

"The rich man was impressed with the boy and took him in," Abrahim continued. "He cleaned him up. He educated him. That boy went to the finest schools and lived like a prince."

"And that boy was you, Abrahim?" Amber asked.

"Yes," Abrahim replied with a smile. "Do you know who that rich man was? Felix Monroe!"

Abrahim's face became twisted with hate as he said, "And he died because of you." He quickly backhanded Amber across her jaw with his left hand and sent her staggering back into a wall. She fell to the ground. His right hand came toward Jeff with a knife in it, heading straight toward Jeff's heart. Jeff's reaction time was slowed by the alcohol, so he barely deflected the knife away from his torso. Instead of stabbing Jeff in the heart, Abrahim planted the blade deep into Jeff's left arm. Jeff could feel the blade hit bone and rip into his flesh. The pain was excruciating, but no worse than what he had felt before.

Instead of protecting his wounded arm and turning away from his attacker, Jeff's training took over and he hit Abrahim hard in the throat with his right hand. If Jeff's reaction time had not been slowed by the alcohol, he would have crushed Abrahim's Adam's apple and killed him on the spot, but the delay allowed Abrahim to move enough to avoid instant death. It did stun the big man and sent him staggering back a few paces. Jeff's next actions were automatic but poorly executed due to the alcohol in his bloodstream and the pain in his left arm screaming at him like alarm bells in a firehouse. He kicked with his right foot into Abrahim's knife hand, sending the knife skidding across the concrete floor past Amber. He then did a roundhouse kick with his left foot right into the center of Abrahim's chest, staggering him back some more.

Jeff's next move would have been a killing blow to Abrahim's eyes or throat, but his maimed left arm made him scream in pain as he tried to move it. He could already feel the warm blood dripping from his left hand as it hung useless by his side. He did another roundhouse kick, this time targeting Abrahim's nose. It was a bad move.

The slight delay was all the time Abrahim needed to recover. He anticipated the kick and threw Jeff off balance. Abrahim grabbed Jeff by his tie with his right hand and pulled him toward the roof's edge. The two men struggled but Abrahim was stronger. He manhandled Jeff to the edge of the building. His left hand grasped Jeff's good arm at the wrist; his right hand was now on Jeff's throat. He bent Jeff's body backwards over the three-foot-high concrete wall surrounding the roof and pushed Jeff toward an eighty-eight-story fall that would surely kill him.

Jeff desperately wrapped both legs around one of Abrahim's legs to prevent himself from being pushed the rest of the way over the edge. Jeff's mind was racing, trying move after move, but nothing was working. Eventually, he would pass out due to blood loss or Abrahim's stranglehold. He had to act fast.

Abrahim smiled at Jeff's struggles and said, "Time to die, Jeff. Then I will deal with pretty little Amber and the rest of the guests at this party. I just had to kill you two first."

Jeff panicked. He struggled harder, tried everything he knew, but he was trapped. The world around him was starting to fog over. The end was near.

Amber had been hurt by the brutal attack but was not unconscious. She heard what Abrahim was saying to Jeff and slowly looked up through the hair that was half-covering her face to see them struggling. She looked around and saw Abrahim's knife a few feet away. She painfully crawled toward it, grabbed it, and struggled to get back on her feet.

Jeff did not have much time. Amber ran forward and plunged the knife into Abrahim's back. He spun around, his left elbow hitting Amber in the side. She let out a shriek of pain and crumpled into a ball on the roof.

Abrahim never let go of Jeff's wrist as he shifted his weight. He no longer had Jeff pinned to the ledge. It was just the break Jeff needed. Shifting his weight, sweeping Abrahim's legs out from under, Jeff toppled Abrahim over him and off the building, but Abrahim did not let go of Jeff's neck right away. His weight pulled Jeff over the building's edge with him.

Amber, still lying on the roof, screamed when she saw the men go over and repeated, "No! No! No!" She tried to ignore the pain in her side as she got up to look over the edge, but her body felt like it was made of lead, and the sharp pain in her side slowed her movement further as she favored it. As she looked over the edge, almost paralyzed with fear, she saw the two men falling and hit the ground.

Amber pushed herself back from the edge of the building and stared in shock for a few moments. Then she remembered what Abrahim had said about killing her and the rest of the guests. She went back to find her purse on the floor, grabbed her cell phone, and called the World Congress security team leader.

"This is Amber van Hosteen. I was attacked on the roof by our host, Abrahim Abdi. He and Jeff Smith are dead. Abdi said he was going to kill everyone in the building. We need to evacuate the building."

"Do you need medical attention?"

"No, get everyone out. Hurry."

"Stay on the roof. I'll have helicopters soon."

The security team sprang into action and began evacuating the guests. Security teams from many countries moved to protect their charges. Some moved to the roof for helicopter extract. Some moved to the elevators for ground transportation.

However, another team was in the building setting other plans in motion. When the alarms were pulled, power was cut to the elevators and nerve gas entered into the building's air conditioning system. The guests, panicking when the elevators shut down, moved to the stairwells. The assassins had planned for this, so nerve gas killed everyone who entered the stairwell heading down.

The only people to escape alive that night were those who headed to the roof.

As Amber boarded a helicopter, she saw a sleek black helicopter approach the building, hover, then leave. The roof must have been Abrahim's escape plan too. Many of the world's champions of freedom were dead, and the Hidden Hand had proved it was not yet defeated. The aliens had been chased away, but the damage they had done to human society remained.

CHAPTER

WARNING

Two years to the day after General Sergeev drove the aliens from Earth's orbit, a new ship appeared uncloaked at the L2 Lagrange point.

Unlike previous visitors, this ship's crew members announced themselves on multiple frequencies to the world. The new World Congress space division spotted them immediately and received their signal. Predetermined alarms were set off around the world warning countries of the aliens' return.

World Congress Admiral Xavier Mendez met with his senior staff to review the message and recommend next steps to the world's nations.

The technical specialist on duty reported, "Sir, the message they sent was short. I will replay it now."

"People of Earth, we are not here to harm you. Not all of our people supported those who were here before us. We will speak to your leaders in two days."

"The message," continued the technical specialist, "was followed by communication and timing details, including a video feed."

"Analysis?" the admiral asked the room.

"The last time they visited, Admiral, they brought a fleet of twenty-six vessels—one Alpha command ship, two Beta cargo ships, six Delta scout ships, and a host of smaller vessels. This time, they only brought one Delta," said the intelligence officer on duty, listing the names the military used to identify the different alien ship types.

"That we know of," said the current commander of all alliance ground forces and the American Commander of the Joint Chiefs of Staff, General Daniel Dawson.

"If they stay where they are and send nothing toward the Earth, I don't see why we can't talk before we shoot," Admiral Mendez said.

"All right. Let's tell them exactly that. We will grant them their meet and greet. However, we will also destroy anything that approaches the Earth or the moon," General Dawson said.

"My thoughts exactly," agreed Admiral Mendez. "If there is no disagreement?"

The room erupted with disagreements.

Multiple people said, "What if this is a trick to locate our leaders and destroy them?"

Admiral Mendez calmed down the room and said, "Our world leaders can take the call from their own countries in places of their choosing as long as it has good communications."

"I know I'll be in a bunker under the Rocky Mountains," said General Dawson.

After a little muttering, there was no more disagreement.

"Very well," said Admiral Mendez. "We will send this exact message in return, Lieutenant. 'We agree to this meeting, but in three days, not two. Be prepared to explain why your people were on Earth.' Attach the communications details required. I will communicate the alien request and our reply to the World Congress."

The admiral caught a lot of flak from the World Congress as he thought he would. Its members were angry that he had agreed to anything with the aliens without their consent. While Admiral Mendez respected civilian authority, he knew the World Congress could not agree on a day to meet in less than a week, let alone what to say and who should be involved. Every day the aliens were in Earth's orbit would cause more panic and give more time for some trigger-happy general to target a nuke on the alien ship and fire on them. The last thing Earth needed was angry aliens hurling asteroids from the asteroid belt toward the Earth.

One day later, Admiral Mendez was woken up when two new ships appeared at the L2 Lagrange point.

As the admiral walked toward his operations room, he was briefed on the situation by an aide. "Sir, two new alien scout vessels arrived at the L2 Lagrange point fifteen minutes ago. They came alongside the Delta already there, sat for ten minutes, and then enveloped the Delta in some form of energy we think is a tractor beam."

"Why do you think it's a tractor beam?"

"It's the same energy signature the Russians recorded two years ago, when the alien scout ships towed their Alpha to the moon."

As they entered the operations room, the commander on duty called attention. "Admiral on deck." Everyone not in the middle of an urgent task stopped what he or she was doing and stood at attention.

"At ease," the admiral said in a loud voice.

As the admiral approached the commander on duty, he said, "I've been informed of the situation up to tractor beams being applied to the original Delta. Has anything changed?"

"The Delta just fired her engines, sir. She appears to be trying to pull away from the scouts."

As the admiral checked the view screens at the command console, an operator called out, "The scouts have cut power to their energy projectors. The Delta has turned off her main engines and returned to station in the exact same spot as before. The scouts are heading toward Jupiter."

One minute later, another operator called out, "We have lost sight of the scouts."

"They probably changed course right after we lost sight of them," Admiral Mendez said.

"We couldn't see the scouts approach the Delta until they were right on top of it, sir," the commander said.

"We've got to improve our sensor technology," Mendez said. "Those scouts are probably headed back to a Delta somewhere in our solar system. Let's hope there isn't a fleet with them. I'll inform the World Congress of this incident."

As the World Congress' leaders returned to their home nations, its military leadership moved to its command bunker under the Swiss Alps. Eight connections were established around the world. One was the World Congress command bunk. The other seven went to the G7 countries—the seven wealthiest and most technologically advanced countries in the world, which financed 95 percent of the World Congress, including its military.

The World Congress' communication technology was a highly secure version of CISCO's Telepresence technology. The audience in each location could see three large video screens. A connected site was assigned to a screen for the other sites to see when anyone at that site spoke. The alien connection was assigned the center screen. The remaining eight locations were assigned with four to the left screen and four to the right. The aliens could only see one video screen at a time, so they would always see the current human site speaking.

Admiral Mendez would lead the conversation, "yielding the floor" to other sites based on requests by secure text message to his aide. A less secure text channel was also available to the aliens, communicating to all participants only one way. Each site displayed two people in chairs at the front of the video feed with a sign behind them that clearly displayed their country's flag. Each site had one primary speaker who would yield the "second chair" to anyone else speaking from that site.

The American room was designed with twelve chairs. All the chairs were full, and ten more people were standing in the back.

By this time, Amber had become the president's press secretary and was fortunate enough to be one of the people standing at the back of the room.

Everyone was nervous. People were saying, "I hope this isn't a plot to kill the world's leaders? What if the aliens declare war? No, the aliens are here to negotiate a truce." It was all a loud buzz in a room designed to amplify every word spoken. There was a lot of nervous laughter. Amber kept quiet and listened. The butterflies in her stomach made speaking too difficult.

As the communications system switched on, the room became quiet. Each site answered a roll call as the connections were tested for the thousandth time. The technology was amazing as it switched from China to France to Great Britain. The video was smooth and clear. Sound lined up exactly with the movement of each person's mouth. The center screen was blank.

At 2 p.m. in Switzerland under the Alps, 6 a.m. in the NORAD command bunker under the Rocky Mountains, and 9 p.m. in a Chinese bunker outside of Beijing, the center screen came to life. Around the world, every site made sounds of shock and horror. To his credit, Admiral

Mendez immediately muted all sites except his own and cleared his throat to make the aliens see him on the World Congress video display.

What they saw was far from human. The aliens had oval bodies, thick in the middle and rounded toward the top. They stood on three massive legs with feet like elephants. A pair of large arms extended off the top of their rounded "shoulders." A bend in the arm formed something like an elbow. At the end of the arm was a hand with what looked like three thumbs and no fingers. There were no fingernails. A smaller pair of arms began to unfold from under the larger arms with delicate hands that looked like they also ended in three thumbs. The little hands came together almost like a priest about to pray. The most alien thing about this creature was its lack of a head. In its place stood three eyes on long stalks. Each eye was huge with beautiful, long eyelashes. The edge of each eye was white, but the center was more like a cat's eye than a human eye. Two of the eye stalks looked forward at the humans while one faced backward.

Everyone in the room was stunned into silence by the alien creature except Admiral Mendez. He said, "My name is Admiral Xavier Mendez. I am from Spain. I command the military branch of the World Congress. May we start with your name?"

After a three-second delay, the alien's eye stalks began to sway from side to side. There was no mouth to signal that it had started speaking but a voice replied in clear English.

"You may call me Cain. I represent what you would call the religious leader of my home world. Her name is Ashzahan." The spelling of their names came over the text channel as he spoke.

"What does your religious leader want to share, Cain?" Admiral Mendez asked.

"I am glad you asked, Admiral. Not all of our people support the ones who came before us. Our world is divided over how to solve our problem."

"Your world is divided. How so?" asked Admiral Mendez. "Are you a different faction of the same political entity or a different political entity? What problem are you trying to solve?"

"Our world has been united for over 100,000 Earth years. There is only one political entity. We represent more of a political party than a faction of our people."

"Why did the scout ships attack you two days ago?"

"That was not an attack. They did not want our mission to move forward so they tried to escort us out of Earth's orbit."

"We noticed you had to fire your engines not to be pulled away."

"The stress of their beams against our engines would have destroyed our vessel. Since no Zalthurian has killed another in over 100,000 years, they were forced to relent."

The text message channel lit up with this revelation. Amber and a few others wrote, "We should use this division to our advantage." Hers received the most upvotes and Mendez was made aware of it. The next highest message said, "What is a Zalthurian?"

"Can you tell us what a Zalthurian is?"

"My apologies. We are from the planet Zalthur. We call ourselves Zalthurians."

"Thank you for the explanation. Can you tell us why you are here and what problem you are trying to solve?"

"Ashzahan does not agree with the way our people have decided to deal with our problem. We fundamentally believe it is wrong, but we were outvoted. We wish to bring you a warning. The fleet you chased away will return with an ultimatum: Surrender or be destroyed."

"Are you threatening us?"

"No, we are warning you. If you surrender, it will minimize the loss of life. Your people will be able to rebuild. If you fight, you risk extinction."

The text message stream lit up again with this revelation.

"Why must you kill us? What problem are you trying to solve?"

"Our people have lived in harmony for 100,000 of your years because of the teachings of Zalthur. Our world was continuously at war for almost 1,000 years when our people finally had enough of central governments, greed, and corruption. Zalthur's teachings swept across our world like a cleansing storm. Soldiers put down their weapons. Workers walked away from munitions factories. The wars ended, and we built a new society. We believe our bond with the Creator is built upon the Creator giving us the spark of life at birth. We nurture that spark throughout our lives by being a positive influence on the world around us, each in measure to his or her capabilities. When we die, we pass a stronger spark of positive energy back to the Creator, increasing the Creator's ability to spread life throughout the universe."

"Are you trying to convert us to your religion?" Mendez asked.

"No, that is not my intent at all. Each individual of any species must make its own choices about its relationship with the creator. It is not our place to dictate this."

"Then why did you tell us this, Cain?"

"This is fundamental to who we are and our problem. A few hundred years ago, a brilliant scientist named Darr created the cure to aging for our people. He made us immortal."

"You cannot be killed?" Mendez asked.

"Any living thing can die, Admiral Mendez. We now no longer die from old age, but children are still important to our race. The creation of new life is precious to us. Unfortunately, our immortality process has a flaw. It makes us sterile after we reach fifty years. It was an unexpected surprise, and now we have almost no children. We have broken the pact with the Creator. The cycle of life has shattered. Through the centuries, our people began to despair. Many have taken their own lives, an unthinkable act that sends the Creator's spark wandering throughout the empty space between life and death. Only 10 percent of our original population remains. The others have ended their own lives."

"Then why come here? Why expend so much effort on trying to take over our planet?"

"We have found a cure to our curse, but it requires an organic acid that cannot be produced by any living thing on our planet. We have searched the galaxy for centuries with robotic probes seeking a species capable of creating this elixir. We found only two species in the galaxy that can make it. One is an herbivore on a planet owned by a xenophobic race that would rather kill us than help us. Their technological superiority and aggressive nature makes obtaining this animal impossible."

"And the other?"

"The other is you humans on the planet Earth."

"How do you justify killing us to save yourselves?"

"The logic behind it is simple. Your race is young and growing faster than your world can sustain. You are not advanced enough to move your people to another planet as you outgrow this planet. By removing five billion humans now, it would allow a reset to your population explosion. You can maintain enough biodiversity to thrive, and perhaps you will better manage your population growth in the future. We would be giving you a second chance."

"You want to help us by killing five billion people?"

"As I have said, we do not agree with this approach, but we are not the majority."

"What is your approach?"

"We believe that reconnecting with the Creator and asking forgiveness for our arrogance will enlighten us to a different path."

"You believe in divine intervention then?"

"Not intervention, more of a divine revelation. We fully expect the need to take action ourselves, just not this action."

"How long have your people been watching us?"

"We discovered your species over seventy Earth years ago. Execution of the harvesting strategy you just thwarted began fifteen years ago."

"Harvesting strategy?" Mendez said in an angry growl.

"I am sorry if that term offends you. Your people were never meant to know we even existed."

"No more human beings are going into your factories while I draw breath."

"This is what we find odd about your people, Admiral. Your own people murder each other by the thousands in your cities each year. Thousands more die on the roads, and even more die in natural disasters. All preventable deaths. Every decade you slaughter hundreds of thousands in wars or through genocide. In the last few centuries, millions died in huge wars. You are so willing to kill your people, but not one will die to help us."

The President of the United States signaled on the shared chat line that he wanted to speak. "Cain, the President of the United States will speak to you next. Mr. President."

"I am William Marshal, President of the United States," the president began. "I am willing to listen and find a way to prevent those deaths you mentioned, but murdering more in those horrible factories doesn't make sense. You said so yourself."

"Mr. President, I am only presenting my people's view of you. I am not defending this as justification for what was done. You must see that from the outside looking in, you do not seem to place very high value on the lives of your people. In fact, it was surprisingly easy to find people on Earth who were willing to kill their neighbors. This was shocking to us."

"I am Helmut Kraus, Chancellor of Germany," said the chancellor, taking over. "What you say is unfortunate but true; however, we are a people governed by laws. The people you speak of broke those laws, and I demand the names of every one of them to be turned over to us for prosecution."

"I will take your request to Ashzahan, Mr. Chancellor, but I do not have the names to give you."

"I am Dewei Zhang, President of the People's Republic of China," said the next world leader. "The factories your people planned in China would have killed more than 95 percent of my country's population. Why did you target China and not Russia or the United States?"

"In short, Mr. President, you have one seventh of the Earth's population and your country's government made it easy to build those factories. The middle layers of your government have no oversight."

China's president shook his head and made notes.

The questions and answers continued briefly until the questions became less germane. Then Cain said, "My time with you has come to an end. I have shared what I can. I will take back your requests to Ashzahan. I do not know if we will be able to return with answers. We borrowed this vessel, and we may not get access to another. I do not have knowledge of our exact plans, but we estimate that our fleet will return in seven to ten Earth years. Please consider everything I have shared with you."

The alien video feed went dark.

The world's leaders argued and debated for a month after Cain's warning. The outcome was never really the question. Earth was going to fight no matter what the alien said. The real question was how much to invest and who would lead the effort. They had at least seven years to prepare. The next invasion would not be silent.

ABOUT THE AUTHOR

Chris Shockowitz was born and raised in sunny California. He grew up exploring the fields, creeks, and hills of northern San Jose before the housing boom. At age ten, he discovered science fiction at the local library, where he read the Lensman series by E. E. Doc Smith and fell in love with the genre.

Chris worked at many different jobs before graduating from San Jose State University with a business degree. Then he worked at Intel for twenty-five years, starting as a software developer and retiring early as a Director of Application Development. At Intel, Chris was recruited to participate in many projects designed to envision future products or services. One of his favorite phrases is, "The best way to predict the future is to invent it."

Chris and his wife Carolyn are blessed with two wonderful children. He loves the outdoors and goes hiking or mountain biking every week. He enjoys writing science fiction and hopes to complete two science fiction series within three years.

Read Chris Shockowitz's Other Books

If you enjoyed *Silent Invasion*,
be sure to read all of Chris Shockowitz's books.
You can find the latest release dates, descriptions,
and much more at:

ShockowitzSciFi.com

Zalthuras Series (2018 – 2150)
    Book 1: Silent Invasion
    Book 2: Earth's Zero Hour
    Book 3: Attacking Zalthuras

Outward Bound Series (2230 – 2500)
    Book 1: Colonizing Trappist
    Book 2: Returning to Earth
    Book 3: Embracing the Galaxy